A LIFE UNEXPECTED

ALISON RAGSDALE

This book is a work of fiction. Names, characters, organizations, places, events, and incidents either are products of the author's imagination or are used fictitiously.

A LIFE UNEXPECTED

For information: info@alisonragsdale.com

ISBN-13: 978-0-9907478-9-5
ISBN-10: 0-9907478-9-1

Also by this author

FINDING HEATHER

THE FATHER-DAUGHTER CLUB

TUESDAY'S SOCKS

PRAISE FOR FINDING HEATHER

"The characters are beautifully wrought and I didn't want the story to end!"
Peggy Lampman, author of The Promise Kitchen and The Welcome Home Diner

"Tugs at your heartstrings. I was totally swept away by this book."
Amazon ★★★★★ *Review*

PRAISE FOR TUESDAY'S SOCKS

"A novel to read, share, and reread – great literary prose."
Amazon ★★★★★ *Review*

"Once I started reading this book, I could not stop. I laughed...and cried."
Amazon ★★★★★ *Review*

PRAISE FOR THE FATHER-DAUGHTER CLUB

"...descriptions.... as sumptuous and lyrical as a travelogue."
"...flowing dialogue...at once complex and believable."
— *Kirkus Reviews*

"...a final chapter that will take your breath away."
Amazon ★★★★★ *Review*

A LIFE UNEXPECTED

CHAPTER 1

Eve Carruthers stacked the last plate into the dishwasher and clicked the door closed. Dinner had been a success despite her limited time to prepare and her husband Ken's forgetting to bring home the wine she'd asked for.

It was the first time that Jess, their twenty-three-year-old daughter, and her new husband, Ram, had been to dinner since returning from their honeymoon in Goa, and Eve had wanted everything to be perfect.

She glanced around the tidy kitchen. Cooking for a vegetarian son-in-law had initially presented its challenges, but Eve had been practicing and, despite several attempts that had been unceremoniously dumped in the bin, she'd mastered a handful of casseroles and some simple, Indian staples. After much unsolicited advice, and ingredient suggestions, Ken had assured her that the dishes were now more than acceptable.

As she lifted an empty wineglass and set it in the sink, a

rattle behind her made her jump. Ken stood in the doorway. His thick, silvery hair was sticking up at the back, and he held an empty bottle.

"OK, love?" He smiled.

"Yep. Fine." She took the bottle from him and smoothed his hair. "Dinner went down well."

"Another triumph, Mrs. Carruthers." He winked. "So what's for dessert?"

Eve tutted.

"*Nada*, nix, *rien*, nuttin." She prodded his rotund stomach. "You certainly don't need any."

Ken frowned. "But I thought you were making ice cream?" He paused. "You know the kids will be expecting something?"

Eve turned away from him. With two sentences he had popped her bubble of culinary accomplishment. Ken's tendency to lecture, that had been evident since they'd met twenty-four years earlier, was aggravating.

Just as Eve was about to respond, Jess walked into the kitchen, her willowy frame slipping easily through the space between her parents. Her long blonde hair was caught up in a messy bun, and several loose tendrils curled around her square jawline. Her blue-grey eyes, duplicates of her father's, sparkled with amusement.

"What're you two up to?" She beamed, dropping four neatly stacked napkins on the counter. "Any dessert, Mum?"

Ken guffawed.

"See, I told you." He lifted a towel and flicked it playfully at Eve's bottom.

"Stop it, the pair of you. There's fruit in the bowl if you

actually have room for anything else." Eve shook her head at the twosome, unable to stop the smile that split her face. "Where's Ram?"

Jess rolled her eyes.

"On the phone again. The surgery's after-hours service. Some patient with a cracked crown."

Eve nodded.

"Right. Well, lucky them, that he's so responsive."

Jess laughed. "Yeah. After a glass or two of wine, I wouldn't let him near my mouth with a high-speed drill." She crossed her eyes.

Eve enjoyed Jess's spontaneous humor, a quality that balanced the more contemplative nature of Ram, seven years her senior.

"He won't be going tonight, surely?" Eve frowned.

"Don't be daft. Of course not." Ken tutted.

Eve winced at the barb. "Right. I knew that." She felt her cheeks burning.

Jess smiled at her mother. "He's just confirming an appointment for tomorrow."

Eve breathed deeply, trying to shake off her embarrassment. She looked over at her husband, and, not for the first time, the coincidence of her daughter's circumstances so closely mirroring Eve's own made her pause.

Jess and Eve had both married relatively young, and to someone quite a bit older. They'd each chosen confident men whose nature was to take the lead. In Jess and Ram's case, the contrast in their personalities, rather than separating them, created a tapestry of qualities that enriched the pair. Where she and Ken were concerned, specifically over the past year, Eve had felt a distance widening between them fueled not only by what felt like over-familiarity, but also by Ken's tendency to belittle her.

The young couple had been talkative at the dinner table, relating details of their trip to Goa and the welcome they'd received from Ram's family in India.

"Mum, it was amazing. His Aunt Nita had about a hundred people at her house. The whole place was decorated with fresh flowers, even on the floor. The music was incredible and the food was magic. There was enough for two armies." Jess had grabbed Ram's hand, and he'd smiled at her as she continued. "They made us so welcome."

"That's wonderful, Shorty." While nodding at her daughter, she'd locked eyes with Ken as Jess talked animatedly about their hotel, their visit to Old Goa, the bus ride in from the family home in Panjim and the wonders of the archeological museum and the portrait gallery.

Both Eve and Ken knew the toll it had taken on their new son-in-law that his devout Hindu parents, who lived close by in Perth, had refused to attend the wedding. Their objection to Jess had caused serious tension, and Ram had apologized over and over, trying to explain his parents' position.

"It's not just the Hindu thing, it's the Brahmin thing too." He'd been sitting on their sofa, with his elegant fingers laced together between his knees. "The daft part is that they love Jess. That's not the issue at all."

Eve and Ken had tried to take in all that he was saying without seeming too defensive of their daughter.

"But they won't come to the wedding?" Ken had been

incredulous, widening his eyes at Eve across the room. "You're their only son. Don't they want to see you happy?"

Ram had shaken his head.

"They do, but they won't come because they don't believe this is a good match. They're disappointed in me for not choosing a Hindu girl, someone from Goa, and moreover, a Brahmin."

Eve had long been fascinated by Eastern religions, having read extensively on Buddhist and Hindu philosophies. The diverse student body that she advised on careers at St. Andrews University had been happy to provide her with much-needed input when Jess had first brought Ram home to meet them. But despite all her research and accumulated knowledge, she still found it hard to absorb the fact that parents could discount their child's choice of partner based on religion, or a social construct.

Now, eighteen months later, the two had been married for six weeks. Ever since their engagement, Ram had become all but estranged from his parents, visiting them only on religious holidays or occasionally attending family get-togethers when his cousins visited from Glasgow. The situation had saddened Ram, and Eve was worried that the new distance between him and his parents could potentially leach out and manifest as resentment toward Jess.

Eve watched Jess drying glasses and sliding them into the cupboard. There had been no signs of any friction between the two. As far as she could see, Jess and Ram were as much in love as ever.

Ram walked into the kitchen, his thatch of black hair almost brushing the top of the door frame as he passed. He moved up close to Jess and kissed her.

"What did I miss? Can I help with the dishes?"

Eve shook her head. "No. You always do them, so you get the night off tonight." She winked at him as she felt Ken's arms circle her waist from behind.

"Aye, but the bad news is, there's no pudding." Ken spoke against her cheek. She could smell garlic, and his arms were heavy about her middle.

Ram's eyebrows shot up. "What?"

Eve slipped from Ken's grip. "Honestly, you've all got hollow legs."

Jess laughed. "Come on, you two, out. Go and see what's on TV. I want to talk to Mum." She gently pushed Ram away. "Go, shoo." She flapped her hands at him.

"All right, I get the hint. We're gone." Ram jabbed his thumb over his shoulder. "Ken?"

Ken nodded.

"Never stay where you're not wanted." He held his palms out and shrugged. "A wee dram, Ram?"

Ram nodded and the two men turned quickly, jostling to see who could get through the doorway first.

Eve lifted a cloth and wiped some water marks from the countertop.

"So, daughter of mine, what's on your mind?"

Jess discarded the towel she was holding and turned to her mother.

"Thanks for the dinner. It was great." Jess slung an arm around Eve's shoulder. "You're the best."

Eve turned into her daughter's embrace.

"Love you, Shorty." The childhood nickname had stuck, despite Jess having surpassed Eve in height by more than three inches.

She felt Jess's arms tighten around her and Jess's chin dig into her shoulder.

"Love you back." Jess stepped back and shoved her hands into her pockets, her collarbones forming shallow cups as she rolled her shoulders forward. Eve recognized the stance as one her daughter always took when she was nervous, or trying to sell them on something she knew they'd disapprove of.

"So?" Eve felt a flutter of nerves and had a flashback to the day when, the previous year, Jess had told her that she wanted to give up her job at the insurance company to help her dad in his specialty cheese shop, in St. Andrews.

Jess cleared her throat.

"Don't freak out, OK?"

"Well, saying that's not going to help." Eve frowned.

"Sorry. OK. Ram and I..." She paused.

"Yes?"

"We've been talking about children. About having a baby."

Eve felt the floor shift under her. "Jess, you're only twenty-three."

"I know, Mum. Just listen."

Eve filled her lungs to drive down the wave of anxiety that was rising. She nodded at Jess.

"Not now, I mean not immediately, but we were talking about it because we have to be careful." Jess stopped.

"What do you mean?"

"Well, because Ram's a cystic fibrosis carrier."

Eve blinked. Had she known that? Had Jess discussed this with her and she'd blanked on such a critical piece of information? She bit down on her lower lip and stared at her daughter.

"Before you say anything, it's not something that would've ever stopped me marrying him, but before we get pregnant, I'm going to get tested. That's why I'm telling you."

As her daughter's voice began to fade, Eve knew overwhelmingly what was coming next. The inevitable line of questioning that she had no answers for – the one she'd been avoiding for over twenty years.

"Mum, are you OK?" Jess slid onto a stool at the breakfast bar and tucked a loose spiral of hair behind her ear.

Eve nodded, afraid to speak in case her voice failed her.

"Look, it's not the death knell, Mum. We just have to make sure there's no strain of CF on my side because if there is, there's a twenty-five percent chance that a baby would have cystic fibrosis. I'm getting tested next week, but I wanted to ask you if we could check with Nan about the family history, you know, in case there's anything else concerning that I should know about."

Jess was smiling at her, but over her daughter's musical voice, Eve could hear rushing in her ears, and her tongue was sticking oddly to the roof of her mouth. Her mind ran through a picture show of opportunities bypassed and avoided, moments when Eve should have told the truth about her own childhood. Now, the initial angst at Jess's question was being replaced by a surge of regret.

"Mum?"

Jess was leaning across the counter.

Eve focused on her daughter's eyes. "Jess, love, we need to talk about that."

"Right, that's what I'm saying."

Eve shook her head. "No, I mean I have to talk to you about something first."

Jess frowned. "What?"

Eve slid onto the stool opposite Jess and reached across the cool marble. Jess slipped her fingers into her mother's and met her gaze.

"It's OK, you don't have to worry. I don't know why I never told you this. It was a mistake, and I'm sorry."

Jess pulled her fingers back.

"What is it?"

Eve took a deep breath.

"Well, I was actually adopted. Nan and Pop aren't my birth parents." Eve felt the rush of words take her balance with them. She pressed her palm onto the counter to steady herself.

Jess stared at her, her mouth slightly open.

After a few moments of silence, Eve could no longer bear it.

"Jess?"

Jess shook her head almost imperceptibly. "Why wouldn't you tell me that? I don't understand." She turned her body away from Eve as if the glare of the deception was too bright to face.

Eve felt her stomach fold over. Why had she kept this from

her daughter? Why had she persuaded Ken not to share this piece of information that was, after all, nothing to be ashamed of? Now, seeing the beautiful face in front of her awash with confusion, Eve was furious with herself.

"I know it was a bad decision not to tell you. Honestly, I don't know why I kept it from you."

Jess swung around to face her again. "Dad knows, of course?"

Eve nodded. "Yes."

Jess snorted. "Well, what a pair. You're as bad as each other then."

Eve felt the sting of the words. She'd deserved that.

Jess's eyes were full as they met Eve's. "Wait. I'm not…" Her voice cracked.

Eve lunged forward.

"No, of course not. You're ours, all ours." She jumped up and rounded the bar, closing the distance between them before she could create any more.

"Darling girl, I'm sorry. I was in the wrong." She wrapped her arms around Jess's shoulders and felt her daughter tense. "I think I was afraid that it might affect your relationship with Nan and Pop or something. It was stupid."

Jess sniffed and nodded against her chest.

"Yes, it was." She sat upright and wiped her nose on her sleeve. "Even if you thought I was too young, initially, you could've told me years ago."

Eve nodded.

"I know." She wiped a tear from her daughter's cheek with her thumb.

Twenty minutes later they sat opposite one another, each cradling a coffee mug. Jess's nose was still slightly pink, and her eyes were glassy.

"So, what do you know about your birth parents?" She lifted her cup and blew on the surface of the hot liquid.

"Nothing." Eve shrugged. "I never asked Nan and Pop much. I don't think I wanted to know." She gave a half smile. "Perhaps I'm just an anomaly. I was never interested in finding them or knowing why they gave me up." She slid the cup away from her, suddenly not interested in drinking the frothy coffee.

Jess frowned.

"But you're so curious about stuff. You always dig down, won't let things go. You're like a pit bull for details" – she set her cup down – "and yet you didn't want to know anything about the two people who made you, then gave you up? The woman who gave birth to you?"

Eve shook her head.

"No. I didn't."

"It just doesn't make sense to me. It's not like you."

Eve nodded. "I suppose not. I know it sounds like the ultimate cliché, but I felt that if I asked them, it would be hurtful, like they weren't enough."

Jess's face softened.

"Now, that I understand." She smiled. "Mum?"

"Yes?"

"I'm sorry I got upset." She reached across the counter. "I was just shocked."

Eve patted Jess's hand.

"You were entitled to. It was my fault for hiding it."

Eve took in the wide-set eyes, the high cheekbones, the streamlined nose, and the small mouth with the one, shallow dimple on the left. How much of this gorgeous face that made up such a large part of Eve's happiness was her own doing, and how much was down to the genetic material of someone, of two someones, she knew absolutely nothing about?

"So, what do we do now? I mean, about family genetics and stuff?" Jess sniffed. "Surely Nan can help us? She must've known the identity of your birth mother, at least?"

Eve shrugged.

"You know, I don't know." She took in Jess's open face. "But we can ask her, certainly."

The women emptied their cups into the sink and joined the men in the living room. The TV was loud, and the father and son-in-law shouted at the screen. Two football teams darted around on a waterlogged pitch, and it was obvious that Ken and Ram were supporting opposite sides.

Jess rolled her eyes at her mother and settled on the arm of Ram's chair.

"Sweetheart, we need to go." She spoke into his ear, her fingers raking the thick hair from his temple.

"Just a minute. We're going into extra time." He patted her thigh and pulled her onto his lap as Eve circled Ken's chair, which was pulled up close to the fireplace.

"How much longer?" She poked Ken's shoulder.

"Twenty minutes or so." He spoke to the TV screen.

Eve sighed.

"I think I'll go up and read, if you two don't mind?" She met

Jess's gaze.

"No, go up, Mum. I'll drag him out of here soon, I promise." Jess smiled.

"There's no hurry." Eve walked over and pecked Ram's cheek.

"Thanks for dinner, Eve. It was cracking." He squeezed her fingers.

"Welcome, love. See you soon."

Jess followed Eve out into the hall.

"So, when can we talk to Nan?"

"Let me give her a ring tomorrow, see when it works for her. I haven't been over for a week or so, so it's time I popped in anyway."

Jess nodded.

"Thanks Mum. Love you."

Eve hugged her daughter.

"Night, Shorty."

After taking off her makeup and showering, Eve could still hear the TV and three voices meshed in a harmony of exasperated groans and excited yelps as the game continued. As she sat on the end of the bed and smoothed on hand cream, she felt a second wind drag her back from the fatigue she'd felt after dinner. She twisted around to see the bedside clock. Ten thirty-five.

Standing up, she moved to the dressing table and dragged a brush through her chin-length hair. She leaned in to the mirror and patted the fine lines that had recently become more visible under her grey eyes. Staring back at her was Jess's nose, the square jaw, and the high hairline. Those parts of her daughter she could at least lay claim to.

She pulled on her bathrobe and walked along the hallway, pushed the door open, and stepped inside her makeshift studio. Photography had been a passion of Eve's since her youth and finally, two years ago, Ken had persuaded her to relinquish the larger of the two spare bedrooms – which was used twice a year at most – so that he could transform it into a space where she could print out and work on her photographs. He'd installed the specific software she needed on her laptop and bought her an expensive printer, which she'd protested about.

Ken had insisted she keep it.

"You never buy yourself anything. This is to you from me." He'd pulled her into his broad chest and kissed her. "No arguments."

Surrounding her, stacked in boxes, pinned to boards in collages, and hanging on the walls in simple black frames, were her pictures. The majority of the shots were black and white, many of local architecture, St. Andrews being saturated with historic subject matter. Dominating the largest board on the far wall, the ruins of St. Andrews Castle, proud on its sandstone promontory, rose into a misty sky as waves kicked white froth up at the base of the cliff below. Eve took in the image, squinting to soften the edges of the composition as she assessed her latest piece of work. The perspective of the shot wasn't quite what she'd hoped for, neither was the light, and as she widened her eyes again, she resolved to go back to the same spot and try again.

On one wall was a series of shots taken by a photographer whom she greatly admired. The woman, who signed herself simply as Grant, specialized in images of babies in outdoor settings. Many of the infants were photographed lying on hay bales, nestled among fresh flowers, or curled up on soft lamb's wool rugs. They were generally asleep, tiny lids resting over their newborn eyes, either with fists tucked under their chins or with limbs splayed out like trusting little starfish. Eve would study the ethereal and yet wholly realistic light that Grant was able to capture – something that Eve struggled with herself. While she knew that the photographs were done for commercial purposes, there was a personal quality to each one that drew her in.

Two years earlier, Eve had been to a large bookstore in Edinburgh where Grant had been signing copies of her latest coffee-table book. Eve had stood in line for half an hour with the hardback close to her chest. When she'd eventually reached the table where the softly spoken, middle-aged woman sat, Eve had become tongue-tied.

"Who should I make it out to?"

Grant had been patient with Eve's mumbled response and had steadily held her gaze until Eve had blurted, "Just Eve."

Eve turned back to the pile of photographs stacked on the work table. Several shots were fanned out across the surface, and as she flicked through them, Jess's and Ram's faces shone up at her.

Jess had asked her to take a set of candid shots on their wedding day, separate from the official photographer's, and Eve had been delighted. After the civil ceremony in the Old Town Hotel, she'd spirited the couple away from the small group of guests to the enclosed courtyard in front of Ken's nearby shop. The setting had been perfect. The wrought-iron tables and chairs that sat on the cobblestones; the crumbling clay pots lined up along the walls on either side, filled with geraniums and trailing ferns; the dark lacquered door of the shop with the bubbled glass bay window – all provided layers of atmosphere to the images.

Jess's dress had been simple: a V-neck, knee-length oyster-colored shift with delicate embroidery around the bottom of the skirt and a floral design in tiny seed pearls across the front. The long chiffon scarf that she'd draped across her collarbones, letting the tails hang down her back, was a nod to Ram's heritage. Her hair had been loosely curled, and she'd worn Eve's pearl earrings – a gift from Ken on their fifteenth wedding anniversary.

Eve picked up one of the photos. Ram looked stylish in his black suit and luminous white shirt. His thick hair was brushed back from his face, and his dark eyes sparkled. He was looking at Jess as she reached down and pulled up his trouser leg to reveal a flash of colorful sock. Her head was thrown back, and there was a look of such pure joy on her face that it made Eve's chest hurt.

As she placed the photo back on the table and picked up another, she revisited her earlier conversation with Jess. The time had come for Eve to speak to her parents, to ask the questions that she wasn't sure whether she'd been avoiding or honestly hadn't wanted to know the answers to, for over thirty years. As she stared down at the picture of her daughter kissing the cheek of her new husband, those unasked questions began spinning around her, floating loose in the quiet of the room. Who was the person who had handed Eve over as a new-born to total strangers rather than care for her herself? What circumstances had made it impossible for that faceless woman to keep her own baby? Eve's fingers tightened on the photograph. The very notion of letting go of Jess, watching another person walk away with her precious child, was inconceivable.

When Mary and Russell Parvin had sat six-year-old Eve down in the living room of their harbor-front cottage and explained how she'd come to be their daughter, Eve had been nonplussed. This was her home and these were her parents. The knowledge that Mary hadn't given birth to her, while surprising, hadn't engendered the shock or identity crisis that her parents had obviously expected. Eve remembered taking in the information and then saying, "OK. But you're my mummy and daddy, right?" in response to which Mary had held Eve's hand and said, "Utterly and completely."

Eve had listened to her father telling her that she could ask any questions she wanted and that she could even tell her friends that she was adopted, if she felt like it.

Now, as she stared down at Jess's joyful face, Eve could still see Russell on that day thirty-three years ago, his weather-beaten forehead creasing and his tanned fingers twisting into knots as he leaned forward in his chair. Having been a fisherman for four decades in the small port of Pittenweem on the East Neuk coast of Fife, her father wasn't a man who was easily unnerved. The sight of her invincible father's hands trembling had been more disturbing to Eve than his words had been. She remembered that, at that moment, all she had wanted was for Russell's hands to stop shaking.

When Mary had pressed her again about having questions, Eve had shaken her head.

"No. I heard you, Mummy." She'd paused. "Can I have a glass of milk, please?"

She could still see the look of surprise on Mary's face as she'd glanced over at her husband before standing up and calmly walking into the kitchen.

Now, a tap at the door made Eve jump.

Ken peeked around the door. "Thought you'd gone to bed?" He stepped into the room in socked feet, his shoes dangling from his hand.

"I'm just looking at the kids." She held out the photo. "Aren't they perfect?"

Ken hovered at her elbow.

"Yes, they're a lovely pair." He shifted several shots around on the table then yawned. "Are you coming to bed?"

Eve shook her head. "Not yet."

He halted his progress toward the door.

"Why not?"

She sighed. "I'm not tired now."

He tutted. "Well you came upstairs a while ago. You should've gone to bed then."

She turned to face him.

"Ken, I'll go to bed when I'm tired."

His eyebrows lifted.

"What's the matter with you?" He squinted at her.

"Nothing." She felt the nut of an untruth clog the back of her throat. As he shrugged and stepped out into the hall, she spoke to his back.

"Actually, there is..."

"What?" He cut her off, the shoes dangling next to his thigh.

"You embarrassed me down there?"

Ken frowned. "When?"

She pulled the edges of her robe tighter around her torso.

"When I asked if Ram was going into work."

He shook his head. "What are you talking about?"

She linked her fingers over her knee.

"Do you even know you're doing it?" She watched as he blinked several times then, seeming to remember the incident, his eyes met hers.

"Sometimes your tone is condescending." She heard the quiver in her voice and willed the tears that were pressing in not to come.

Ken rolled his eyes. "You're over reacting. I didn't mean anything by it."

Eve stood up.

"But you make me feel small when you speak to me like that in front of people. Especially the kids." She pulled her shoulders back and then her hurt abruptly turned to anger as, rather than answer, he turned away.

"Ken?"

He wafted the shoes above his shoulder as he ambled down the corridor.

"I'm off to bed."

CHAPTER 2

Jess rolled onto her side and buried her head in Ram's neck. "You smell good." She kissed the warm skin.

Ram pulled her close.

"That was good fun tonight." He spoke into her hair. "Your mum did a great job with dinner."

"She went to a lot of trouble." Jess draped a leg over Ram's thigh and circled his chest with her arm. "I asked her if she'd talk to Nan, about the family medical history."

He nodded.

"She dropped a bit of a bombshell." Jess felt him tense under her arm.

"What?" He jerked himself up against his pillows. "Is there CF in your family?"

She sat up next to him and looked into the mahogany eyes that, just two years ago, had captured her heart as she'd nervously waited in the dental surgery for a crown to be fitted. Ram had a way of calming her when she let her anxiety get the better of her, but now, as she scanned his face, she saw once again the angst that he carried along with the CF transmembrane conductance regulator gene. The full descriptor was a complex mouthful, but when he had explained the implications to her, and after her own extensive research, Jess felt that it needed an even more sinister label.

She smiled at him. "No, love. It's something else. Something I didn't know."

Ram looked startled.

"Something else? As in something worse?"

She wound her fingers through his.

"No. It's just that Mum doesn't actually know her family's medical history." Jess watched Ram's brow gather. "She told me that she was adopted." She pushed the hair from her face and leaned back against the headboard.

Ram blinked.

"Adopted?"

"Yes."

"And you didn't know that?"

Jess sighed. "No. I had no idea."

"God." Ram whispered. "A bombshell indeed."

Jess nodded.

"So what do we do now?"

"Mum's going to talk to Nan to see what she can find out about her birth mother." She hesitated. "Nan's not her birth mother. It doesn't seem real." She hesitated. "And Nan's not technically my real nan." She frowned as another layer of her mother's deception settled on her. "It's crazy. I don't know what to feel about it. I can't believe she kept that from me."

Ram, seeming to have regained his composure, twisted around to look at her.

"It must've been really hard for her to tell you that."

"I know. I was pretty upset though. I mean, why would she keep that secret for my whole life?" Jess sniffed, reliving her initial, emotional response to Eve's revelation. "The fallout affects me too." She watched as Ram nodded slowly and then reached over and took her hand.

"Jess, there's bound to be more to this." He paused. "Your mum is one of the most selfless people I know, and I doubt she'd have hidden it for any other reason than to preserve your relationship with your Nan and Pop."

Jess felt her face growing hot. Sometimes Ram's good heart reminded her that she could be a selfish wretch. Feeling suitably corrected for her moment of narcissism, she leaned in and put her head on his shoulder.

"I know. You're right." She sighed. "I suppose we'll find out more when Mum talks to them. I've got so many questions though. I hope she lets me go with her."

"I think it might be easier on your mum if you weren't there, just initially. Who knows how that first conversation might go, and you don't want to make it harder than it has to be, right?"

Her husband's advisory way of speaking to her sometimes chafed. She'd seen a similar pattern between her parents and, occasionally, had caught Eve rolling her eyes at Ken's tendency to overexplain or dismiss her opinion. Jess believed the behavior came from a protective instinct that both men possessed, but it irked her when she saw it in Ram. In this instance, however, she knew him to be correct.

"You're probably right." She said. "Anyway, I'll be ready to go if Mum wants me with her. It's my fault that she has to talk to Nan about it at all. I feel bad about ever bringing it up." Jess nibbled at a hangnail.

"No, my love. It's not your fault." Ram exhaled. "It's mine."

The following morning, Jess rolled out of bed and tiptoed into the living room. Ram seldom slept in, but this was Sunday, and the whisky he'd had with her dad after last night's dinner would keep him under the covers for a while longer. She found it amusing that her husband was a lightweight when it came to alcohol. Ken would laugh and say fondly, "One wee dram and Ram is anybody's."

She drew the heavy curtains and looked down at the street. Their flat, above the wool shop in the center of St. Andrews, had been Ram's when they'd met. Located equidistant between his surgery on South Street and her dad's shop off Church Street, it was the perfect location for the couple.

She'd moved in a few months before the wedding. With Ram's blessing and the addition of a few carefully chosen pieces, she had turned it from a starkly furnished bachelor's space into a warm home with an eclectic mix of ethnic and traditional furniture that respected the history of the atmospheric building but still suited Ram's more modern taste.

She glanced down at the bookstore across the street. The windows were dark, as were those of the bank next to it. In the past, she'd often looked up at these flats when walking in Market Street and wondered who was fortunate enough to live in them. They were among the three-story sandstone buildings that made up a large part of the city center, and Jess would wander past them, inhaling the saltiness of her hometown as she listened to the myriad foreign accents that passed her in any given hour.

Turning her back on the window, she went into the kitchen. Two large café-au-lait cups sat next to the coffee jar, and a dish of strawberries was neatly covered with a square of kitchen paper. Seeing the crimson hearts, she smiled. Ram had obviously laid these out last night before collapsing into bed. He'd been nagging her about eating more fruit.

She pulled back the paper and popped a strawberry into her mouth. Nothing tasted quite like the local berries at this time of year. As she crushed the summer fruit against the roof of her mouth, Jess could taste the soil, spring water, and sun that had helped create her breakfast.

With a cup of coffee and a handful of berries, she walked back into the living room. She set her cup down and picked up her book from the ottoman. Then, pulling her long T-shirt over her knees, she settled into a corner of the sofa.

The summer weather in St. Andrews was always unpredictable, but this year was being kind to them so far. Their plan for the day was to take a picnic and walk along the links at the Old Course. Jess often spent time around the golf course, where she'd watch the passersby – local people walking dogs, tourists with impressive cameras and players pulling golf bags on trolleys. When she'd see an older couple, Jess imagined that she was looking into her future with Ram.

Thinking of their future and the children they might have, an image of Eve came to her. The look on her mother's face the night before had been that of a startled deer. Jess felt a resurgence of guilt. She hadn't meant to cause any hurt with her reaction to the truth that Eve had shared, but now as she considered it again, the weight of the shock was heavy. The idea that she wasn't linked by blood to her beloved Nan and Pop, a major part of the foundation of her world, was undeniably painful.

Having let her thoughts meander through various *what-if* scenarios, Jess took a deep breath and blew the sense of betrayal she was harboring out into the cool room. Above all else, regardless of what they did or didn't find out about Eve's birth parents, Jess was determined not to let this new knowledge come between her and her mother, or her and her grandparents. The one thing Jess knew to be true, which shone steady and beacon-like, was that Russell and Mary had been Eve's true parents. No matter what the genetics, nothing would change that.

CHAPTER 3

Eve placed her phone back on the kitchen table. Mary had been delighted that her daughter was coming and hadn't asked the reason for her visit or why she wasn't going in to work. Eve still didn't know how she'd broach the subject after all this time and was concerned about her parents' reaction.

As she moved in close to the sink, Eve caught her reflection in the kitchen window, ghostly against the dark green of the lawn and the rows of waxy leaved camellias lining the fence. The garden was Ken's pride and joy, and while she had little interest in the making of it or the work it took to maintain, she appreciated everything he put into it.

She glanced at the clock. She wasn't due at her mum's until 2:00 p.m. so, filling a tall glass with water, she let herself out the back door and made her way along the pea gravel path. The July sun was tepid, but in their garden, which was surrounded on all sides by tall hawthorn trees, it was pleasant enough not to need a jacket this morning.

Eve sat at the mosaic-topped table and slipped her bare feet out of her shoes. The stones felt rough under her toes, and the smell of the closely cut lavender bushes surrounding her was pungent. Behind her, the sandstone bungalow sat low and long on the property that she and Ken had bought the year after Jess was born. She'd been nervous about the purchase, as the house had been more expensive than she was comfortable with, but Ken had persuaded her that it was a great investment and, with their growing family, a wise move. As usually happened when they were faced with a major decision, she had deferred to him, and, despite some lean times, they'd managed to live comfortably since moving in.

As Eve considered the years they'd spent trying to have another baby after Jess, she felt the familiar press of sadness that always accompanied this train of thought. There had been no medical explanation for her inability to become pregnant again, but it had never happened. She'd always wanted Jess to have siblings, but for some reason the universe had seen fit for her daughter to remain an only child.

She squinted into the morning sun, looking down toward the end of the garden. There on the grass was the pair of doves that visited every year around the same time. When she saw one, she automatically looked for the other and would worry until she spotted the two together. The twin birds often made her think of herself and Ken, one seeming to need the other in order to function. Seeing the matched pair, she exhaled. The sky was a mid-blue, marred by only a few straggly clouds. She closed her eyes and let the sun bathe her face.

Thinking of the day ahead, her mother's image floated into

her mind – the small, round face, bright blue eyes and ever-present lipstick under a sphere of carefully styled honey-colored hair. Russell, still impressively upright and strong for his age, towered over Mary these days. They were both becoming hard of hearing, and consequently most conversations inside their home were shouted rather than spoken now.

Her parents lived in the same tiny, whitewashed cottage that they had all her life. It had a red pan-tiled roof and matching leaded windows, and the dark-green front door opened directly onto the harbor near the West Pier of Pittenweem. As a teenager, Eve had loved to walk up the hill behind the village and look down on the stepped rooftops as they tumbled toward where Russell kept his boat. She'd try to pick it out among the cluster of bright hulls, looking for the red lines of the Mary-Anne in the collection of wooden bodies lined up like colorful fins against the sea wall.

Now that her father had officially hung up his fishing nets, they both walked miles every day around the villages and surrounding countryside of Fife. At seventy-three and seventy-one respectively, Eve thought Russell and Mary were remarkable.

As she watched, a cloud slid over the sun, turning the grass from lime green to emerald. She checked her watch. Just over two hours until she had to face her parents with her question. She crossed her legs, feeling the metal of the chair bite into her back.

Mary stood at the kitchen table, her pillar-box-red shirt and matching lipstick a splash of color against the pastel-green of the room. She'd arranged several biscuits onto a plate and then tucked the tin away in a cupboard. Russell was hovering by the stove, waiting for the kettle to boil.

As Eve looked around the cozy room with the green Aga stove that she'd burnt her hand on at age six, and the same wooden table where she'd done her homework for years, she felt a tug of nostalgia for the simple days of her childhood. This was the place she'd grown up and where she'd felt wholly loved, at home, exactly where she belonged. It was also the place where she had first brought Ken to meet her parents. She had been almost sixteen when she'd met him, and her father had disapproved of the relationship from the start, becoming tyrannical about curfews and rules for her going out with a boy four years older.

As Mary fussed with some paper napkins, another memory jolted Eve. It was of a subsequent meeting she and Ken had had with her parents in this very room just four months after the initial introductions. It had been gut-wrenching. Eve getting pregnant had been the ultimate shock to them all. Ken had proposed immediately, but her parents were devastated that their clever daughter, the thoughtful girl they'd brought up so carefully, who wanted to go to university, could have been so naïve and irresponsible. As she recalled the humiliating and painful days leading up to their hasty marriage, Eve grimaced. That had been the only time when she'd ever truly questioned whether her parents might stop loving her.

Russell's gravelly voice snapped her back to the moment.

"So, what's new, love?" He smiled, his tanned face wrinkling. "Any scandal for us old fogeys?"

Eve laughed. "No scandal, I'm afraid. Just much of the same."

Her mother passed behind her and slid into a chair.

"How's wee Jess doing?" Mary patted Eve's arm. "Still happy?"

Eve smiled at her mother. "Yes, Mum. Still happy."

Russell and Mary had been concerned about their granddaughter marrying so young. Eve understood those concerns but, despite her own similar worries, was determined to support Jess's decision one hundred percent.

Russell filled the teapot and then placed it on the tablemat that Mary shoved toward him.

"I know." He winked at Eve. "After fifty-eight years, I think I know to use a mat."

Mary tutted and indicated the chair at the end of the table. "Oh wheesht, man, and sit down."

Suddenly nervous about her mission, Eve defaulted to a safe question. "Any good gigs coming up, Dad?"

Russell was quite a local character, his love of playing the fiddle having become his trademark in the community. He would often be called on to play for ceilidhs and weddings while Mary would hold court at a table at the back of the room, tapping her toes to her husband's reels while soaking up the jollity around her.

Russell shook his head.

"Nothing for the moment. Probably more in August. More weddings, you know." He nodded. "So, what brings you to sleepy Pittenweem?" He poured tea into three cups and then slid one across the table toward Eve. "Not that we're complaining."

"Well, it's been a while. I was off today and just felt like a visit." Eve added milk to the cup and stared at the circling liquid, avoiding her mother's penetrating stare.

"Uh huh." Mary stirred her tea.

Eve never could get a lie past her mother.

"OK. It's not just that." She looked up at her father. "I need to talk to you both about something."

Mary audibly sucked her breath in.

"Are you ill?"

"No, no, Mum, I'm fine. We're all fine." Eve reached over and covered Mary's hand with her own. "It's something else."

Russell shunted his chair in closer to the table and picked up a biscuit from the plate.

"We're all ears, lass."

Eve swallowed.

"It's more about Jess, actually." She flicked her glance between her parents, who had locked eyes. "She came to me the other night and asked something about the family medical history." Eve lifted her cup and sipped some tea.

"Oh aye?" Russell frowned. "Like what?"

Eve took a breath, hoping for some divine inspiration as to how she might couch this. Deciding to dive right in, she continued.

"She wanted to know if there was any history of cystic fibrosis in the family, because it turns out that Ram is a carrier."

"Oh, Eve." Mary exhaled the words. "Is that dangerous?"

Eve explained the implications of the gene mutation and the need to understand both familial lines in order to avoid passing the condition on to a child.

"Surely they're not pregnant yet?" Mary sounded shocked.

"No, Mum. That's exactly the point." Eve tried to keep her

voice level, despite the angst that was clogging her chest. "Jess is getting her blood tested and they'll know before they get pregnant, so that if there are two strains of the CF mutation they can take measures to avoid…" She halted.

"Avoid what?" Mary was frowning.

"Avoid having a child with cystic fibrosis. Apparently, where both parents are carriers, there's a twenty-five percent chance of the child being born with CF." Eve pushed the cup away. Her throat was too tight now to swallow.

Russell coughed.

"So, you're saying that if this gene mutation is in your bloodline, and if Jess has it too, it could affect her having children at all?"

Eve shook her head.

"Not at all, she just needs to be as informed as possible before they get pregnant. But it's not just about the CF. She had questions about other aspects of family health history." Eve paused. "Which, of course, I couldn't answer." She eyed her parents. "So I had to tell her I was adopted."

Mary pursed her lips.

"Well, of course." Russell held his cup in midair. "How did she handle it?"

"A bit emotionally. She asked me why I hadn't told her years ago."

He nodded his tacit agreement.

Eve lowered her voice. "That was a decision I took, Dad, right or wrong." She leaned back in the chair. "We've talked it through and she understands now, I think."

Mary pulled a tissue from her sleeve.

"Is she upset with us for not saying anything either?" She looked anxious.

"Not at all, Mum. She knows it was absolutely my decision. And she's quite determined that it makes no difference to how she feels about the pair of you. She adores you. You're her grandparents. End of story."

Mary nodded and then dropped her gaze to her lap, where her fingers plucked invisible fluff from her skirt.

Russell shoved his chair back, the wooden legs screeching against the flagstone floor.

"So, what is it you want to know in particular?"

Mary made a small, choking sound.

"Are you OK, Mum?" Eve laid her hand on Mary's back.

"Aye. Just taking it all in." Her voice was little more than a whisper.

"Well, what I suppose I'm asking is, can you tell me anything about my birth mother?" Eve tasted the words, sour on her tongue. "I mean, just basic stuff like her background, where she came from." She took a breath. "Do you know her name, or whether there's any way we could contact her, just to get medical info?"

She took in the pained expression on her father's face. Silence blanketed them all for a few moments and then Mary spoke, her voice stronger again.

"I knew you'd ask, eventually. I wasn't sure when, but I knew you would."

Eve took in the watery film that had covered her mother's eyes.

"Mum, it's not for any other purpose than what I've told

you." She squeezed Mary's fingers. "Honestly."

Mary nodded.

"I've got some things I can show you, if you want?"

Eve caught a movement in the corner of her eye. Her father was shaking his head at his wife.

"Russ, it's OK. She's asking." Mary patted the air. "It's fine."

Russell blinked several times and then gave one nod, dipping his chin toward the table.

"Aye, right then." His eyes bore into Mary's. "Do you want me to come too?"

Mary shook her head.

"No. I'll do it." Her voice was firm now.

Russell held his wife's gaze for a few seconds, stood up, and then lifted the teapot and put it into the sink.

Eve followed her mother down the narrow hall, past the living room and into the tiny bedroom that had been her childhood lair. While the curtains were the same floral print she'd chosen in her teens, the single bed was gone and a dark wood table sat against the wall, laden with patchwork squares in a variety of patterns. On the tall shelves where Eve's books and dolls had stood were small stacks of material cut into neat squares and reels of thread in myriad colors, covering the entire spectrum. Mary's impressive sewing machine was plugged into the wall and a swath of lemon fabric was draped across an ironing board that stood under the window.

"You're really getting on well with the quilt, Mum." Eve smiled at Mary, who was pulling a small box from an upper shelf.

"Aye, well, I want it to be ready for when Jess…" She paused.

"What?"

"I was going to say, has her first baby."

Eve walked over and circled her mother's narrow shoulders with her arm.

"She's going to have babies, Mum. One way or another, nothing will stop her." Eve laughed softly. "You know our Jess well enough to know that's true."

Mary turned to her and nodded. The dark-blue shoebox she was holding sagged in her hands.

"Right." Mary swallowed. "I'm not sure what to do now." She looked down at the box, then back at Eve. "How to do this."

Mary's expression made Eve's heart crack.

"Let's sit down. Whatever's in there won't change a thing. OK?" Eve held Mary's hand as Mary sank onto one of the wooden chairs next to the table.

"I hope that's true." Mary's eyes were now brimming.

"Mum, please. Don't get so upset. I wish I didn't have to ask this. If it was just for me, I wouldn't want to know, ever." She sat down and raked her hand through her hair. With all the emotion that was tugging at her mother's face, Eve was startled that her own nerves had suddenly ebbed away.

Earlier in the day, when she'd been playing this scene over in her mind while driving along the coast road and the familiar lanes of Pittenweem, she'd been preparing for all manner of emotional turmoil. Now that the critical moment was here, she felt oddly numb. She'd been steeling herself for whatever Mary had in that box but, overriding everything else she was feeling was regret for the obvious discomfort she was causing these people whom she loved so deeply.

"It's all right. You should've known about this a long time ago." Mary settled the box on her lap and eased the lid off.

Eve leaned forward, straining to see inside as Mary lifted a piece of paper folded neatly in two and a small object that Eve couldn't make out.

"Before I show you this, I need to tell you something." Mary held the articles on her lap.

"OK." Eve frowned. "I'm listening."

Mary shifted awkwardly, pulling the box back up the slope of her lap.

"Your birth mother didn't give you up for adoption in the usual way."

"What do you mean?"

"She left you in a safe place and..." She paused. "She ran away."

Eve was watching her mother's mouth, the words sounding like garbled code. Eve's heart was pattering.

"Ran away? You mean she abandoned me?"

Mary carefully placed the box on the table.

"She was very young. The authorities eventually identified her as a runaway. Apparently she'd taken a bus to Braemar to hide her pregnancy from her parents."

Eve held her breath.

"She stayed there for a few months." Mary paused. "Some of the community in the village seemingly helped her out until she had you. Then, one day, she just disappeared."

Eve shook her head trying to take in what she was hearing.

"She was a child, Eve. She obviously panicked, and the responsibility was just too much." Mary licked her lips. "Do you want me to go on?"

Eve nodded.

"She left you somewhere where the people had been kind to her – somewhere she knew you'd be found quickly."

Eve blinked, finally finding her voice.

"Where?"

"It was at a wee tea shop in the village. It was summer, and apparently she left you outside the place."

Eve felt her eyes burning. Outside. Left like a pile of grass clippings or a bag of leaves for collection. Inexplicably, the word *outside* seemed to cut deeper than the words *left you* had, and Eve blinked to clear her vision.

"Are you all right, darling?" Mary's voice was breathy.

Eve closed her eyes and nodded. "Go on, Mum. I'm listening."

"She left a note, pinned to your baby basket, and this broach."

Eve opened her eyes to see her mother extend a quivering palm. On it was a long, narrow silver broach in the shape of a thistle. Eve reached out to take it and noticed that her own hands were shaking as badly as Mary's. She lifted the delicate item. The clasp was broken, so the long pin swung open as she held it up to look at it. The top of the broach was the head of the thistle, the silver cleverly formed into the familiar brush that would hold the color purple out on the moor. Cupping that was the pear-shaped base of the bloom sporting rows of slash marks, imitating prickles. The long stem had three jagged silver leaves sticking out of it, two on one side, one on the other, and then it tapered away at the bottom into the little circle of silver that should have held the pin closed.

Mary sniffed again, making Eve's eyes snap back up to meet her mother's.

"Shall I go on?" Mary tried to smile.

"Is there more?"

Mary nodded.

"Yes. The note." She held the yellowed paper out to Eve. "Do you want to read it?"

Eve took the note as if it were spun of spider silk and might snap in her fingers. She let her hand drop to her thigh, the weight of what she held suddenly overwhelming.

"Here, let me read it to you." Mary leaned over and slipped the paper from Eve's hand. "Ready?"

Eve nodded, mute again as Mary whispered the words. *"My darling daughter. I'm very sorry. You were so loved, but I was afraid. I will always miss you. Mummy."*

An hour later, sitting awkwardly in the living room, the threesome was silent. Eve had gone for a brief walk along the harbor, and when she got back, Russell had poured her a brandy. Her glass was now empty, and her quaking stomach was settling. The thistle broach and note were on the coffee table, forcing their intrusive presence into the quiet space.

Mary fluttered her hands on her lap, yanking her skirt over her knees and then tapping her fingertips on the arm of her chair. Eventually, not being able to handle the unaccustomed silence, Eve spoke.

"So, I have a question." She glanced from one parent to the

other. “Why didn’t you ever tell me the whole story?”

Russell sucked his cheeks in, a gesture he performed when he was preparing for a bold statement. As he began to speak, Mary cut him off.

“We both felt that it was enough to have a six-year old understand that she was adopted, let alone left under a table.” Mary’s face was flushed.

“Under a table?” Eve frowned.

Mary blinked several times.

“Your basket was left under a table in the garden at the café, in Braemar.”

Eve caught her breath.

Mary looked exhausted and Russell stood up abruptly from his chair and walked to the window overlooking the street. Eve could see from the set of his shoulders, his hands linked behind his back military style, that he was upset.

“I’m sorry, it’s just a lot to take in.” She watched her mother drag a hanky out of her pocket and dab her eyes.

“We probably should’ve told you. We were just afraid that it might be too hurtful, that final stab.” Mary folded the hanky and shoved it back in her pocket. “We agreed that we’d tell you the minute you asked, but that we wouldn’t volunteer the information if you didn’t. Right, Russ?” She addressed her husband’s back as he nodded silently at the window. “Then as the years passed and you didn’t ask us anything at all, it sort of became less important.”

Eve noticed her mother’s tone become slightly defensive. Eve hadn’t wanted to sound accusatory, especially as her own actions in not telling Jess about her adoption had echoed her parents' choice to keep this information from her. She took a deep breath and acknowledged that she had played a large part in this entire mess, with her own lack of inquiry.

"Look. I don't blame you at all. I know I never asked you about it." She paused." But wasn't there a time when it would've made sense to tell me?" She flicked her gaze between her parents. "Dad?"

Russell's face was dangerously red and he was staring at her mother, as if afraid she might implode. He caught Eve's eye and held up a wrinkled finger.

"We did what we thought was best, and there's an end to it." He sounded hoarse as he lowered his hand and turned his back on her again.

Eve stared at her mother, seeing the full effect of her questions.

"Look, I don't want to hurt you both or make this any more difficult than it has to be." She forced herself to smile at Mary, who smiled back, relief flooding her lined face. "It'll just take a while to sink in, that's all."

Russell turned around and faced them.

"It made no difference to us how you came to us. You were the child we'd prayed for, and when the child protection people in Edinburgh called us in, we didn't need to ask questions, we knew that you were our daughter from the moment we saw you." Russell's eyes were glittering. "There was nothing we wouldn't have done for, and still wouldn't do for you, Eve. Perhaps we persuaded ourselves that you didn't need to know." He looked over at Mary, who was nodding. "Maybe that was a mistake, but we wanted to protect you."

Eve stood up and walked over to her father.

"I know, Dad. I know that."

Russell accepted the hug she gave him, then gently pushed back from her embrace. He held her fingers in his.

"Your mother and I both believed that it was about where you belonged, rather than where you came from – and you belonged with us."

Thirty minutes later, Eve guided her car toward home, passing the Castle Links. Even in the twilight, she could make out the pale stretch of sand far to her right, the narrow strip of beach she had walked on so many times that she'd lost count. Her parents had often brought her here for picnics, and with a striped wind-screen and a basket full of sandwiches, they'd wrap themselves in blankets, huddle together, and count the white horses curling in to the shore. At the memory, Eve smiled. Her life then had felt light, unencumbered. How odd it was that one seemingly simple question from her daughter had catapulted her down a veritable rabbit hole. Much of what she knew about her life had become a half-truth, and now some of the seeds of questions she'd had about herself had taken on a larger form.

Suddenly tired, Eve indicated and pulled off the road. She was on Abbey Street, a familiar stretch of park on her right and a row of stone terraced houses on her left. She turned off the engine and leaned her head back against the rest. As she closed her eyes, seeking a moment of quiet in her mind, she was jolted by a memory. As the picture clarified itself, she pressed her fingers into her eyes.

She'd been twelve. It had been the night after her birthday and she'd been restless, tiptoeing along the dark hall back toward the living room where her parents were watching TV. She was hoping for a glass of milk, or better still a sliver of the cake her mother had made the day before.

The swish of a passing car forced her eyes open and made her heart flip-flop. She shivered, closed her eyes again, and tried to focus on the scene, the smell of the harbor-side cottage, the feel of the dark carpet under her bare toes. Gradually she slid back into the memory.

That night, as she'd approached the living room door, she remembered hearing her father speaking over the sound of the television. Her mother was shushing him but, after a whisky or two, Russell's voice generally gained volume. Eve had leaned into the doorway, careful not to let her shadow creep up the wall inside the room. Mary had sounded odd, as if she was afraid. Russell had obviously been pacing around the room, and Eve had followed his voice back and forth, trying to discern how angry he'd be if she stepped inside, having been sent to bed almost an hour earlier.

Now, as she sat in the dark car, Eve waited for the words she'd overheard to come back to her. Something was keeping them down, buried under years of blissful calm, but as she clenched her teeth, she could hear her father again.

"It's time she knows, Mary. She's not a wean anymore."

Mary had shushed him again.

"Wheesht, Russ, she's just down the hall."

Eve remembered seeing her father's shadow approaching the door. Panicking, she'd scurried back to her bedroom, and as she'd closed the door silently, not letting the lock click in the frame, she'd felt a small knot forming in her stomach. She'd not been sure what it had meant at the time and, as children are capable of doing, she'd wrapped herself in the warm flannel sheets that smelled of toast and pushed it aside.

Eve's eyes flew open. The car was getting colder, and now she felt the press of the same knot under her ribs. She'd been able to squash it numerous times in the past but tonight it was years older, having grown like a tumor. As she let her breath out, finally giving it even more room, she knew that there was a truth inside the knot that she needed to confront.

Eve turned on the engine and pulled away from the layby. She wanted to talk to someone, and sitting here was getting her no closer to home.

As she drove past the Holy Trinity Church, she saw the glint of the tall Gothic windows set high up in the fascia. The roads were quiet and, breathing easier again, she fell into a rhythm of gear changes that felt comforting. She reached a small roundabout and rather than go straight, she turned right. After a few moments she drove into Market Street and pulled to a stop outside the dark windows of the bank.

Surprised at herself, she glanced up at the lemon light glowing behind the curtains in the bay window above the wool shop.

CHAPTER 4

Jess heard the doorbell and jumped. She was focused on her laptop screen, having been home for a little over an hour. Ram had gone out straight from work with a friend and so she'd eaten an apple rather than cook. Eddie Reader was crooning in the background, and the glass of water that she'd been drinking was sweating onto the table next to her, forming a puddle on the wood. She closed the laptop, grabbed the glass and dumped it in the kitchen before trotting to the door. She checked her watch. It was 6:25 p.m. and she wasn't expecting anyone, so when she opened the door and saw Eve standing there, her face flushed, Jess was instantly alarmed.

"Mum, what's wrong?"

Eve looked embarrassed.

"Oh, Jess. I'm sorry, I should've called." She stepped back from the door.

"Not at all. Come in." Jess tugged her mother's sleeve,

pulling her inside the door. By the look on Eve's face, Jess knew that she needed to reinforce the welcome.

"Ram's out. It's just me. What's up?"

Eve walked through the kitchen and into the living room. Jess closed the door and followed her mother.

"You look upset."

She waited for Eve to speak, but instead she just shrugged, and the sight of her mother's distress wrenched at Jess's chest.

"Mum, please. What's going on?" She directed Eve to a chair and gently eased her back into the leather cushions. "Can I get you a drink?"

Twenty minutes later, Jess knelt at her mother's feet. She held one of Eve's hands, absently patting the back of it as she spoke.

"So, you're a foundling? That's what they call it, right?"

Eve nodded.

"I suppose so. It's nicer than saying abandoned." She looked up at the ceiling.

"God. I mean, I don't know what to say." Jess swallowed, feeling useless in light of her mother's revelation. "So they have no idea who your parents are?"

Eve lowered her chin.

"Well, they have some information. The broach I told you about could be a clue, and the note." She paused. "It seems that some people in Braemar kind of took her under their wing."

"Well, that's something." Jess could picture a close community rallying around a young girl hiding from her family to conceal a pregnancy. The notion was somewhat romantic, even TV-movie-esque, but the reality, far from being romantic, was extremely sad and stark. Her mother had been dumped as an infant, left under a table. Jess blinked the image away and focused on Eve's face.

"So, what are you going to do?" She sat opposite Eve on the sofa. "I mean, do you want to *do* anything?" She didn't want to pressure her mother, but Jess's natural curiosity was piqued. How could they not try to find out who this person was who'd walked away from her baby? How could they not dig a little, see if they could find out why, or what had driven her to that unimaginable act?

Eve shrugged.

"I don't know yet." She rubbed her eyes. "I'm sorry, love. I should've waited a few days to tell you."

"No, you shouldn't." Jess shook her head. "We've always told each other everything." The moment she'd said it, Jess wanted to snatch it back. She needed to release Eve from any further guilt over this whole situation. "Well, until this week, we have, anyway." She leaned over and poked Eve's knee, hoping that the levity of the gesture would break the tension in the room.

Eve looked startled. "I know. I can't apologize enough."

Jess tutted.

"I was kidding, Mum. Just let that go." She frowned. "We're fine."

Eve was studying her, and Jess felt the heat of her mother's scrutiny.

"What?"

"I just can't help wondering, when I look at you, how much of you comes from me and your dad, and how much…" Her voice faded.

"Oh, stop. I'm you and Dad. Beyond that, what does it matter?" Jess took both of Eve's hands in hers. "Winding yourself up about what-ifs will drive you round the bend. So just try not to, OK?"

Eve dropped her chin to her chest.

"I don't deserve you, Shorty." She squeezed Jess's fingers.

"I know. I've been telling you that for years."

At that, Eve laughed, a watery sound but an undeniable laugh.

Jess exhaled. "Right, wine or brandy?"

Eve shook her head. "Tea, please."

Jess tutted. "Wine it is."

The three of them sat in silence. Ram looked a little shocked but was doing a good job of hiding it, and Jess loved him even more deeply for his sensitivity to her mother.

"So, does Ken know?"

Eve shook her head.

"No. I'm embarrassed to say that I came straight here from seeing Mum and Dad, and then of course I had the glass of wine, so I didn't want to drive. Are you sure it's no trouble?"

Ram shook his head.

"Of course it's no problem. I was the designated driver tonight anyway, so I'm teetotal all the way." He smiled at Eve. "Do you want to call Ken and let him know I'm bringing you home now?"

Eve nodded and walked into the kitchen to retrieve the bag she'd dropped when she'd arrived. As soon as she left the living room, Jess stepped in close to Ram, rose onto her tiptoes, and whispered in his ear.

"Can you believe this?" She lowered herself onto her heels as Ram shook his head. "I can't believe that she never asked them about this stuff. All those years. Poor Mum." She mouthed the last two words just as Eve came back in, the phone pressed to her ear.

"I know. Sorry. I should've let you know sooner, but Jess and I got into the wine and my bag was in the other room. I didn't hear the phone." She grimaced at Jess, indicating that she was in trouble. "Yes, Ram's bringing me now. Can you drop me over in the morning to get my car?" She nodded. "Thanks, love. See you in a bit."

Jess circled the sofa and helped Eve with her jacket.

"Don't worry. Dad's fine. As soon as you tell him what's going on, he'll understand."

Eve nodded. "I hope so. He sounded cross."

Jess patted the air. "He's a kitten. Just tell him how much you love him and he'll forgive you anything."

Ram held the door open for Eve, then turned to Jess.

"See you in half an hour or so." He leaned down and kissed her. "Wait up, OK?"

Jess nodded. "It's a date."

Jess watched as the car pulled away from the space directly across the street. Ram would never be that lucky when he got home and might have to park quite a bit farther away from the flat, as he usually did at night. The taillights disappeared around the corner and she picked up the empty glasses and took them into the kitchen.

The more she thought about her mother's predicament, the more convinced she became that they had to investigate. The health history aside, there was something horribly fascinating about the fact that Eve, in one short day, had gone from being good old predictable Mum, fruit of wholesome Nan and Pop, to being not only adopted but a foundling with a mysterious past that could have implications for all their futures.

Jess pulled the living room curtains closed and made her way to the bathroom. As she wiped the mascara from her eyes, she caught the reflection of Eve's distinct bone structure staring back at her. While she was desperate to know more, tempering Jess's curiosity was the knowledge that however unwittingly, with her seemingly simple question, she was responsible for sending her mother into an unnerving spiral about her past. For that, Jess felt the undeniable weight of responsibility.

Behind her, her phone chirped. She picked it up. A text from Eve read *Thank you. Don't know what I'd do without you xxx*. Jess typed back *Ditto*.

CHAPTER 5

Ken was waiting for her in the living room. He sat close to the fire, his feet up on the coffee table, and looked tired as she flopped into the chair opposite him.

"So. Quite the day then?" He lifted his eyebrows, his expression eloquent.

Eve sighed, recognizing that it had been an odd decision to go straight to Jess.

"Yes. Definitely not what I expected." She thumped the cushion behind her and settled back in the chair.

"So are you going to tell me what happened?" He dropped his feet to the carpet and leaned forward. "Unless you don't want to?"

Eve frowned. "Why wouldn't I want to?"

He shrugged, his eyes questioning.

As Eve related the information Mary had given her, Ken moved gradually across the room. He eventually perched on the edge of the coffee table and took her hand.

"I'd never have thought they'd keep something like that from you."

Despite recognizing his predictable solidarity with her position, Eve disliked the implication that Mary and Russ had done anything wrong.

"It's mostly my fault, because I never asked them anything about my past. I did my usual ostrich act, and they were just taking their cue from me." She got up from the chair.

Ken stood up and followed her.

"I didn't mean to criticize them, but you'd think they'd have told you at some point." He shook his head. "Well, I would have, at least."

Eve leaned against the back of the chair that separated them.

"Well, we can't judge them based on what *we* might or might not have done." She swallowed. "We did, after all, keep the fact that I was adopted from Jess too."

"Aye, and I always said that was a mistake." Ken nodded to himself and shoved his hands in his pockets.

Eve felt her face grow hot.

"Yes, I know. You've told me that numerous times." She turned and lifted her coat from the sofa.

"Just a minute. Am I not allowed an opinion now?" He was behind her, his hand firm on her arm as he turned her to face him.

Eve felt the press of tears.

"That's not what I'm saying." She swiped her cheek. "You just like to remind me of things like that, like you need to reconfirm that I was wrong."

Ken dropped his hand and stepped back. "What's got your goat tonight?"

Eve shoved the hair from her forehead.

"I just found out that I was literally dumped somewhere, as an infant. So I'm a little upset. I think that's understandable." She watched him cross the room, back to the fireplace.

"But we knew you were adopted. This doesn't really change things that much." He spoke over his shoulder.

Eve took in what he was saying, a rushing sound dulling the clatter of her heartbeat.

"How can you say that?" She squeezed the back of the armchair, her fingernails digging into the leather.

Ken swung around and stared at her.

"It could potentially affect Jess." She felt a cold trickle on her top lip. "You can't dismiss this, Ken. It's like a hole has opened up in my past. A new tear in the fabric of who I am, or who I thought I was." She swallowed a sob.

Ken frowned and made to come toward her. Eve held a hand up, stopping him in his tracks.

He patted the air. "Just calm down. You're being a bit dramatic. I don't see why you're so upset. It makes no difference to me. I mean, does it really matter whether you were left somewhere or simply given to a social worker?"

Eve felt her jaw loosen. She scanned the face that she knew so well, puzzling over the blinkered perspective she'd just been presented with. Had he really no idea of how seminal this discovery could be?

"Ken, you can't wipe this one away. My history isn't spilt milk." She swept a hand down her body.

He stared at her, jingling the loose change in his pocket.

Eve sighed, forcing out her disappointment.

"Oh, never mind. I'm going to bed." She turned toward the hall. "Turn off the lights, please."

CHAPTER 6

Eve hung up the phone.

"Excellent." She slapped the top of the desk then walked to the window. Outside, the late-afternoon sky was tinged with purple as the surrounding slate rooftops of St. Andrews shone, and the glass fascia of the Union Center opposite speared up toward the clouds.

To her right, behind a tidy hedge, was the dark-blue pedestal sign honoring the original owner of the house that now was host to the University Careers Center. Thomas Rodger had been the first professional photographer in St. Andrews, living and working in the city in the mid to late 1800s. He'd constructed the building to serve as both his home and world-renowned studio. Each day, as Eve passed the sign, she would nod at the irony of Rodger's profession being aligned with her own treasured hobby. It felt entirely fitting that she worked in this particular building.

Her position as a careers adviser was demanding, and her days were often varied and unpredictable. With all the resources that her department provided to support students in their transition from academia to the working world, the most rewarding part of her role was when she heard that a student whom she'd advised and coached through the interview process had successfully landed the job. The young man she'd just been speaking to had told her exactly that, and it had made her somewhat frustrating day a touch more pleasant.

As a bus slid past on the street, she glanced behind her, the desk calendar of Grant's photographs catching her eye. The July baby was wrapped in muslin and lay in a shallow oval fruit-crate, a large sunflower tucked in next to its cheek. The crate was set in a field, with long furrows of ploughed earth stretching away like rail tracks from its base. The light was bouncing off the bloom, giving the baby a gilded glow as dust motes hung in the air, glittering around the tips of the yellow petals. This mastery of external light was something Eve was determined to figure out. In her mind's eye she saw again the image of St. Andrews Castle that she'd taken a month earlier, dull and flat by comparison to what she was looking at here.

She walked over and sat at her desk deciding that if she had time in the coming week, she'd go back and try the shot again.

Eve tipped the screen on her laptop back, focusing on the schedule for the following week. Aside from those postgraduate students who were working on theses or research projects, the majority of the student body was normally absent now, enjoying their long summer holiday. The sixteen weeks or so between May and September generally provided Eve with the time to plan for the next semester, but more students than usual were still around, and things had been hectic over the previous few days.

As her schedule seemed to jump around before her eyes, Eve's mind wandered again.

Ever since her meeting with her parents and then her subsequent visit with Jess, Eve was finding her customary controlled focus somewhat elusive. She kept rerunning the surreal conversation she'd had with her mother, seeing the words on the fading note and feeling the weight of the thistle broach, which she now carried with her each day. Picturing the jagged shape again, the etched prickles and sharply angled leaves, she reached down and pressed her pocket. She wasn't sure why she was putting it in her pocket or in her handbag each morning before she left the house, but somehow it had become a habit. Without it, she'd begun to feel less than fully dressed and even as she acknowledged that fact, it felt ridiculous.

When Ram had dropped her off a few nights ago, after their argument, and her departure for bed, Ken had followed her upstairs. He'd been contrite, asking her to tell him more about the startling information that she'd been given. His rumpled shirt and sagging eyes had melted her anger, and they'd stayed up late into the night, talking.

"Well, information is power, I suppose. So what's the next step?" He'd paced across their bedroom, his pajama bottoms trailing on the carpet.

Eve hadn't been sure.

"Um, I suppose I have to contact the child protection people, see if there was any official record of the girl, and if they have an idea of how we might find her."

Ken had nodded, crossing his arms over the round of his

stomach that was distorting the logo on the Rangers T-shirt she'd bought him for Christmas.

"Makes sense."

As was his way, the following day, Ken jumped into the driver's seat and said he'd try to locate a phone number and a website that might help her find what she was looking for. She'd bitten her lip, letting him do it, not saying that she'd prefer to be allowed to figure this out for herself.

Despite him pushing her to start the search, she still had not used the information he'd written down. The web link and phone number were scribbled on a sticky note that had been smouldering in her handbag ever since she'd tucked it in there. She was afraid to start a process that had a totally unknown outcome. There were so many questions roiling inside her now, where previously there had been calm acceptance. What if they traced the woman and she was dead? What if they found her and she had no interest in meeting Eve? What if they never found her? What if there were other children, a slew of half siblings that Eve had no idea existed? How would that change her own family dynamics? Would they soon be inviting half-cousins and faceless aunts and uncles into Jess's life? All of these potential scenarios had been keeping Eve awake at night and now, as she watched a young man walking past the window, she yawned. There was nothing for it. Jess needed answers, so Eve must continue asking questions.

Her handbag was full of so much unnecessary rubbish that she frowned, her fingers pressing down to the bottom, feeling for the note that she'd stuck to a packet of travel tissues. Locating the soft rectangle, she pulled it out. Ken's handwriting was bold, much like his character, which she valued and occasionally even envied. He wasn't easily flustered, and right now, despite her reluctance to have him direct her in this search – which felt intensely personal – she was grateful that he'd helped. She pulled the note from the surface of the packet and stuck it to the desk. Now was as good a time as any.

Ken had cooked. The minute she walked into the house, she could smell fried onions.

"Hi, love." She tossed her keys into the dish on the table, slung her bag over the bannister, and made her way into the kitchen.

He was wearing an apron with a kilt and sporran on the front which always made her laugh.

"How's my hearty Highlander today?" She wrapped her arms around him.

"Unhand me, woman. I'm in the middle of a culinary experiment." He kissed her and then nudged her gently away with his stomach, his hands held up in front of him like a surgeon.

"Oh, what's on the menu?" Eve peered over his shoulder. "Can I help?"

He shook his head. "Nope. I'm making stovies. My mum's old recipe." He jabbed at the frying pan with a spatula. "Something's wrong though."

Eve tutted. "What've you done?" She looked at the mess of sausage and potatoes.

Ken shrugged.

"I dunno. I did what it said." He turned to her, his tongue sticking out comically. "Oh, well. We'll just have to use lots of ketchup."

Eve went to the dresser and pulled out two placemats.

"What time did you get back today?" She shoved the fruit bowl out of the way and laid the mats on the pine tabletop.

"A bit early. Around three." He stirred the pan, his shoulder moving in small circles with the spoon. "Jess said she'd close up, because she was later in today than usual."

Eve frowned. "Why?"

Ken shook his head.

"Not sure. I think she said the doctor."

"Again?" Eve moved in next to Ken and picked up the salt and pepper grinders. "She was just there the other day."

Ken glanced at her over his shoulder.

"Aye, right enough. So she was." He frowned. "Well. I'm sure she's fine." He turned back to his task. "OK. This looks like crap." He dropped the spatula and pouted. "Fancy fish and chips?"

Having saved the stovies with a little beef stock and some grated cheese, Eve sat opposite her husband. His plate was empty, but hers was still half full. Her appetite had seeped away as she mulled over the information that she'd been given on the phone earlier.

"So, I called child protection today." She pushed the plate away.

"Oh, good."

"There's quite a bit of procedure to go through."

"Unsurprising."

"I think I'll have to go in to the Edinburgh office, see if

they'll let me look at the records of my adoption, etcetera."

"Right, right." He paused. "I'll come with you."

Eve felt a rush of new nerves.

"Ken, I'd rather you didn't. Just initially." She watched as his eyebrows arched.

"Are you sure?"

Eve nodded.

"Just initially, until I see how the land lies." She paused. "Once I know what this whole thing entails, we'll figure the rest out. OK?"

He assessed her as he rose, then picked up their plates and dumped them in the sink.

"Just don't take it all on by yourself." His voice was low. "You'll need some moral support."

Eve smiled at her husband.

"I won't. I mean, do it all myself." She stood up and met him as he walked toward her. He circled her waist with his meaty arms.

"I thought I'd ask Jess to come with me," she whispered, and then felt his back stiffen.

He stepped back and looked at his feet. "OK."

"She's the one with all the questions, after all."

In Ken's silence, Eve felt the ground shifting under her argument. While she wanted to make it clear that she intended on navigating this uncharted course herself, she'd hurt his feelings, which was the last thing she'd intended.

"For some reason, this feels like something Jess and I need to do together."

"Is this about the other night?" He frowned. "I thought we'd got over that."

She shook her head.

"No. It's not about that. It just feels like a mother-daughter thing – literally." She paused. "Two generations' worth."

Ken met her gaze.

"That's fine. I understand." He nodded, but she saw his lip protrude.

"Do you?" She watched him turn to the sink.

He tossed a dishcloth onto the counter and looked at her. She knew he was wanting to step into his customary role of adviser, but that wasn't where she needed him right now, and getting him to understand her need to do this her way felt paramount.

"I think so." He shrugged.

Eve crossed the room and slipped her hand into his.

"It's not a slight or a vote of no confidence in you. This is about me."

He enclosed her in his arms.

"OK. I get it." He patted her back.

She spoke into his chest. "You're the best, Ken Carruthers."

"I am. There's no denying it." His breath was warm as she lifted her head to kiss him.

The following morning, Eve stared out of the window and the phone was heating her cheek. Jess had asked her to hang on while she served a customer, and Eve was flicking her gaze between the clock and a crow pecking at the thick worms that were surfacing on the lawn after the rain. Ken was on his way in to the shop, and Eve wanted to have this conversation with her daughter before her husband arrived at the other end.

"Sorry, Mum. All quiet, then three people came in at once. Typical." Jess sounded breathless. "What's up?"

Eve scanned the lawn for the crow.

"I wanted to ask if you'd come to Edinburgh with me. Next week."

"Oh." Jess laughed. "Is that all? Of course I will."

"I'm going in to the child protection office to see what they can tell me about my adoption." She paused. "Well, if they know anything about before I was placed with Mum and Dad."

After a few moments, Jess sounded tentative. "I'll come. Of course. Is Dad going?"

Eve shook her head in the quiet room.

"No. I thought this was something you and I could do together. Just us girls."

Eve waited, hearing the cogs of Jess's mind grinding. Her daughter might be young, but she was extremely sensitive and compassionate. She'd see the potential for this to hurt her father, and Eve wanted to reassure her that Ken was on board.

"Dad's OK with it. I've explained that it's about mothers and daughters, for now." When Jess didn't respond, Eve exhaled. "He's all right, Jess."

"If you're sure."

Eve nodded. "I am."

After they settled on the following Tuesday for their trip, Eve picked up her camera and headed for the door. She'd taken the day off, and St. Andrews Castle awaited.

CHAPTER 7

Jess knew that her driving made her mother nervous. She'd tried to stay aware, but the more they talked the heavier her foot became on the pedal, and before she knew it, she was speeding again.

"Jess. Please." Eve sighed. "Take it easy."

They'd been on the road around an hour and the giant red cat's cradle of the Forth railway bridge was visible ahead. Both the old and the new, suspended road bridges ran parallel to the more interesting, cantilevered railway bridge, and Jess had always loved to stare at the towering structures as they'd crossed the firth on road trips.

"Here come the bridges." She smiled over at her mother.

Eve nodded. "Same as ever."

"Well, I always say that." Jess pouted. "Won't stop now."

Eve laughed. "I wouldn't ask you to."

The car slowed as the traffic built up ahead, road works

slowing the flow of the lanes accessing the bridge.

"So, what's the name of the person we're meeting again?" Jess eased the car in front of a lorry that had stopped to let her merge.

"Helen something." Eve leaned down and lifted her handbag onto her lap. Jess glanced over as Eve felt around inside the bag, eventually pulling out a crumpled note. "Helen Fields."

"Right." Jess nodded. "We're making good time, too."

"Uh huh."

"The appointment is twelve thirty, right?" Jess braked as the car in front of her halted.

"Yep." Eve was looking inside her bag again and frowning, then Jess noticed her pull out an envelope and turn it over in her hand.

"What's that?"

"It's from your dad." Eve flapped it.

"What's in it?" Jess laughed. "Directions in case the GPS fails? Your blood type, name, and address in case you get lost?"

"I know. He's a bit of an old woman." Eve pulled a piece of paper from the envelope. She paused. "It comes from love, though."

Jess enjoyed the way Eve often defended Ken, even when Jess was only teasing. She'd noticed Ram doing the same for her recently, and it felt good to be so loved. However, with this last statement, her mother had sounded as if she were reassuring herself of her father's motivation.

"What does it say?" Jess switched lanes. Below them, the expanse of silver water separating North Queensferry from South Queensferry stretched into the distance.

Eve unfolded the paper.

"Dear E, Don't let Jess speed and remember to take the North Bridge and then turn left onto the Royal Mile so you can park near the council offices. Here's a wee something so you can have a nice lunch somewhere. Call me when you get there. Love the pair of you. K."

Eve flapped a twenty-pound note.

"Wahoo. We're going to partay." Jess laughed.

Eve tutted. "All right, Shorty."

Thirty minutes later, they walked under the high stone arches of an arcade and crossed a cobble-stoned quadrangle. In front of them stood the grand sandstone building housing the council offices.

"It's quite impressive in person." Jess tipped her head back.

Eve nodded absently, studying the paper with the details of her meeting.

"Mum?" Jess reached over and touched her mother's shoulder. "It's going to be OK."

Eve turned to look at her, and Jess caught a flash of anxiety clouding the usually calm grey eyes.

"I know. I just never thought I'd..." Eve's voice caught, and with the truncation of the phrase, Jess flinched. Once again she was bitten by the thought that if it hadn't been for her, her mother might have lived out her life in blissful ignorance of the details of her birth, and her abandonment.

"You know, we don't have to do this." She pulled back on Eve's shoulder, stopping her progress across the quadrangle.

Eve met her gaze.

"We can walk away. I'll get all the blood test results soon, and anything else we don't know about won't hurt us." Jess waited as Eve licked her lips. Despite their closeness, her mother could be hard to read sometimes, and today, in this odd moment, Jess was at a loss.

Eve chewed her lower lip and then shook her head abruptly.

"No. It's not just about that anymore." She frowned. "It's about me too now."

Helen Fields's office was dark. Located on the second floor and on an inside leg of the building overlooking the Royal Mile, its narrow window was shaded by the wall of the section next to it. Helen, a small, rotund woman with a tight red perm and what Jess's grandmother would call solid ankles, had left them to retrieve some files, a mild lilac scent floating in her wake.

Jess looked around the room as Eve fidgeted in her chair. There were several photos of ruddy-cheeked children on the desk, and Jess leaned over and picked up one of the frames.

"Do you think they're all hers?" She smiled at Eve, who was frowning.

"Put it back." Eve pointed at the desk, her voice a forced whisper. "Please."

Jess set the photograph down and rolled her eyes.

"We're not in the headmaster's office, Mum."

Eve obviously registered Jess's teasing tone, and she saw her mother's face relax.

"Sorry." Eve smiled. "She's younger than she sounded on the phone." She nodded toward the open door just as Helen walked back into the room, a beige file held across her chest.

"So, there's not much really, but we've got a few documents

here, Mrs. Carruthers. Shall we go through them?" She shunted her chair up close to the desk and spread one of the folders out across the surface.

"Yes. That's fine." Eve mimicked the move, pulling her chair up to the edge of the desk.

As her mother twisted the piece of paper she'd been holding into a narrow rod, Jess wanted to reach out and calm the nervous hands, but doing so would only draw more attention to Eve's anxiety.

"I've made copies of the things I'm permitted to share with you." Helen held a few pages out to Eve, who took them, letting them drop to her knee without looking at the contents.

Helen lifted a flimsy sheet of paper from the folder.

"So, first of all we have the registration of your arrival into the care system in 1977." She looked over the edge of her reading glasses.

Eve nodded mutely.

"According to this, as I'm sure you know, you were initially brought to a foster family here in Edinburgh, having been found over in Braemar."

Jess noticed a pinkening of Helen's cheeks as she leaned back in her chair, suddenly seeming uncomfortable with her choice of words.

"Found, yes," Eve whispered.

"Sorry, I..." Helen faltered.

"It's fine. Go on." Eve's weak smile yanked at Jess's heart.

Helen cleared her throat.

"So, it says here that you were found in a tea shop garden by a woman on holiday. You were in a baby basket."

Eve nodded and Helen, taking the cue, continued.

"The local social worker in Braemar was told, perhaps by the person who found you, or more likely some of the locals, that your birth mother had been in the village for some time when she gave birth. It also says here that it was believed she came from the Fort William area."

Eve's eyes widened.

"Really? How did they know that?"

Helen shrugged. "Apparently, based on that info, they tried to contact social services in Fort William at the time, but there was no way to trace the mother."

Eve flicked a glance at Jess, then shifted her focus back to Helen.

"So then there's the record of your placement in the foster home here in Morningside, with a Mr. and Mrs. Wheeler, for eight weeks, after which you were placed permanently with Mary and Russell Parvin of Pittenweem, Fife."

Eve nodded. "Yes, my parents."

Helen smiled. "Well, you know the rest then."

Jess swallowed. Her mother's profile was sharp in her peripheral vision, the strain showing across Eve's shoulders. This was harder than Jess had anticipated. For some reason, hearing the information, even the part they'd already known, stated somewhat clinically here in this stuffy office made it sadder, heavier to bear. Jess uncrossed her legs and leaned in toward her mother.

"All right, Mum?"

"I'm fine. Please, Ms. Fields, go on."

The woman smiled broadly, revealing a row of white,

uneven teeth.

"Call me Helen, please." She dipped her head, squinting at the papers in front of her. "Well, that's really all we have here. Most of the rest of it is just internal processing forms and a copy of your birth certificate, which I'm sure you've seen?" She lifted a yellowed document that had been folded several times.

Eve sat up straight.

"Actually, I haven't." She shook her head slowly. "Oddly enough."

"Your parents didn't give it to you?" Helen frowned. "What about when you got married? Didn't you need it for the license?"

Jess felt a jolt to her middle. What Helen had said was true. How had Eve managed that?

"Well, my mum took care of it. She went to the registrar with Ken, my husband." Eve blushed. "I was in school."

Helen's eyebrows lifted.

"Ah. That makes sense then."

"May I?" Eve leaned forward, her eyes on the paper in Helen's hand.

"Of course." Helen held it out. "There's a copy of it included there." She pointed at the documents lying across Eve's lap.

"Oh, thanks." Eve opened the certificate gingerly with her fingertips, as if it might disintegrate with every move to unfold it.

Jess watched as her mother studied the dark print.

"Birth date June 24th, 1977. Mother unknown. Father unknown." She lifted her eyes and turned to Jess. "That's bizarre, isn't it?"

Jess swallowed and pushed the hair out of her eyes. "Yes, it is."

"So how would they know that?" Eve's voice was stronger now. "That that is my exact birthdate?" She eyed Helen across the desk.

Helen reached for the paper that was now quivering in Eve's hand.

"Well the date would have been determined by the doctor who examined you immediately after you were surrendered."

"So it was a guess?" Eve sounded shocked.

"Not a guess, Mrs. Carruthers. An estimation made by a medical professional who saw you shortly after your birth. And I'm sure there would have been local testimony too, from the people in Braemar."

For the first time since they'd arrived, Jess heard a trickle of irritation enter Helen's voice. She reached over and squeezed Eve's arm.

"I think medically, they can be pretty accurate with that stuff, Mum." She waited for Eve to turn to her, but instead her mother continued to stare ahead as if she wasn't fully present in the room.

"Right, I suppose so." Eve sounded dreamy.

"As I mentioned on the phone, I think you'll have more luck with Family Connections." Helen placed the certificate back in the folder, closed it, and laced her fingers across her stomach.

"Thanks for helping me get that appointment." Eve ran a hand through her hair.

"You're going this afternoon, correct?" When Eve remained silent Helen glanced at Jess for confirmation.

"Yes. Three o'clock." Jess smiled. "To see a Mr. Patterson, right, Mum?"

Eve was standing up, sliding her handbag up onto her shoulder.

"Uh huh."

"Well, I wish you the best of luck." Helen stood and extended a fleshy hand. "These cases can be hard, but Daniel is an excellent resource. He'll steer you right." She shook Eve's hand and then reached for Jess's.

"Thanks, Helen." Jess smiled at the woman who had given them little more than confirmation of what they already knew. Mother, unknown. Father, unknown.

The restaurant on Cockburn Street was busy. Jess had chosen an Italian place, enjoying the potential for a rare meat-centric lunch that she wouldn't feel guilty about eating. The smell of garlic was heavy in the air, and their tiny table was tucked in close to one of the windows overlooking the street. Eve sat across from Jess, her face flushed and her eyes darting around the room.

"How's the spaghetti?"

"Good, nice." Eve forked a twist of pasta into her mouth.

"Ram would love this. Us chowing down on carnivorous treats." Jess took another bite of ravioli, the rich red sauce trailing down her chin.

"Shorty, really." Eve tutted and pointed at her own chin. "Dribbling." Eve's face melted into a smile as Jess wiped her face with a napkin.

"So you'd really never seen your birth certificate?" Jess

reached for the spoon and sprinkled more Parmesan on to her pasta.

"No. Nan went and got the marriage license, and I never thought to ask for it at any other time." Eve shrugged. "Another of my ostrich impersonations, I suppose."

Jess swallowed her mouthful and shook her head.

"Not an ostrich, exactly." She paused, wanting to divert the conversation away from any more of the self-flagellation that Eve was prone to. "Why would you ask for it? I mean, you only gave me mine when we got married, right?"

Eve nodded.

"So it's understandable then." Jess lifted her wineglass.

Eve laid her cutlery on the empty plate and pushed it away from herself. "That was great. Far too much for lunchtime, really, but worth every calorie." She dabbed her lips.

Jess wiped the remainder of the meat sauce up with a piece of bread and popped it into her mouth.

"Thanks for offering to drive back." She grinned, speaking around the bread. "I really fancied a glass of vino."

Eve laughed. "Yes, I got the hint."

As much of the lunch crowd began to filter out, Eve and Jess sipped their cappuccinos. The Family Connections office was close by on New Street, an easy walk from where they now sat. Eve had just explained that the private organization worked with people to help them trace their birth parents and family members when the cases were particularly challenging – where there was a lack of information or if the individual had a somewhat less-than-orthodox route into the care system. Jess had been skeptical at first, asking if they were like a detective agency.

"No. They just help track down information in more obscure case histories. Seems like they help you uncover paper trails, dig up old records, access electoral roles, census information, etcetera – things that might give a clue to the past."

Jess nodded. "So they charge you for the help?"

Eve shook her head. "No, it's a charitable group. They work from donations and grants."

"Ah, right." Jess licked some froth from her top lip. "So this Patterson guy. Have you talked to him yet?"

"No. Just his assistant, when I called to confirm the appointment." Eve paused, and Jess saw a frown split her forehead.

"What?"

"Nothing really." She pulled her mouth down at the corners. "What if he says I'm wasting my time? Or he's no help at all? We could be on the proverbial goose chase."

Jess reached over and patted Eve's fingers, halting their plucking at the tablecloth.

"It'll be fine, Mum. Just breathe."

Forty minutes later, having made their way up the gradual incline of the cobbled street, they left behind them the staunch outline of Edinburgh Castle high on its rocky pedestal. The afternoon sun was warm on their backs and the fascias of the tall buildings they passed on either side curved concavely with the bend in the road, as the smell of ground coffee followed them up the gentle hill.

The building they were looking for was tucked behind another, and it had taken them a few minutes to figure out the location was in an alley rather than on New Street itself.

The reed-thin, middle-aged woman who'd greeted them had been pleasant, offering them water before disappearing down a corridor, leaving them hovering in a musty reception area.

"We're not late, are we?" Eve shoved her shirtsleeve up to look at her watch.

"Not at all." Jess shook her head. "Bang on." She leaned over and gently bumped Eve's shoulder with her own. "Ten out of ten for timeliness."

Eve laughed, swiping the hair away from her forehead with her index finger, the movement a perfect duplication of one Jess performed several times a day.

As Jess dropped her handbag onto the floor, a tall, slim man in his mid-forties with startling blue eyes walked into the room.

"Mrs. Carruthers?" He looked directly at Eve. He was suntanned, and his thick hair was greying slightly at the temples. His smile reminded Jess of a poster on the wall in Ram's surgery, the teeth almost too perfect. She tried not to stare.

"Dan Patterson. Pleasure to meet you."

As Jess watched, Eve stood up, and to Jess's surprise, her mother blushed as she took the man's hand.

"Yes, lovely to meet you too."

CHAPTER 8

Jess had been quiet in the car on the way home. Eve, her mind reeling as she tried to focus on the implications of her conversation with Dan, kept looking over at her daughter, who was staring pointedly out of the window.

"Jess, is everything OK?"

"Yep." She sounded sniffy – a term Eve used when Jess's nose was out of joint.

"What's up? It went well, I thought." Eve negotiated her way around a car that was going under the limit.

"He was a bit annoying, didn't you think?" Jess glared at Eve. "So full of himself." She sounded sulky, and the childish tone caught Eve off guard.

"What? He was perfectly nice."

"All that stuff about him living in France and giving you his entire life story. I mean, who cares?" Jess tutted. "Today wasn't about him."

Eve smarted at the edge in Jess's voice. What had started out as a pleasant if somewhat angst-ridden day together was suddenly deteriorating. As she took in her daughter's profile, the slim nose and softly rounded cheek, the long fair hair falling heavily over one shoulder, Eve felt her eyes prickle. That had been happening more often recently, her emotions seeming to crouch directly under her skin since the question of her history had been raised.

"You sound cross. He was just being friendly." Eve braked hard as the car in front of her slowed.

"I'm not cross."

Eve took a deep breath. "Look, Jess, this is difficult stuff. If you're feeling…"

Jess cut her off. "It's not that. It's you."

Eve glanced sideways. "What on earth do you mean?"

Jess yanked the seatbelt away from her throat and shifted in the seat, turning her hips toward Eve.

"You were all fluttery, totally flirting like a teenager. It was a bit embarrassing." Her face was flushed.

Eve frowned. Jess's words cut her, and yet, swimming around under their implication, Eve felt a sliver of acknowledgment. Dan had been charming, forthcoming, kind, attentive, and undeniably attractive. Was it abnormal to have responded as most women would to a man like that? Eve studied the wing mirror as she maneuvered the car into the middle lane. Jess's accusation may have been harsh but, as Eve replayed the scene in the Family Connections office, she knew that she'd been less than her usual collected self.

"I think flirting is a bit of an exaggeration, don't you?"

"Not really." Jess shook her head. "You should've seen yourself."

Eve felt the tiny cube of guilt she'd just acknowledged dissolve. Whatever the truth, Jess was very rarely disrespectful.

"Don't speak to me like that, Jess." She paused. "You're totally overreacting."

Jess sniffed, her hands going into her hair as she twisted the long tresses into a knot, forming a makeshift bun.

"Perhaps I was a bit over-friendly, but he was taking an interest and helping me. Helping us." Eve swallowed. "There was nothing more to it than that." Even as the words came out, Eve doubted their authenticity. If she were completely honest, the details of their conversation with Dan had not been the only thing occupying her mind since leaving his office. She'd also been thinking about his magnetic eyes, the cultured way he'd spoken about having lived in France while doing his master's degree and the way he described the cottage he owned in the Dordogne. As she acknowledged that, Eve was freshly ashamed.

Jess was staring out her window again.

"Look, sorry if I seemed a bit fluffy in there." Eve spoke to the back of Jess's head. "But he's an impressive man, and I was just nervous."

Jess nodded and then turned to look at Eve.

"Honest?"

"Oh, of course. You know me. I'm useless with good-looking people. It took me about a month to talk to Ram without stammering."

Jess let out a laugh. "God, yes. You were useless."

Eve smiled, the tension between them dissipating.

"Jess, you know I love your dad, right?"

"Yes, but you two seem to be a bit prickly with each other these days." She paused. "It's not like you."

"Let's just forget all this, OK?"

After a moment's pause, Jess nodded.

"Right. Sorry." She shook her head, releasing the hair from the knot at the back of her neck. "I didn't mean to…"

Eve reached over and patted her thigh.

"It's OK. We're both a bit wound up today. Understandably."

"Do you think he can really help us find them?"

Eve shrugged. "Well, he has more ideas and resources than we could ever come up with ourselves, so if he can't – I'd say no one can. I wouldn't have known to list myself on the Adoption Contact Register."

Jess nodded. "And you want to go to Braemar to ask around like he suggested?"

Eve considered the question. It made sense that she go to where it had all begun, but she really had no plan of what she'd do once she got there.

"Yes, I want to. Probably soon, too, before term starts."

Jess pulled her phone from her bag and checked for messages. "Can I come with you?"

Eve studied the road ahead. The thought of spending more time with her daughter was irresistible, regardless of the unpredictable reconnaissance mission they'd be on.

"Oh, yes, would you? I'd love that." She smiled.

"Will Dad be OK in the shop without me, do you think?"

"I'm sure he'll manage." Eve nodded. "He's a big boy."

After dropping Jess off at home, Eve pulled into her driveway and saw Ken's dark-green Audi crouched in front of the garage.

"Hi. I'm back," she called from the hall as she heard pots clanking.

"In here."

She checked her reflection in the mirror. Her hair was windblown from driving with the window open, so she smoothed it back, running her fingers through the knotted waves that had formed behind her ears. Leaning in, she wiped mascara smudges away from under each eye and took in the thin lines that were emerging around her mouth, like matching brackets. Her freckles always came out in the summer, as did Jess's, and the sight of them scattered across the bridge of her nose was reassuring – they were testament to another undeniable connection with her daughter. For some reason, those tiny threads were taking on greater importance now.

Ken walked into the hall and came up behind her. His arms circled her waist as he addressed her in the mirror.

"Hello." He kissed her cheek. "How did it go?"

"Oh, well, I think." Eve turned into his embrace, rose onto her tiptoes, and kissed him. "Come on, I'll tell you all about it."

Ken finished cooking dinner as she sat at the kitchen table and recounted the day's events.

"So, this Helen didn't really have anything new?" He stirred the risotto.

"Well, the only new thing we learned was that someone told

the social worker in Braemar that the girl came from around Fort William."

"Really?"

Eve shrugged. "Helen thought that the person must've known her."

He nodded. "Aye, makes sense, I suppose." He served steaming risotto onto two plates and set one in front of Eve. "So what's next?"

Eve dusted the rice with Parmesan shavings and handed the spoon to Ken.

"Well, after speaking with Dan Patterson at Family Connections, I think I have to go to Braemar." She hesitated. "He said that because there's so little documentation about her, going to ask members of the community if they knew her might help." She forked some rice into her mouth.

Ken cranked the grinder, covering his food with black pepper.

"Hmm, I suppose so. Seems a bit archaic though, in this age of technology." He topped up her glass. "We should probably take a few days. I can get Jess to mind the shop and we'll make a trip of it." He was smiling.

Eve swallowed, feeling her throat suddenly thicken around the fragrant rice.

"Can we talk about that?"

Ken frowned, his tan cheeks pulsing as he chewed. "Talk about what?"

"About Braemar."

He eyed her over his glass. "And?"

Eve dipped her head, avoiding the heat of his scrutiny.

"I was thinking that Jess and I should go, you know, finish

what we started." Even as she said it, Eve knew that this was another barb in Ken's side, but for some reason she couldn't help herself. She had only just knocked the top off of this search and, whatever form it might take, the desire to see it through without him directing her was overwhelming.

When she finally looked up, his expression was sullen.

"But I thought we agreed that I'd help you, once you'd been to Edinburgh?"

"I said we'd see how it turned out." There was a slew of questions in his eyes. "Ken, for some reason this feels like something I need to do without you." She forced herself to swallow. "I don't want to exclude you though." She paused.

"Well, it sounds like you do." Ken shoved some rice into a heap. "Why can't I help?" He eyed her once again.

Eve shook her head. Watching him digest what she'd said, she followed her own trail of questions. Did she really want to take this on without him – the man who'd been her best friend and biggest supporter for her entire adult life? She saw his eyes cloud over as her silence extended itself across the table. She owed him some kind of explanation.

"I think it's that you're always fixing things for me, finding the lost, replacing the broken." She waited for some sign of acknowledgement in his face, but Ken's frown had only deepened. She took a breath. "Sometimes, when you're just being you, plotting our course and taking care of everything, I feel like I'm not capable of certain things, so I just take a back seat."

Ken's mouth opened slightly.

"What are you talking about?" He shoved his plate away and leaned forward on his elbows.

Eve frantically tried to garner her argument, to clarify in her own mind what she needed him to understand. As she recognized her desire to go on this journey without him, she considered that for as long as she'd known Ken, he'd been shielding her from the unknown or the unpleasant, putting himself in front of life's blows so that she might not hurt as much. Perhaps because she'd been so young when they'd married, he had assumed the role of protector. If she was honest, there were times when she'd felt excluded from the fullness of her own life by his gatekeeping. It might be late in the game, but it was time she found out, for once, if she could handle a challenge without him.

She studied his face, the familiar eyes, the shock of greying hair, the slightly lumpy nose that had broadened with the years. Suddenly, Eve couldn't see his face for tears.

"You've always been there for me, holding me up, filling in the gaps, making things better. But for once, I need to figure this out myself." She paused. "I rely on you too much. You're like my connective tissue."

Ken stood up and lifted his half full plate. "I don't mind that, Eve."

"That's exactly it." She felt a cold trail running down her upper lip. "I know it might sound clichéd, but I feel like I need to prove myself capable of figuring this out."

Ken dumped his plate in the sink.

"Capable?" He turned and stared at her. "That's the daftest thing I think you've ever said."

Eve finally wiped her nose with her napkin. "Don't do that. Don't make it sound small."

"You're more capable than anyone I know." Ken walked back to the table and hooked his large hands around the back of his chair. "Is there something else you're not telling me?"

Eve shook her head. "No, honest. I just need you to trust me."

Ken was watching her as she ran a thumb under each eye.

"Why are you crying?" His voice had softened.

"Because I don't want this to hurt you."

He circled the table and crouched down at her side, his broad stomach supported by his denim-clad knees.

"Give me your hand." He reached for her fingers.

Eve let him close her hand in his.

"You know that I trust you."

She nodded.

"You can do this whatever way you want to." He stood up. "Just don't shut me out completely."

Eve met his gaze.

"I won't. I promise."

Ken walked to the counter, came back to her and exchanged the soggy napkin in her hand for a dry sheet of kitchen paper.

"Use this. That one's waterlogged."

Eve felt a tiny bubble of laughter catch her by surprise. Ken had a way of making her laugh even when she thought it impossible.

"Thanks." She smiled at him. "I love you."

Ken nodded.

"Aye, and I love you back."

CHAPTER 9

Jess wrapped the sheet of wax paper around the wheel of cheese. As she reached up to tuck her phone tighter under her chin, she caught her fingertip on the wire cutter that was curling over the broad wooden board.

"Damn." She stuck her finger in her mouth.

"What's up?" Ram laughed in her ear. "What've you done now?"

She tutted. "Cut my finger again."

The door to the shop opened and Ram walked in. Jess grinned and switched off her phone.

"What're you doing here?" She peeled off the nitrile glove, wrapped her finger in a tissue, then skirted around the glass-fronted display cabinet and hugged him. "Nice surprise."

Ram kissed her neck.

"Missed you, so I thought I'd see if you could have a bite of lunch." He reached over her shoulder for a sliver of brie that

Jess had laid out on a platter for customers to taste.

"Hey, that's not for you." She tapped his hand. "Dad's not here, so I can't leave." She walked behind the counter. "But I can make us something."

Ram hunched over the misty glass case, examining the contents. He pointed at the haunch of prosciutto.

"I'll have a chunk of that."

Jess laughed. "That's pork, you loon."

Ram crossed his eyes at her.

"So, I'll have some Anster, a slice of Blue Murder, and some of that Isle of Mull." He pointed to a slab of crumbly golden cheese. "Throw in some French bread and some chutney too – wench."

Jess clicked her heels and saluted, then worked quickly making two cappuccinos and assembling a plate for them to share. She stopped to serve a customer before joining Ram at one of the wrought-iron tables in the courtyard.

She pushed the plate toward him and he took a huge bite of bread as she broke a corner off the triangle of blue cheese. She popped it into her mouth and followed it with a dried apricot, the combination something she'd recently discovered that she adored.

"So, when's the Braemar trip again?" Ram watched her pull some dark grapes from the cluster.

"Not sure exactly, but I think Mum wants to go soon." Jess licked her fingers. She hadn't realized how hungry she was until she'd started eating.

"Makes sense." Ram nodded, spearing an olive with his fork. "And your dad's OK with not going?"

"Mum says he is."

Ram nodded, but something in his face was giving Jess pause. She could often read his mood by the set of his jaw, the flicker of his eyelids, and the way his nostrils flared slightly when he disapproved of something.

"What? Do you think I should check with him?" Jess frowned, a grape suspended in front of her mouth.

Ram eyed her over the rim of his cup.

"Well, I'd be surprised if he's not a bit upset." He shrugged. "They do everything together."

Jess felt the truth of the statement. She'd been concerned about Ken too, but when Eve had assured her that he'd be all right, Jess, despite her misgivings, had not pursued it. Now, the idea of Eve excluding Ken from something as important as this took on weight. Perhaps there was more to this decision than Eve was sharing.

"Damn, I knew I should've talked to him." She popped the grape into her mouth. The skin burst, sending a spurt of tart dew across her palate. She closed her eyes and let the flavor soak her tongue for a moment, enjoying the warmth of the sun on her shoulders.

She looked at Ram.

"Talk to him when he gets back. I think he'd appreciate it."

She nodded, reaching for another piece of cheese.

"I will. I'm worried about them. They seem off at the moment."

Soon after Ram had returned to his surgery, Ken arrived with three large cheese rounds tiered up like a wedding cake. As he carried them into the shop, Jess could smell the pungent scent of coffee.

"Did you get more Isle of Mull?" She lifted the top round from the tower in her father's arms and placed it on the counter.

"Yep, and another coffee cheddar and an Anster. Can't keep that one on the shelf." He smiled at her. "Everything OK?"

Jess cut the string off the wax paper that covered the Anster, a peppery cheese that was made locally in St. Andrews.

"Yep. Ram popped in and we grabbed a quick lunch."

Ken nodded. "Oh, shame I missed him. How's the boy?"

"Great."

She shifted some produce around inside the display cabinet, making room, and then piled the remnants of the previous wheels on top of the new ones.

"Good stuff." Ken deposited the rounds he held onto the marble slab behind the counter. "Did he take a bit of Blue Murder home? He likes his Blue Murder, does the boy."

Jess tutted.

"He ate enough of it here." She closed the sliding door on the cabinet. "We'll have to watch it. We're both putting weight on." She patted her stomach. "A minute in the mouth etcetera." She smiled at her father, who had opened the tall drinks fridge and pulled out a bottle of spring water. There was something in his body language that bothered her. He seemed deflated.

Having served three separate couples, Jess cleared the courtyard tables of dishes. With the empty plates lined up precariously along her arm, she walked back inside.

Ken was staring out of the window, a melancholy aura hovering around his broad shoulders.

Jess set the dishes on the counter. "You OK, Dad?"

He jumped, turning to face her. "Aye, I'm fine."

"You looked miles away." She watched him reach behind his back and tie on one of the long white aprons that he liked them both to wear when they were serving.

"Yes, I was." He shrugged. "Probably just a bit tired."

Jess assessed him. His face did look slightly paler than usual, and he had dark shadows under his eyes. How had she not noticed this earlier that morning?

"Is it Mum?" She moved behind the counter, squeezing past Ken.

He looked surprised by the question.

"Why would it be about Mum?" He waited as Jess filled the coffee grinder with fresh beans from a burlap sack, the silky beads cascading through her fingertips.

"Well, this whole Braemar thing." She spoke over her shoulder but could feel the waves of his discomfort permeate her back. She turned in time to see his jaw jut out.

"I suppose it's bugged me a bit." He paused. "But I understand her need to do this, with you." He met Jess's gaze.

"Are you sure?" Jess moved toward him. "I feel a bit weird, but Mum said you were fine with it."

Ken nodded, shoving a basket of long baguettes back into a corner.

"I *am* fine. I mean, I'm getting used to the idea." He shrugged. "She and I've always been partners in crime so to speak, so it's a bit disconcerting. But I'll get over it." He winked at Jess, but she saw no true mirth there. It was obvious that he was hurt, and so she felt her role in the current situation more keenly.

"I don't think there's anything to it, Dad. She just felt it was…"

"Jess, I'm all right." Ken cut her off. "She'll involve me when she's ready. I'm a big boy, I can cope." He tipped his head to one side, a gesture Jess often made herself, and recognizing that made her smile.

She leaned her shoulder in to meet his. "I'll bring you back a bag of caramels."

Ken laughed. "Oh jeepers, don't spoil me too much."

The afternoon passed with a steady stream of customers, some buying cheese to take away and many sitting in the courtyard to eat and enjoy the afternoon sunshine. Jess had watched the flow taper off toward 5:30 p.m. as the sky turned a pale pink above the rooftops and the gloaming settled over the city. She'd washed down all the counters, filled the coffee grinder again, wiped the tables, and stored the fresh food in the fridges. Ken was cashing out the register as she hung up her apron and picked up her handbag.

"I'm off, Dad."

He nodded.

"Right-o. Say hello to Ram." He sounded distracted as she made for the door.

"Will do. Give Mum a kiss from me."

He waved at her without looking up, so she turned and left her father to his thoughts.

Ram was waiting in the car on Church Street. She saw the headlights flash as she emerged from the lane. Waving, she darted toward the little Ford. It was cooler outside now, the unpredictable early August evenings often becoming chilly in St. Andrews as the breeze blew in from the sea.

Ram leaned over and opened the passenger door.

"Hi." She ducked inside the car and kissed him.

He looked over his shoulder and pulled away from the curb. "Fancy eating out tonight?"

Jess nodded. "Absolutely. The Twisted Vine?"

The restaurant on South Street had become a favorite due to the extensive vegetarian menu. Jess and Ram generally ate there midweek and, being regulars, would often be given a table without a reservation. Their favorite table, under a section of vaulted ceiling, was tucked in close to a heavily carved wooden screen, allowing them a view of the restaurant but still feeling private.

The place was surprisingly quiet for a Friday.

"Not too busy tonight." She scraped up some lentil daal from the bowl with a scrap of naan. When she looked up, Ram was smiling at her.

"What?"

"Nothing." He laughed. "Enjoying that?"

Jess felt herself redden.

"So? I'm hungry. I enjoy my food. What's the crime?" She knew she'd sounded petulant, so she followed the statement by crossing her eyes. Frowning, she drained her water glass. She'd need to get a grip if she didn't want to gain the infamous newlywed pounds that she'd read about. One article she'd recently seen had been titled "The Weight of Contentment," and when she'd read it, she had dismissed it as nonsense.

Ram shook his head and finished his raita.

"So, what did your dad say about Braemar?"

Jess wiped her mouth. "He says he's fine but he's obviously a bit put out."

Ram nodded slowly. "Not surprising." He stacked their empty plates and reached for Jess's hand.

She wound her fingers through his.

"Maybe he and I could spend some time together while you ladies are away?" Ram caught the waitress's eye and mimed signing something.

Jess felt her heart lift. "That'd be great. What could you do?"

Ram shrugged.

"I'll think of something. Perhaps we can squeeze in a round of golf, or maybe there's a new girlie bar opening or something?"

Jess laughed loudly. "Just you dare."

Walking back to the car, Jess leaned into Ram's shoulder. "Do you think this is a good idea, the whole search thing?"

He pulled her closer.

"I think it must be the right thing to do, especially if your mum is so keen to pursue it."

"But once we get the blood tests back, we'll know the most important things anyway. I tried to give Mum a get-out-of-jail card in Edinburgh." She waited for Ram to weigh in, but he just nodded silently. "Perhaps if I told her again that we don't need her to do this?"

Ram stopped at the edge of the pavement, gently turning her to face him.

"Jess, this has become a much deeper issue. The fact that you kicked it off is almost irrelevant."

She knew it to be true. Eve had told her as much herself.

"I know." She ran a finger under her fringe. "It just feels like I've created a monster somehow, and I'm worried for Dad." She paused. "And Mum."

CHAPTER 10

Eve put the last of her clothes and her compact camera in the small suitcase. She'd packed for three days, and the bed and breakfast in Braemar had confirmed that she could extend by up to two more if she needed to. She'd booked a twin room for her and Jess, and while Eve was naturally looking forward to their few days together, there was a strange, new staccato quality to her breathing which she was putting down to a combination of excitement and nerves.

Ken was being stoic, but she had been tiptoeing around the subject of leaving for the past few days. He'd kissed her and wished her luck when he'd left for work earlier that morning, and now, as she zipped the case closed, Eve couldn't wait to get on the road.

The drive into town was short, and with good traffic-light Karma, she was outside Jess's flat within fifteen minutes. The sandstone buildings looked dull today, their customary pink glow washed out as the sun hid behind a thick layer of rain-threatening cloud.

As she watched, the lights came on in the dark bookshop to her right and a silhouette moved around inside, opening blinds and gradually illuminating the long shelves that stretched like runways deep into the belly of the narrow building.

The passenger door opened, making her jump.

"Sorry, I was grabbing some snacks for the road." Jess dumped a rucksack onto the back seat and they kissed each other's cheeks. Eve smelled toothpaste, coffee, and a trace of the musk aftershave that Ram used. Jess's hair was loose, splitting over her shoulder like long golden curtains.

"That was nice of you, to make snacks." Eve wiped away the trace of lipstick she'd left on Jess's jaw.

"It's nothing much. Just some samosas from last night and a couple of oranges." She smiled. "Ready to hit the road?"

Eve nodded. "Let's go."

They wove through the slow buildup of morning commuters and, once clear of the town, headed for the Tay Bridge. The route was one that Eve had taken hundreds of times, but today, despite the struggling light, the long hedgerows bordering the road between Guardbridge and Leuchars seemed a richer green than usual. The familiar inn that huddled low on their right, far out on the sandy flat at the river's edge, looked brighter than usual, the white of the pebble-dash glowing in fierce contrast to the surrounding pastures.

"That place is so pretty." Jess spoke Eve's mind.

"It is. We've never been in there, you know. In all these years." Eve smiled. "We're such creatures of habit, your dad and

I." The words out, Eve felt a jolt of recognition. She and Ken had become exactly that, rarely breaking the mold of what their life had become. As the realization permeated, Eve wondered if Ken felt the same.

Jess was staring at her, and Eve felt the scrutiny of the clear blue eyes against her cheek.

"Well, that's easily changed." Eve could hear the frown in her daughter's voice so she stroked the hair out of her eyes and focused on the road.

"Your dad doesn't like change, but things and people *do* change, and we need to learn to grow with it."

After their speedily organized marriage, she and Ken had been inseparable throughout her pregnancy. They'd shared their dreams, secrets, her tiny bedroom at her parents' cottage in Pittenweem, and their hopes and fears of parenthood. Then, when Jess had been born, she'd immediately become their focus. Their everything. While it was rightly so, Eve mourned the lack of uncomplicated time that they might have had as a couple. It had all been too fast, and now, almost in their forties, there were gaps in their knowledge of one another that were surfacing more frequently.

When Jess had moved in with Ram, Ken had thrown himself into the gardening, spending his entire days off outside, clearing, weeding, planning, and planting. She had been happy that he was so obviously enjoying it, but despite her appreciation of this new time to herself, underlying that had been her growing loneliness. He'd used the garden as an escape to fill the void Jess's departure had created, and in turn she had retreated to her camera, watching the world outside of their lives take place through a lens.

When she glanced back over, Jess was frowning and Eve instantly wished she could edit her last remarks. With everything that was going on, all of the new uncertainty around their family history, she had chosen a bad moment to blurt out an unfinished thought. Jess was a free spirit, but Eve knew that deep down her daughter needed the reassurance that all was well with the foundations of her world.

After a few moments, Jess turned and looked out of her window.

"What would you do differently, then?" She spoke to the glass.

Eve pressed her foot down on the accelerator, wanting to gather speed and move them through the momentary awkwardness she'd caused.

"I'm not saying I would change anything, maybe just shake us up a little. Get us out of our comfort zone now and then." Eve glanced at the back of Jess's head. "We could make more effort."

Jess swung around, and Eve caught a glimpse of her daughter's loose mouth.

"What do you mean, more effort? In what department?"

Eve felt a heat creeping up her sternum. The more she elaborated, the pricklier Jess was becoming.

"Never mind. I was just thinking out loud."

"No, tell me. Are you two really OK?"

Eve felt the tip of the question, like a splinter piercing her chest. This was the first time that she'd put words to something that had been nibbling at her.

"Of course we are." She turned to see Jess redden.

"Honestly, just forget I said anything."

Jess chewed at the skin around her thumb.

"Well, I think if you're bored, you should make the first move. Tell Dad you want to break out a bit. You know he'd do anything for you."

Eve blinked as a splash of sunlight split the cloud ahead, spearing down toward the road. Jess sounded sullen. If ever there was any conflict between her parents, Jess would generally defend Ken. Rather than be upset with Jess about that, Eve had registered the way Ken would use their daughter's support as leverage to get his way.

Eve forced herself to take a breath. "I'm not pointing fingers, Jess, I just think that both of us could be more open to new things. Maybe go abroad for a break somewhere, or even just try a new restaurant, go into Edinburgh to the theater once in a while or take ballroom dancing lessons. I don't know."

Jess snorted. "Ballroom dancing? You two? You've got four left feet between you."

Eve forced a laugh.

"Well, maybe not that, but something." She paused.

"So, what're we going to do about Dad?" Jess finally smiled. "How are we going to shake up the old stick-in-the-mud?"

As they laughed together, the sound of their melded voices snapped the string of tension that had stretched between them.

They spent the next half hour in silence. Jess had her nose buried in her phone, apparently scrolling through pages of what Eve guessed were texts from Ram.

"Missing you already?"

"Oh, sorry. I'm being antisocial." Jess slipped the phone

back into her handbag.

They had already crossed the River Tay and left Coupar Angus behind. This was the section of the journey that Eve was looking forward to, as the stretch of whitewashed bungalows in the village of Blairgowrie hugged the quietening roadside. She'd always loved the row of one-level homes with their immaculate gardens, and walls draped with Virginia creeper. Had she and Ken not chosen St. Andrews, she was convinced that this village would have been where they'd have settled.

"I love those cottages." She nodded over her shoulder.

Jess glanced out her window. "Yep, kind of picture-postcard perfect."

Eve heard a faraway quality to Jess's voice. "You OK, love?"

Jess twisted her hair into a rope.

"Yep, just hope Dad's not going to mope for three solid days." She stuck her bottom lip out comically.

Eve sighed.

"We'll call him every day. Make sure he feels involved." Eve consciously pushed away the press of guilt that threatened to spoil her mood. This was her time with Jess, and she didn't want to waste it regretting her decisions up to this point.

As they crossed into Aberdeenshire, the A93 wound due north, taking them through the moss-green valley of the Cairnwell Pass, at the head of Glenshee. The undulating landscape on either side of them slid away from the road, gradually rising steeply on their left toward The Cairnwell and Carn Aosda peaks and on the right to Meall Odhar and Glas Maol. The stunning Cairngorms' jagged fingers were tinged with purple as the early heather bloomed on the upper slopes.

As she navigated the gentle bends in the road, in her peripheral vision, Eve caught the glint of Shee Water. The river followed the line of the road, slicing the green carpet between their car and the mountain in two.

"Do you remember when we came here skiing?" Jess's voice cut into the silence, startling Eve.

"Yes, of course. You were seven." Eve smiled at the memory. "You were telling the instructor what to do after two lessons."

Jess laughed. "Sounds about right."

Eve recalled Jess's face under a red pompom hat, her long golden plaits trailing down her back as she stomped around in the tiny pink ski boots they'd rented. She'd become so attached to them that she'd wanted to take them home. Her inherent stubbornness had brought on a tantrum and only after Ken had patiently persuaded her that while they were very pretty, she'd soon be too grown up for them had Jess given up on the notion.

As was happening frequently now, Eve's examining the elements that made up both her daughter's and her own character reminded her that she had no idea who she took after. Her birth mother could have been an empath, a mild-mannered person or, for all Eve knew, a shrew. She sucked her cheek in, feeling the sharp edge of her teeth bite into the flesh. What had her father been like? Why had they decided to let her go? As the road wound away ahead of her, she wondered what lay around the next bend.

Eve had looked at several B&Bs online, but something about the face of this house had pulled her in. It was a former Victorian shooting lodge with twin bay windows below and three ornately corniced dormers above the stone facade. The house was set in a beautiful, formal garden just on the edge of Braemar, and Eve hoped that the reality would live up to the photographs she'd seen on the website.

As she pulled the car into the gravel driveway, far from being a disappointment, the reality surpassed the cyber-beauty of the images she'd seen at home.

As the tires crunched over the stones, Jess sighed. "Oh, it's gorgeous, Mum."

Eve beamed. "Well, I thought, why not treat ourselves?"

"Too right." Jess grabbed her rucksack from the back seat and climbed out of the car. "We deserve it."

The owner of the B&B, Mrs. Atchison, was a rotund woman in a faded kilt and mint-green twinset. She was standing on the doorstep as they approached the house, her glasses dangling on a chain between her heavy breasts.

"Welcome. You must be Mrs. Carruthers?" She held out a blotchy hand.

"Yes, good to meet you, Mrs. Atchison." Eve gestured toward Jess. "This is Jess, my daughter."

"Call me Mrs. A. Keeps things simple." She dipped her chin. "Hello, Jess."

"Hello." Jess smiled, but hung back.

"Did you have a good drive over?" Mrs. Atchison assessed their bags, and Eve caught the hint of a frown as their host spotted Jess's tatty rucksack.

"We did. No problems." Eve stepped sideways, positioning herself between Jess and Mrs. Atchison, whom Eve noticed smelled slightly of bleach.

"Come away in then." She walked ahead of them into the cool hallway.

After a quick rundown on the various house rules, which had made Jess's eyes flare, Mrs. Atchison beckoned them to the stairs.

"I'll show you to your room then."

They followed obediently up the wooden staircase, Eve widening her eyes at Jess when she pulled a face at the broad, kilted behind, all but obscuring the light streaming in from the window on the landing at the top of the stairs.

Jess nudged Eve's elbow and she glared at her daughter, mouthing, "Stop it."

"This is our only twin." Mrs. Atchison opened the door and let them pass. "The Glenduggan Room. You were lucky we had a last-minute cancellation. This is our busy season, with the Braemar Gathering next week. Her Majesty comes every year, you know." She glared at Eve.

Eve picked up on what sounded distinctly like a scolding from the older woman. Deciding to let it go, Eve set her bag down and walked past the high twin beds, taking in the matching wooden headboards and thick yellow quilts. She stood at the wide-paned window and looked down at the splendid garden. Surrounded by a lush hedge, the lawn was manicured and the flower beds were expertly shaped, trimmed, and brimming with a tumble of English-country-style summer color. A table and chairs sat at the far end on a flagstone patio, and a green umbrella fluttered in the midday breeze.

"Oh, your garden is exquisite." She turned to smile at the grey-haired proprietress, who was holding the large brass room key on an incongruous purple climbing carabiner.

"Thanks. Hubby and I spend hours out there." She patted her stomach. "It's great exercise. Keeps us in shape."

Eve shot a glance at Jess, just as Jess closed her hand over her mouth and walked into the small en-suite bathroom.

"Feel free to sit outside if you'd like. The no-smoking rule applies in the garden too, I'm afraid."

Eve shook her head. "We don't smoke."

Mrs. Atchison didn't seem to have heard her the first time when Eve had said the same thing downstairs.

"Breakfast is from eight to nine thirty and, once again, we close the front door at nine p.m. You'll need the smaller key to get in after that time." She jiggled the keyring, and Eve stepped forward and took it.

"Right. Thank you."

Mrs. Atchison stepped out into the hall.

"If you're still here at the weekend, it's the Jacobite 1715 reenactment, and then there's a concert at St Margaret's too." She nodded.

"Oh, sounds lovely." Eve hoped she sounded suitably interested. "But I don't think we'll be staying that long."

"Well, if you need anything, just ring the bell downstairs. I'll be around and about." She smiled.

Eve met the older woman's gaze, noticing that despite her slightly crisp manner, Mrs. Atchison's pale eyes were kind. Eve wondered where "hubby" was and what kind of life the couple led as innkeepers. As she pondered the amount of work running a place like this would take, she was suddenly rewarded by the image of "hubby" in his matching kilt, digging out weeds as Mrs. A directed him this way and that. Eve forced down a laugh.

"Mrs. A., I was wondering if there's a café in the village that backs onto the river?"

Mrs. Atchison's eyebrows shot up, as if she hadn't expected to be needed quite this soon.

"Oh, well, yes. There's the Garden Café on the river. It's just a wee place but does decent coffee and cakes. Light lunches too." She nodded and folded her arms across her stomach as if protecting herself from said baked goods.

"Right. Does it have an outside sitting area?"

Mrs. Atchison nodded. "Yes, that's the one."

Eve smiled. "Thanks. I think we'll go for a walk and see if we can find it."

"Just go down Invercauld Road, you can't miss it."

With that, she closed the door and was gone.

Jess came out of the bathroom, her face pink.

"What a character." She patted her stomach theatrically. "Keeps us in shape, my foot."

Eve tutted. "Jess, stop. She's very pleasant."

Jess nodded and crossed her arms under her breasts. "The no-smoking rule applies in the garden too, you know." She grimaced.

Eve laughed despite herself. "OK. Enough now. I want to check the Adoption Contact Register again, then let's unpack and head into town."

Jess tossed her rucksack onto one of the beds and then spread her hands out like fans.

"That's me unpacked. Let's go and get something to eat. I'm starving."

CHAPTER 11

Jess carried the plates out to the narrow terrace that overlooked the river. Eve had snagged a table near the railing and was leaning over, looking down at the water, her camera against her eye.

"Here you go." Jess set the plates down.

"Thanks." Eve slid her sunglasses onto the top of her head and set the camera on the table.

Jess flopped into a chair and bit into her sausage roll.

"So do you think this is the place?" A tiny flake of pastry floated out with her words.

Eve nodded and sipped her coffee as Jess looked around. There were eight tables, all with the same wooden slatted chairs around them. While it was well past lunchtime, the café was still full and the low hum of voices floated across the flagstones, while below them was the constant burble of the river sliding over time-smoothed rocks. The long wooden planter boxes lining the patio were filled with fuchsias hanging their heavy pink heads. Jess put her head back and breathed in deeply. The air smelled different here than it did in briney St. Andrews.

Eve had been quiet since they'd arrived at the café, but Jess knew that this was often her mother's modus operandi when she was working up to something.

She eyed Eve across the table. "So, what's the plan then, Sherlock?"

Eve set her cup down. Her face was serene, eerily devoid of emotion.

Jess's humorous jibe having fallen flat, she tried again. "Mum?"

Eve blinked at her as if processing a reply.

"I'm going to ask inside if they know anything about the story." She shrugged. "I know it's donkey's years ago, but I've got nothing to lose."

"Right." Jess nodded. "Do you want me to come with you?"

Eve pushed her barely touched food away and nodded. "Yes, please."

Jess pulled her mother's plate toward her and lifted the sandwich.

"Jess, really?" Eve laughed.

"What? It's a waste to leave it." She took a huge bite and then crossed her eyes at Eve, who was shaking her head. Sensing that the proverbial iron was hot right at this precise moment, Jess dropped the rest of the bread onto the plate. "OK, let's go." She spoke clumsily around the food, causing Eve to close her eyes and shake her head again.

Inside the café there were a further six tables, all of which were occupied. Across the room, Jess spotted a wood-burning stove with a bench in front of it, and in another corner, two leather armchairs were pulled up close to a low table. The air was heavy with cinnamon and bacon, and even though she had just eaten a giant sausage roll, and part of Eve's sandwich, the wonderful smells made Jess's stomach rumble.

Eve moved ahead, making her way toward the long counter where the woman who had served Jess earlier was refilling a glass-domed cake stand with fresh scones.

"Excuse me." Eve sounded apologetic.

Wanting to bolster her mother's resolve, Jess moved up next to Eve and wound her fingers around the loose hand.

"Yes, how can I help you, pet?" The woman's auburn curls framed her freckled face and Jess guessed that she was in her mid-thirties, by the bright eyes and smooth skin.

Eve cleared her throat, and Jess gave her mother's fingers a squeeze.

"This might be an odd question, but do you know who owned this café thirty-nine years ago?"

The woman threw back her head and laughed.

"Well, that's not what I expected." She smiled at them. "Heavens above."

Eve laughed nervously and swiped the hair out of her eyes.

"Sorry, I know it's a daft thing to ask but I…" She paused. Her fingers went up to her throat. "Something happened here in 1977 and I was wondering…"

The woman cut her off. "Did you say 1977?"

"Yes, I know it's a long time ago."

"Uh huh." The woman nodded. "So what was it that

happened?" The ready smile was gone, and she looked curious now.

Eve leaned in closer to the counter and lowered her voice.

"A baby was left here, abandoned here." Her voice cracked. "Outside on the terrace, I think."

The woman's eyes were wide now.

"Oh my god."

"Someone found the baby and handed her in to the authorities."

The woman nodded mutely.

"I'm trying to find anyone who might have known about the incident, or maybe knew the child's mother." Eve paused, turning her glassy eyes to Jess.

Jess stepped forward.

"We're hoping that we can trace the girl, through some of the community here in Braemar who apparently helped her at the time." Jess smiled. "Is there anyone we can talk to who might know what was going on around then?"

The woman frowned and carefully set the glass dome she'd been holding, over the pile of scones.

"1977. Well, the only person I know who was definitely here, and who knows everybody's business, is Scot Kerr." She winked at Jess. "He's a gardener over at The Old Hall. He'd be your best bet." She pushed her lower lip out. "He's a bit of an old duffer, but I'd start there if I were you." The woman glanced back at Eve and, seeming to sense her discomfort, smiled warmly. "I hope that's helpful?"

Eve snapped back to life and nodded vigorously. "Oh, yes. That's great. Thank you very much."

Jess reached over the counter and extended her hand. "Yes, thank you. Where is the hall?"

Her stomach was jumping, any residual appetite having disappeared. They had their first lead, and she had to admit it was exhilarating.

The woman lifted a tea towel and wiped her hands on it before shaking Jess's.

"On the way out of the village, on Old Military Road, before you get to the castle." She jabbed a thumb over her shoulder. "It's got a big green sign and black gates."

"Thanks again." Eve patted Jess's shoulder. "Let's go."

The Old Hall was set far back from the road, perched on a rise with expansive lawns disappearing under a dense row of pines. Out in the middle of the largest lawn to their left was a fountain where two dolphins leaped, nose to tail, forming a perfect circle under the spattering water.

As they drove into the parking area, Jess craned her neck, looking up at the impressive building. The tall Gothic arches and carved baronial stone facade, with crow-stepped gables and narrow turrets, reminded her of childhood fairy stories.

"It's like something out of a book." She wound the window down farther and stuck her head out. "Smells good here, don't you think?" She looked over at Eve.

"It does." Eve nodded. "Like cut grass."

The double-fronted door had an ancient iron ring in the center and a long metal rod mounted on the stone at the side that Jess guessed operated the doorbell. The sign said to use the side door for reception, but Jess couldn't help herself so she reached out and pulled the iron rod.

"Jess, I swear." Eve sounded exasperated. "Can you just behave?"

Jess stepped back. "God. Relax, Mum."

Eve flashed her an angry look, and Jess felt her cheeks warming.

"OK. Sorry. Let's go round the side."

The reception area was noticeably cooler than outside, the narrow slats of windows cutting out a good portion of the daylight. Jess squinted until her eyes adjusted, focusing on the broad wooden desk ahead of them. There was a smell of mothballs that made her think of her grandmother's house. Jess smiled.

"What?" Eve was looking at her.

"Smells like Nan's."

"Yes. It's camphor." Eve reached over and squeezed Jess's hand. "Thanks for doing this with me."

Jess nodded just as a young blond man in a dark suit emerged from a paneled door behind the desk.

"Good afternoon. What can I do for you young ladies?" His tone was patronizing.

Jess felt her hackles go up. She hated to be talked down to, especially by someone who looked to be no more than her own age. Not waiting for Eve to speak, Jess stepped forward.

"Yes, we'd like to speak with Mr. Kerr please. We understand he works here." She did her best to sound imperious and it obviously worked, as Eve's head snapped over her shoulder in Jess's direction. Undeterred, Jess went on. "We've been told that he's a gardener here."

The young man looked startled as he flicked his gaze from mother to daughter.

"Em, yes. May I ask what it's concerning?"

Eve stepped forward and extended her hand.

"Hello, I'm Eve Carruthers. We'd like to talk to Mr. Kerr about something that happened here many years ago." Jess saw her smile at the man. "Apparently he's considered the local authority on all things Braemar."

The young man smiled broadly at Eve as he grasped her hand.

"I'm Graham."

"Nice to meet you, Graham."

Jess felt bad for her clipped tone. She took in her mother's gentle profile, the fair hair tucked behind one ear, the smooth jawline and high forehead so reminiscent of her own. Eve had a magical way of making people relax and of diffusing awkward situations. She was non-threatening, a listener, and Jess often felt that her mother could feel what she, Jess, felt – almost be inside her skin. While it could be unnerving at times, she envied Eve those qualities. Jess felt she was lacking in her ability to sense others' moods or read the emotional map of their mannerisms and gestures. Her tendency to leap before she looked often landed her in hot water. That was why Ram was such a great match for her. Jess felt a pang of loss. It had only been half a day, but she already missed her husband.

"True enough. Old Scot's a right encyclopedia of the goings on around here." Graham laughed. "Never a dull moment."

Eve gestured toward Jess.

"This is my daughter. We're just here for a day or so from St. Andrews, so is Mr. Kerr here today?"

Graham nodded.

"He is. I can try to call him. That's if he's got the mobile with him." He rolled his eyes. "He does like to leave it in the shed."

Letting go of her ire, Jess let out a laugh, picturing an old codger in a holey sweater and muck-stained trousers tutting at an annoying phone that tracked his movements.

After making a call that went unanswered, Graham led them out into the gardens. If the lawns in front had been impressive, as they rounded the huge hall, the sight that awaited them behind the Gothic structure was staggering. Jess caught her breath as stretching out ahead of them, a network of stone paths meandered between densely planted beds of lavender and heathers. Swaths of yellow and white daisies lined the outermost edges of the beds, which were hugged by thick hedges, manicured to form a wall of green. To their left was a wildflower garden. A tumble of colors and heights, tall feathery plants sat next to small-petaled petunias and thick clumps of purple thistles. At the far end of the central path was a round clearing, in the center of which sat a gazebo. Several stone containers lined the outer circle filled with fragrant sweet peas and trailing shrubs that dribbled over their edges, looking artfully unplanned. The effect was spectacular and Jess, knowing how her mother liked to sit out in her own garden, watched as Eve's mouth went slack.

"Oh my goodness." She turned to Jess. "Have you ever seen anything like it?"

Jess shook her head. "It's like bloody Versailles." She pointed at a cluster of pale-pink blossoms. "What are those?"

Eve shrugged. "Geraniums, maybe. Your dad would know."

Graham paced ahead of them, circling the gazebo. They

trotted to keep up with him, mother and daughter glancing around themselves and then back at each other as the gardens went on, extending far behind the summer house and eventually ending at a row of three greenhouses.

"He'll likely be in there." Graham pointed to the first structure, a long narrow house with several glass panes missing and an orange wheelbarrow leaning against the front.

"Scot, you in there?" Graham poked his head inside the open door. "Scot?"

Moments later, a stooped man appeared. Much to Jess's amusement, he was the epitome of the crusty caricature that she'd visualized.

"Aye, I'm here. What d'ya want?" The old man wiped his hands on a filthy cloth, his fingernails black with soil.

"These ladies would like to talk to you." Graham gestured toward Eve. "Have you five minutes?"

Scot's face was so wizened that Jess couldn't tell whether he was squinting, frowning, or indeed smiling at them.

"No' really. What's it aboot?" He eyed Eve, then tucked the corner of the towel into the waistband of his trousers.

Graham turned toward her, and Jess noticed that he was blushing.

"I'll leave you to it." Passing Jess, he whispered. "Good luck."

"Thanks, Graham." Jess rewarded him with a smile and noticed his color deepen.

Eve had moved closer to the old man.

"Hello, Mr. Kerr. I'm hoping you can help me." She let her handbag slip off her shoulder. "I understand you know a lot about what goes on here in Braemar?"

Scot coughed, the wet rattle of mucus making Jess cringe.

"Aye, I know some." He shoved his cap farther back on his head. "What are ye' askin' aboot?"

Eve repeated the question she'd asked the woman in the café and as Jess watched, the old man's eyebrows did a dance.

"A baby, you say?" He narrowed his eyes. "Aye, I do remember that. Not every day a wee bairn gets left alone for an'bdy to find." He shook his head and shoved his hand deep into his pocket. "Damn shame, so it was."

Eve glanced at Jess before continuing.

"So, did you know the young girl?"

Jess could hear the excitement in Eve's voice. As a few seconds passed, Jess willed the man's head to nod, for Eve's and for her own sake. Eventually he complied.

"Aye, I knew her a bit. Quiet wee thing." He shifted his feet, his boots leaving clods of earth behind as he moved.

"Oh." Eve's eyes were wide, and Jess thought she could almost feel the sparks of anticipation coming from her mother's back.

"What was her name again?" Scot closed his eyes. "Fae oot west somewhere." His eyes sprang open. "Fiona, that was it. And just a bairn herself'."

Eve stepped back and reached for Jess's hand. Jess tried to force herself to breathe slowly. He knew the girl. He knew her name. Jess could feel Eve's pulse under her fingertips, the vein jumping at an alarming rate.

"So, her name was Fiona. Did you know her surname?" Eve's voice was shaky.

"Naw. She didn'y talk much. Understandable, mind." He

shrugged. "Sad wee lass."

Jess watched as Eve blinked several times, obviously trying to gather her thoughts.

"Is there anything you can tell us, or anyone who might know more about her?" Jess heard herself ask the question, her mind teeming with possibilities.

Scot stared at her, as if her asking questions was more of an intrusion than Eve's doing so.

"Who's askin' anyway? Who're you?" He scowled at her.

Apparently having rallied, Eve jumped in.

"I'm the baby. It was me." Her face was scarlet now.

Jess hadn't expected Eve to share that much information with a complete stranger. It was uncharacteristic for her quiet and immensely private mother.

"Christ alive." The old man's eyes flared. "Y'er not." He shook his head, removed his cap, and wiped his bald scalp with the dirty towel. "In the name o' the wee man."

As he moved, Jess caught the scent of wet soil and smoke.

"I am. It was me." Eve pressed a hand to her chest. "I'm trying to find out anything I can about my birth mother."

Jess swallowed. This was brutal, emotional, and thrilling all at the same time. She took in the set of Eve's jaw and willed something good to happen. Jess didn't know what a negative outcome or a dead end might do to her mother.

Scot shuffled his feet again, forming a pile of soil behind himself.

"She worked at the wee bakery on Evans Road. Just off the High Street." He jabbed a thumb over his shoulder. "They sorta took her in."

Eve nodded.

"I don't suppose the people there now would know anything, it's been so long." She shook her head.

"It's the MacPhersons' place. The mither had it then, the daughter has it noo'." He put his dirty hand over his mouth and hacked three times. Thumping himself in the chest, he took a deep breath. "Ailene MacPherson's her name, the daughter."

Jess could see Eve's shoulders quivering.

"You can ask her, or her mither'd maybe tell you'." He paused. "I think the wee lass lived somewhere around there too."

Jess, feeling suddenly lightheaded, made her way slowly around to the side of the greenhouse. She laid her palm flat on a warm glass panel. This was all becoming real, perhaps too real.

Eve had pulled a small notepad out of her bag and was writing something down.

"Will they be there today, do you think?" She spoke to the paper, her pen moving rapidly.

"Naw. Closed th' day. It's Mond'y." He frowned. "T'morra morning now."

Eve nodded, clicked her pen closed, and dropped the items in her bag.

"Thank you very much, Mr. Kerr." She extended a hand. "I'm so grateful."

The old man wiped his palm down his trouser leg and then grasped Eve's hand. Jess watched as he appeared to take in Eve's face for the first time. He cleared his throat.

"So, ye'r all right then?" He stepped back from Eve and squinted. "You had a good life?"

Jess felt herself slipping. Her head was spinning, and as she tried to focus, her heart was beating like a snare drum. The voices were becoming farther away, and then the sound of the ocean in her ears was the last thing she heard before sliding to the ground.

Eve dabbed the damp washcloth on Jess's forehead. Their room at the B&B was cool, the open window sucking in the evening breeze as Jess lay on top of her bed.

Seeing her daughter slip to the ground had been terrifying, and Eve had shouted Jess's name, a disembodied sound that she hadn't recognized as her own voice.

Old Scot had been marvelous, calling up to the hall for help and getting Jess some water from his flask. Jess had quickly come around, looking deathly pale as tiny beads of sweat had bloomed on her forehead. However, despite Eve's protestations, when they arrived back to the hotel, Jess had refused to be taken to the nearby medical practice to be checked out.

"I'm fine, Mum. I just got dehydrated and I think I was overexcited." She'd grinned at Eve. "Honestly, I'm fine."

Eve patted her daughter's thigh, rewet the cloth in the bathroom, and then laid it on Jess's forehead.

"Do you want some tea?"

"No thanks." Jess sat up. "I could eat something though." She frowned at Eve. "Surprisingly."

Eve chuckled.

"Well, if you're hungry, that's probably a good sign." She perched on the end of the bed. "What do you fancy?"

Jess shoved her bottom lip out.

"Chips?" She looked so young, her damp hair in disarray with baby blonde strands curling around her hairline.

"You're not serious?" Eve laughed again. "Healthy options are off the menu then?"

Jess nodded. "We can be healthy tomorrow."

Eve picked up her handbag and searched for the car keys. "Do you think we can sneak out without seeing Mrs. A.?"

Jess laughed. "Mum, you are awful. I thought you liked her?" She was up and brushing her hair at the dressing table mirror.

"I do, I did. She's fine. I just have so much on my mind I don't feel like exchanging niceties."

Jess tossed the brush onto the table. "I know. It's amazing that old Scot knew the girl. Her name. Where she worked. Fiona." She paused. "What are you thinking?"

Eve shrugged. "I'm excited. Scared. Want tomorrow to come and not to come." She shook her head. "It's all so much, Jess."

When they'd arrived back at the hotel, Eve had left Jess to rest and gone downstairs to call Ken to fill him in on the day's progress. Jess had made her promise not to tell him she'd fainted, and Eve had agreed. There was no point in worrying him, especially as Jess seemed fine now.

Ken had been bright on the phone, almost slightly forced.

"That's great. So, you actually know her name?"

She'd sat in the quiet guest living room, closely watching the swing door to the kitchen in case Mrs. A appeared. They'd talked for ten minutes, and she'd told him of her plan to go to the bakery the following day.

"So you think this bakery woman might remember her?"

"Well, the current owner's mother might, according to Scot."

Ken had laughed. "Oh, so Scot said so, did he?"

Eve smiled. "He's about eighty and smells like manure."

Ken tutted. "Well, stranger things have happened."

She shook her head in the empty room. Ken liked to pretend at jealousy, but this time there was a point to his teasing that felt sharper than usual. She knew that he wasn't jealous of any one person, more of the situation that had taken her away from him so she'd diverted the conversation.

"You should see these gardens, Ken. Absolutely stunning."

His silence had been eloquent until finally, he'd replied.

"Well, we'll need to go back there together then."

"Yes, we will." She was grateful for the olive branch. "We will."

Jess held the greasy paper up under her chin. The chips were piping hot, and she'd soaked them in vinegar before heading back to the car. Eve licked her lips, tasting the crusted salt. They'd decided to eat and then go back to the lodge in case Mrs. A objected to the smell of chips in her lovely house. They were parked in Invercauld Street, and the overhead streetlight cast an orange glow over the pavement as several customers wandered into the shop.

Jess finished her meal and crumpled the paper into a ball.

"So, shall we do a drive-by? Check out the location of

the bakery?"

Eve shoved the messy papers into a plastic bag and tied it closed. "Yes. Let's."

Within just a few minutes, Jess was pointing out the window. "There it is. On the left."

Eve pulled over and switched off the engine. The Bakery had a broad bay window that pouted over the pavement, and blinds had been half pulled down to hide the empty shelves inside. The weather-worn sign above the window had once been dark green with gold lettering. Now, it read, "Th akery" and there was a "closed" sign hanging in the glass pane above the letterbox.

Eve took in the face of the place that had once been a sanctuary to the mother she'd never known. There was a distinct warmth to the little shop, despite its obvious worn edges.

She stared at the door and pictured a young girl, pregnant, scared, twisting the brass handle, going inside and asking for help. The idea of her darling Jess being in that situation, in her early teens, made Eve shiver.

"You OK?" Jess touched her shoulder.

"Yes. Fine." Eve shoved the hair away from her forehead. "Can I ask you something?" She turned to Jess.

"Uh huh."

"If you'd got yourself in trouble, I mean, if you'd fallen pregnant in high school or something, would you have told me?"

Jess frowned. "Of course. I tell you everything."

Eve nodded, knowing it to be true. "You wouldn't ever have thought that we wouldn't have supported you?"

Jess shook her head. "Well, if I'd been super young, I know

you'd have been angry and disappointed. But you'd never have turned your back on me. You or Dad."

Eve nodded. "No, we wouldn't."

She watched a young couple holding hands as they walked past the car.

"I just can't imagine what she must've been feeling." Eve frowned. "So young, pregnant and totally alone. What kind of parents must she have had?"

Jess shrugged. "I know. I'd hate any child of mine to be too scared to tell me the truth. I'd consider that a huge failure on my part."

Eve assessed her daughter's fine profile. The pride she had in Jess was growing with the years. The more she saw the compassion and depth of the young woman she and Ken had created develop, the more she marveled at the universe gifting them with such a daughter.

"You're exactly right, Jess. It would be a failing indeed."

They passed a disturbed night in the hotel. Jess had been restless and Eve, unable to sleep, her mind in overdrive, had lain and watched her daughter toss the covers off, pull them back on, thump her pillow, and sigh repeatedly. Even though she knew Jess to be awake, she hadn't spoken, as if to do so would promote their wakefulness to a new level.

The light outside the window was purple, a reflection of the heavy cloud that had descended by the time they'd got back from the village. Eve stretched her legs out, feeling for the cool spot at the corner of the mattress. She glanced at the bedside clock. 5:17 a.m. Only two and half hours until she could get up, have breakfast, and make her way back to the bakery in time for it opening at 9:00 a.m.

She had imagined the scene in various ways: The owner of the place denying any knowledge of her mother or Eve's abandonment and the search ending abruptly, or, in contrast, them acknowledging their involvement in rescuing the young girl by helping her to hide. She'd even imagined a scenario where they would tell her that they had kept in touch all these years, and did she want Fiona's address? At that, Eve had tutted, the likelihood being so remote that it was ludicrous. The best that she could hope for was that the current owner's mother might be able to shed more light on Fiona's story. If that were possible, even if she never found Fiona, Eve believed that she would be satisfied.

The time crawled by until she could no longer stand staying in bed so a little after 6:00 a.m., she got up and tiptoed into the bathroom. Jess's breathing was now slow and even, and Eve didn't want to disturb her after a sleepless night.

When she emerged from the shower, Jess was standing in the middle of the room looking at Eve's phone.

"Morning." Eve smiled. "Did I wake you?"

Jess shook her head. "You had a missed call. An Edinburgh number." She held the phone out and frowned. "Who's that then?"

Eve pulled the towel tighter around her chest and took the phone.

"Can't think." She shrugged. "No voicemail, so it couldn't have been important." She tossed the phone onto the bed and began dressing.

Two hours later, they left the small dining room and headed for the car. Jess had eaten a good breakfast, and her color was back to normal, so Eve had resolved not to dwell on the previous day's faint. Young women had all manner of reasons to pass out, and if she remembered correctly, she had done so herself a couple of times, in her twenties, for no particular reason.

Jess was talking to Ram as they rounded the bend on Evans Road.

"We're there now. The Bakery." She nodded. "Yes, the café woman said the current owner's mum might remember the girl. Uh huh. Fiona." Jess looked over at Eve and widened her eyes. "Yes, that's what I said." She grinned at her mother. "I know that. We're not getting our hopes up too much. Just going to see if there's any more info we can gather."

Eve could picture her son-in-law's gentle face as he fretted over them potentially being disappointed.

"Give him my love," she mouthed at Jess.

"Mum says to stop bugging us." Jess laughed.

"No, I didn't." Eve shouted. "That's not what I said, Ram."

Jess's eyes glittered. "She sends her love."

The Bakery was open. There were a few customers already in line as Eve and Jess walked inside. A small bell tinkled as the door opened and closed, reminding Eve of a wool shop in Crail that Mary had sometimes taken her to when she was a child. As Mary had searched for wool, Eve would spend the time walking in and out of the door, imagining the bell summoning the seaside fairies who lived on the shelves, hiding between the balls of wool and stacks of knitting needles. Mary would eventually scold her, telling Eve to stop before the patient shopkeeper lost her temper.

The warm bakery smelled wonderful. It had a floury aroma that once again made Eve think of her mother. Realizing that Mary must be frantic, knowing they were on this mission, Eve made a mental note to call her parents when she got back to the hotel.

The line moved forward, the locals picking up loaves, pies, and rolls to take home in brown paper bags. Eventually, Eve was next to the counter. The woman behind it was tall, willowy, with a raven-black ponytail heavily streaked with grey. Eve assessed the pleasant face. The woman appeared to be around fifty, with elongated green eyes and a wide smile.

"What can I get you?" She eyed Eve.

Eve clamped her fingers around the thistle broach in her pocket.

"I was hoping you could help me with some information. Do you have a moment?"

The woman nodded.

"Aye, I suppose so."

"I was told that thirty-nine years ago, your parents owned this bakery?"

The woman looked startled.

"Yes, that'd be true."

Eve nodded.

"I'm asking because I think your mother helped a young girl." Eve paused. "She was probably a teenager when she worked here. Then she had a baby."

The woman glanced over Eve's shoulder at an elderly man

who was waiting in line behind her.

"Can I just serve this gentleman, then we can talk?" She caught Eve's eye. "It won't take a sec."

Eve nodded, immediately embarrassed that she hadn't thought to check behind her before speaking. As she sidestepped to let the man move up to the counter, she scanned the shop for Jess. Eve hadn't noticed her step away as she'd approached the woman a few moments earlier so she walked to the window and looked out at the street. The car was parked opposite, but there was no sign of her daughter.

Just as she was beginning to be concerned, a familiar flash of blonde hair caught her eye, and Jess trotted past the window and back inside the shop.

"Where'd you go?" Eve took in Jess's flushed cheeks.

"Just nipped outside for a bit. It's hot in here." She flapped a hand at her face and smiled. "All good now."

Unconvinced, Eve frowned. "Are you sure you're all right?"

Jess crossed her eyes.

"Absolutely fine. So, what did she say?" She jutted her chin toward the counter.

"She's going to talk to me now. Just helping that man first."

The woman beckoned them over. Her expression was a little more reserved now, and Eve felt herself moving into her professional mode.

"Sorry to bother you at work, but we're only here for a day or so. I'm Eve Carruthers and this is my daughter, Jess."

The woman nodded at them in turn.

"Ailene MacPherson. So, what was it you wanted to know?"

Eve repeated the question, grateful for Jess's reassuring

presence at her shoulder.

The woman squinted at Eve.

"I do remember something about a girl. A runaway, I think." She paused. "Mum talked about it, many years ago."

Eve felt a lift in her diaphragm.

"I don't suppose we could talk to your mother?"

Ailene chewed her cheek.

"We won't take up much of her time. It's just that..."

Ailene interrupted. "Why do you want to know, exactly?"

Eve felt herself cornered, and unlike the ease with which she'd told old Scot about her history, she reluctantly shared it with Ailene.

"Oh, my goodness. Well, I can understand you wanting to know about her." The warm expression was back. "Mum's getting on now. Very hard of hearing, but if you want, I can ask her if she'll talk to you."

Eve felt Jess lean in to her and caught a faint smell of vomit. At the sour odor, Eve's eyes snapped to her daughter's profile.

"Yes, please." Jess said. "If it's no trouble."

Ailene asked them to wait while she went upstairs to check with her mother.

"If anyone comes in, just tell them I'll be back in a tick."

She disappeared behind the counter and the shop fell into silence around them.

Eve pulled Jess round to face her. "What's going on? Were you sick?"

Jess dabbed her top lip with her jacket sleeve.

"Just a little. Must've been the breakfast. Heavier than I'm used to." She shrugged.

"You're going to the doctor the minute we get home, young lady." Eve tucked a strand of hair behind Jess's ear. "No arguments."

Jess nodded as Ailene reappeared behind the counter.

"If you want to come upstairs, she's fine to talk to you now."

Eve's face split into a grin. "Oh, that'd be wonderful. Thank you so much."

The flat above the shop was surprisingly bright. In the living room, two sash windows overlooked Evans Road below and the large, dark oak sideboard and heavy-legged coffee table were reminiscent of Eve's parents' taste in furniture. There was a smell of coffee, and as she inhaled, Eve thought she detected old smoke, as if years' worth of tobacco had indelibly permeated the floral wallpaper and dark-brown carpet.

Ailene gestured toward the sofa. "Sit yourselves down and I'll get Mum."

Eve and Jess obeyed, silently taking in the room around them. A few moments later, Ailene emerged from another door with a tiny, white-haired lady clinging to her arm.

"This is my mum, Jean." She helped the old woman into a wingback chair, gently tucking a pillow down behind the diminutive back.

Ailene raised her voice, "Are you all right if I leave you for a few minutes, Mum?"

The old woman nodded.

"Aye, off you go. I'll be fine." She patted her daughter's hand.

Ailene turned to Eve. "Just speak up, she's struggling with this new hearing aid."

"I will, thanks." Eve nodded.

Jean MacPherson had remarkably few wrinkles for her obvious age. As the woman assessed them, Eve tried to calculate how old she might be. Judging by her best guess, Jean was well into her eighties, which fit with the rounded back, the stiffness of limb and the milky eyes that Eve saw behind the thick glasses.

Jean cleared her throat. "So, you want to know about wee Fiona?"

Eve leaned forward on the sofa. "Yes. So she worked for you, almost forty years ago?"

Jean blinked several times, not taking her gaze from Eve's face.

"While she was pregnant." Eve paused.

Jean licked her lips, knotting her distorted fingers in her lap. "Uh huh, that's right, she did."

Eve tossed a look over her shoulder at Jess, who was nodding enthusiastically.

"Can you tell me anything about her?" Eve pressed her excitement down, trying to sound casual.

Jean reached for a glass of water Ailene had left on the side table near her chair. The few seconds that elapsed while she drank were agonizing until, the glass replaced on the coaster, Jean spoke.

"Ailene says you're her bairn." She eyed Eve.

"Yes, that's true."

"She was a good lass. Hard worker. Came here one afternoon, out of the blue, asking for work."

Eve felt her face growing warm.

"We didn'y have a need, but just one look at her and we knew we had to help her." Jean nodded. "Jock and I took her in. Jock was my husband."

Eve was afraid to speak and stem the flow of information, so simply nodded.

"We gave her some work in the back, cleaning up and helping Jock with the ovens. After a few days, she asked if we knew anywhere she could rent a room. Turned out she'd been sleeping in our shed." Jean shook her head. "Awful shame, so it was."

Eve leaned farther forward, her elbows digging into her knees.

"We had an old caravan down near the river. Never used it much, so Jock said she could live there until she got on her feet." Jean pulled the glasses from her nose and wiped them on her cardigan. "She'd been with us about two months before we kenned she was expecting."

Eve shifted on the sofa, her barrage of questions held back by pure willpower.

"She'd started to show, so I took her shopping for something that'd fit her. All the time she was with us, she never talked about her family. When we asked where she was from she just said near Fort William, but never more than that." Jean hesitated. "We should've asked more, but she was so frail, seemed so delicate, like she'd fall down in a breeze. I didn'y want to press her."

Eve nodded.

"So, we took care of her. Fed her up a bit, paid her enough to live on." Jean frowned. "Then she had the bairn."

Eve pressed her lips together and felt the broach dig into her thigh.

"She'd been delivering a basket to the café when the pains came. Mrs. Ferguson over there called the doctor, and Fiona had the bairn in their upstairs room."

Eve's chest fluttered. Just the day before, she'd been standing in the building where she'd been born. The irony of the situation was sharp. She glanced at Jess, whose mouth was slack.

"So, after a couple o' days, we brought her back to the caravan. The bairn…" Jean halted and then the gentle face folded into a smile. "*You*, were awf'y bonnie."

Eve felt the prick of tears.

"We settled her in, got her a few bits of baby clothing and nice wee basket for you. Jock and I talked about things and decided to offer Fiona a home here as long as she needed." She jabbed a thumb over her shoulder. "She didn'y really say yes or no, and we didn'y want to press her about it. So we checked on her every day until one day, she wasn't there."

Eve shifted her leg, relieving the pressure of her elbow digging into her thigh.

"T'was a Thursday, and Jock'd popped over to the caravan with some fresh bread and eggs." Jean coughed, a deep rattle that gave her away as the former smoker Eve had wondered about earlier. "The van was empty. Clean like, as if she'd never been there." Jean shook her head. "We thought she'd gone for a walk, so it wasn'y until the next day, and still no sign of her, that we started to worry."

Jess was nodding, her focus intent on Jean's mouth, as if lipreading. "So what happened?"

Jean glanced over at Jess.

"You're a bonnie lass yourself." She smiled. "Like mother like daughter."

Grateful for the compliment, but not willing to let Jean stray from the story, Eve cleared her throat.

"Thank you. So then?"

Jean nodded, as if redirecting herself.

"Aye, well it was two days later that we heard in the village that you'd been found, outside the café."

Eve waited.

"It was a tourist who picked you up. A lady from London, so we were told. Mrs. Ferguson was right upset, but the only thing to do was call the police."

"Right," Jess whispered.

"The local bobbie came and they took you away." Jean stuck her chin out. "We kept trying to find out what had happened to wee Fiona, but all they'd tell us was that you'd been handed over to the care people." She lifted a tissue and wiped her nose. "Heartbreaking, so it was."

Jess pulled her phone from her bag and started tapping. Eve was distracted by the movement but wanted to get to the end of the interview before Jean got too tired to continue.

"So, you never heard from Fiona again? Never found out what happened to her?"

Jean shook her head.

"Not for a long time. We were all worried about her, but we presumed she must've gone home." She lifted a hand to her mouth and coughed. "A few months later I got a letter from her. No return address of course. She said she was sorry for running off. She said she was fine and she thanked us for all we'd done for her." Jean paused. "That was the last we ever heard from her."

Eve nodded, sensing that this was all she could hope to learn from the kindly woman.

"Mrs. MacPherson, I can't thank you enough. It's been so many years I was worried that no one would remember what happened, or be willing to talk to me."

Jean was smiling.

"This is Braemar, pet. We help folk out here, and we're not afraid to keep their secrets either, when we have to."

Eve eased forward on the seat and gathered her handbag from the floor.

"I'm glad you were taken care of." Jean's voice had thickened. "Such a wee bairn to be left on your own."

Eve smiled. "I was lucky. I had the most wonderful parents anyone could hope for."

Jean's smile widened. "Well, they were lucky to have you too."

Having passed back through the bakery, and thanked Ailene for her help, they let themselves into the car. As Eve put the keys in the ignition, her hand was shaking.

"God, Mum. It's amazing."

Eve leaned back in the seat, and the pressure of the headrest against her skull seemed to reground her.

"She actually had me in the café. Lived in a caravan by herself." She felt her throat closing.

"I know. It's sad, and yet so lovely that she found good people to help her," Jess said.

"Yes, she was lucky there."

Jess lifted her handbag from between her feet. "Do you think we should go to the police station? See if there's anything on record about that day?"

Eve's eyes locked on to her daughter's.

"I never thought of that." She bit her bottom lip. "Nothing to lose by asking."

The small, stone police building looked like an unremarkable railway ticket office. The blue-and-yellow-checkered Land Rover sitting outside was the only indication that they'd found their destination until Eve pulled into one of the empty parking spaces and she spotted the small, distinct blue-and-white "Police" sign propped up inside one of the windows.

"Is this it?" Jess peered out the window. "It's tiny."

Eve turned off the ignition. "Looks like it."

While they'd made the short drive from the bakery, the sky had become heavy with grey-tinged clouds, and now, as she opened the driver's door, heavy droplets of rain began spattering on the windscreen.

"Better make a run for it." Eve jumped out and dashed toward the door. Jess was behind her in moments, and together they pushed into the compact station.

A high, L-shaped desk enclosed the opposite corner, and behind it, a tall man in a crisp, blue uniform shirt looked at them over his glasses.

"Hello there." He put down the papers he'd been holding.

Eve wiped her palm on her leg and extended her hand.

"Hello." She moved in close to the desk. "I was wondering if you could help me."

CHAPTER 12

Jess stood in the hall outside their room. She was whispering on the phone to Ram while Eve dozed on her bed. Jess could picture Ram in his office, the desk perpendicular to the door and the framed photo of them on their honeymoon next to the phone. His office smelled slightly of cardamom, and she'd sometimes wondered if he chewed on the fragrant pods between appointments.

"We went to the police station this afternoon. They found an old record of the baby, of Mum, being handed in to them on that day, and then all the report said was that she was taken by the local authorities."

"Uh huh. So now what?"

Jess shrugged.

"Dunno. Next would be to go to Fort William, I suppose, but we'll come home and regroup first."

She moved to the far end of the hall and looked out the

landing window to the gardens below.

"So are you coming back tomorrow?" Ram sounded tired.

"Yes. Are you OK?"

"Yep. Just don't sleep well without you."

Jess smiled. "Neither do I."

Down in the garden, Mrs. A was walking across the lawn with a shallow basket slung over her arm. Jess squinted, trying to see what was in it. Long fronds of green hung over the edges, and as Mrs. A turned, Jess caught sight of what looked like turnips. With no warning, she felt a wave of nausea, took a deep breath and leaned against the wall.

"Has anything come in from the doctor yet?"

"Not that I've seen." Ram paused. "Should be any day now."

Jess nodded, the sick feeling beginning to pass. "I think I might need to get a checkup when I get home."

"Why, what's wrong?"

"Nothing really. I'm just feeling a bit peaky. I threw up yesterday." She watched Mrs. A lean down and pull a jagged weed from a tidy flower bed.

"Oh, really?" Ram sounded more curious than concerned.

"Yep. Silly really. Probably overdid the fried food." Jess turned to check that the bedroom door was still closed.

"So, you were sick?"

She could hear what sounded like a smile in his voice.

"Yes. So?"

"Jess, you don't think you could be…?"

She sucked in her breath.

"Oh my god." She pressed her head back against the wall.

"What if I am?"

"Well, it's not ideal, until we get the test results, but if you are you are..." He paused. "It'll be all right. It'll be great."

Jess felt her stomach heave and tried to calculate how many steps it was to the bathroom. Of course Ram was right. How could she not have seen it? The constant eating, the fainting fit, and now the nausea. How dense was she not to have clicked right away?

"I'm so stupid." She felt the press of tears. "Sorry, I have to go. I'm going to be sick again."

Without waiting for Ram's goodbye, she hung up, clamped a hand over her mouth, and dashed for the room.

Eve jumped as Jess flew through the door and thundered into the bathroom. Having emptied herself, she slid to the floor. The tile was pleasantly cold under her hips as she pressed her face into a washcloth she'd run under the tap.

As she stared at the white toilet next to her, she ran through various scenarios in her mind. How could she be pregnant when they'd used protection? She knew nothing was a hundred percent fail-safe, but with that, coupled with Ram's increased chances of a low sperm count as a CF carrier, she'd never considered that they were at serious risk. She looked down at her flat stomach. Could it be possible that there was a tiny nugget of a someone in there? She laid her hand across herself. The whole question of the cystic fibrosis gene, which had been hovering on the horizon as a potential concern for their future, now felt terrifyingly close. If this was happening before they knew for sure that she wasn't a carrier, there was a chance that the child could be affected. She pressed her eyes closed and, for the first time in years, prayed.

Eve was knocking on the door.

"Jess, let me in." She sounded panicked. "Jess?"

Jess stood up slowly and checked her face in the mirror before opening the door.

Once inside, Eve held her arms open. "What's going on, darling?"

Jess stepped into her mother's embrace, feeling the strength of the arms that she had relied on all her life circle her back.

"Oh, Mum. I think I'm pregnant."

An hour later, with a cup of water and a few salty crackers in her fist, Jess walked behind Eve out to the garden. There was no one using the patio, so they settled themselves at the table. Eve had draped a pashmina around Jess's shoulders.

"So, we need to get you a test."

Jess felt Eve's eyes on her as she nibbled a cracker.

"Maybe we can pick one up so you can do it in the morning?"

Jess shook her head.

"No. I'll do it when I get home. I want Ram there."

Eve blushed slightly. "Oh, of course."

"Sorry. I'd just rather be with him when I find out." She glanced at her mother. "Just in case."

Eve's eyes lifted from her lap. "In case of what?"

"We haven't had the blood tests back yet."

Eve nodded. "I understand. But Jess, I'd think the chances are very slim that you're a CF carrier."

Jess sipped her water, some salty flakes of cracker having stuck in her throat. "Let's hope so," she croaked.

The sun was setting behind the house, and Jess felt the dry biscuits doing their job. Her stomach had stopped jumping, and the evening breeze felt good on her warm cheeks. As she watched a shadowy shape move in one of the flower beds, Jess's mind raced. She pictured their flat in St. Andrews with a crib at the end of the big bed. She saw bottles strewn across the countertops and tiny white onesies folded into squares and stacked inside the deep dresser drawer. She saw Ram pacing the floor in his pajamas with a blanket-wrapped bundle held close to his neck, whistling softly as he did whenever Jess was ill and he was taking care of her. The images came fast, stacked closely behind each other like a slideshow. She blinked to focus on Eve's face.

"Mum?"

"Yes, love."

"If I am, and there's something wrong…"

Eve shook her head.

"Jess, don't do this to yourself. We'll go home tomorrow. You and Ram will get a test, then you'll know for sure. You might even have the report from your doctor by then, and then you'll have all the information in hand."

Jess heard the sense in Eve's words, but the feeling of motion sickness was rising again with her nerves.

"How sick were you, with me?" She bit into another cracker.

Eve laughed. "Well, it was pretty bad. To this day, I don't know why they call it morning sickness." She smiled at Jess. "It'd hit me any time of the day or night. I got caught out more than once."

In the fading light, Jess focused on Eve's grey eyes.

"Once I was in the supermarket. It was about three in the afternoon, and I was just standing in the queue to pay."

Jess sipped some more water.

"There were three people behind me, and I panicked. I couldn't go back to get past them, so I bolted. I left my handbag on the belt, ran out the front door, and just made it to the waste bin on the pavement."

Jess laughed. "Bloody hell."

"I know. I couldn't have cared less who saw me though." Eve shrugged. "I wiped my face, calmly walked back into the shop, paid for my stuff, and left."

Jess pulled the edge of the pashmina up over her shoulder.

"There were a few open mouths in the line, but the checkout girl was lovely. She handed me a tissue and a mint, not caring that the folk behind me were muttering." Eve paused. "She told me that she'd been so sick with her third baby that she hadn't been able to work for the first few months."

"Really?" Jess shivered. The darkening sky was dragging the temperature down quickly.

Eve nodded. "I think that once you've been there, experienced pregnancy yourself, you become so much more understanding. It's a sisterhood of the most profound kind." She leaned across the table and patted Jess's hand. "One you'll be joining soon."

Jess felt the hairs on her arms rising to attention. "Can we go in, Mum? It's getting cold out here."

Eve wrapped an arm around Jess's shoulder as they walked across the garden.

"Don't be scared. What will be will be, and whatever

happens, we're all here to support you."

Jess leaned her head on Eve's shoulder.

"Thanks, Mum. I know."

CHAPTER 13

Since getting home from Braemar, Eve had been restless. This morning, unable to settle to any particular task, she'd already gone for a walk, vacuumed downstairs, sifted through her wardrobe, and put several things in a bag for the charity shop. It was Sunday, and Ken was pottering in the garden. Jess hadn't called yet, and the anticipation of hearing from her was painful.

Having decided to clean them, Eve knelt at the French doors. The August sun was warming the glass and, as she wiped it with vinegar and hot water, she lost herself in the repetitive circular motions. The pull in her shoulder muscles felt good and the sharp scent of the cleaning solution made her think of her mother.

Mary had sounded subdued on the phone, asking few questions about the trip, when Eve had called her the night before. Eve sensed that Mary was nervous about overstepping and, feeling bad for her mother, she had promised to go and see them the following afternoon. Mary had brightened at that.

"Lovely. I've made some gingerbread. I'll keep you some. Will Jess be with you?"

"No. It'll just be me."

A zap of pain in her back made Eve stand up. She rubbed at her knees, the skin dark pink and mottled where she'd been kneeling. She glanced at the clock. Eleven fifteen and still no word from Jess.

Eve tossed the damp cloth into the sink and lifted her phone, checking for missed calls. The same Edinburgh number had come up three times now and each time, the person hadn't left a voicemail. As she scrolled through the list again, she paused at the 131 number and was on the point of blocking it when the phone rang, making her jump.

"Hello?"

"Em, hello. Mrs. Carruthers?"

The voice was deep, not one she recognized immediately.

"Yes, who's this?" Her response was clipped.

"It's Dan Patterson. Family Connections."

Eve blinked as gradually an image of the prominent jaw, the mesmerizing eyes, and the full smile came back to her.

"Oh, yes. Dan. Hello." She smiled. "It's you."

Dan laughed.

"*Oui, c'est moi.*"

Questioning herself even as she was doing it, Eve spun around to check if she was alone in the kitchen.

"How are you? I've been keen to know how it went in

Braemar." Dan's voice was warm.

Eve looked out the window and spotted Ken's round back bent over a flower bed at the far end of the lawn. As she caught sight of her reflection in the glass, she smoothed her hair, then frowned at herself.

"I'm fine, thanks. It went well. Actually, really well."

"That's great. Care to share?"

She considered the question and then, picturing Dan's face, she nodded.

Fifteen minutes later, she glanced out of the window again. Ken was nowhere to be seen, and having talked to Dan about her trip in more detail than she had her own husband, Eve tasted the tang of disloyalty.

"So, next step is Fort William?" Dan sounded enthusiastic. "You're making great progress, Eve."

She lifted a cloth and wiped the already clean surface.

"Yes. I think I'll go early next week. I'd like to get this done before term starts."

"Right."

She sensed there was more he wanted to say.

"You know, if it's not imposing, I'd be happy to help. Maybe even come with you. I won't interfere. Just offer moral support. It's not my first rodeo, you know." He laughed. "I don't want to intrude though. These things are intensely personal."

Eve felt the jolt of his offer high under her ribs. Come with her?

A movement caught her eye. She watched as Ken crossed the lawn dragging a full brown bag of clippings and weeds behind him. He looked up at her and waved. She waved back, for some reason feeling like a traitor.

“Is your daughter going with you?” Dan’s voice snapped her back to the moment.

“Um, no.” Eve heard herself say the words. When had she decided that she was going to Fort William alone? As she watched Ken dump the matted clippings into the compost container, Eve thought about Jess and her potential pregnancy. In the handful of moments that it had taken her to answer Dan, she had resolved that until they knew for sure what was happening, it was for Jess’s own good – to stay at home. Eve turned her back on the garden and closed her eyes.

“She’s a bit under the weather at the moment. She needs to rest. I’m just going to go on my own.”

Ken wiped his forehead with a grubby hanky. He’d pulled off his boots and set them on the edge of the patio. Eve’s salad was wilting, and the sandwich she’d made him was beginning to curl at the edges.

“Come and eat.” She sat at the table. “I need to get off to Mum and Dad’s soon.”

“Aye, right.” He sat opposite her and yanked the plate toward himself. “The camellia was full of dead branches. I hope it comes back OK.” He bit into his sandwich. “The geraniums might give us another bloom, too.” He spoke around his mouthful.

“Uh huh.” She shoved the lettuce around her plate. “The roses have been gorgeous this year.”

Ken nodded happily.

“Must be that tomato supplement I used.”

Eve watched him assess his pride and joy. The three rosebushes were clustered close together next to the fence that separated them from their neighbors' garden. Over the summer, Ken had babied the plants back from some disease or other that she couldn't name. When they were in bloom, the scent was glorious, a pungent perfume that carried on the skin and lingered inside her nose when she sniffed the purple-pink blooms. Ken would occasionally cut one perfect flower and bring it inside for her.

"So, what's the plan for Fort William?" He chewed. "Jess all set for the next phase?"

Eve had not talked to Ken about Jess's belief that she was pregnant. It felt disloyal to share that information before Jess was sure, and the last thing Eve wanted to do was get Ken's hopes up prematurely. She knew how excited he was about grandchildren. The significance of the word made Eve pause. A grandmother. They'd be grandparents. She'd be to Jess and Ram's baby what Mary was to Jess. While thirty-nine was young to be a grandparent, there was part of Eve that felt much older than that these days. The new knowledge surrounding the circumstances of her birth while fascinating, felt cumbersome and the realization that it felt like a burden, surprised her.

"I was thinking I'd go alone this time."

"Why?" He glared at her.

Eve shrugged.

"I think Jess is tired, and she needs to be here with Ram. They're still newlyweds, Ken. I feel bad taking her away again." She wiped her clean knife on a leaf of lettuce and crossed her cutlery, her meal untouched.

"Tired? She's barely done a full day's work this past week. Is she OK?" He frowned.

"She's fine. But she's got things to do here."

Ken dipped his chin.

"I sometimes wonder if we did the right thing, letting her come to work at the shop." He wiped his mouth with the back of his hand.

Eve tutted.

"Now, don't. We agreed to support that decision. She was miserable at the insurance company." She lifted their plates and stood up.

Ken shoved his chair back. "So, you want to go on alone?"

She heard the question and also the others that lay beneath it.

"I think I do."

Ken nodded.

"Sorry, it's just…" She watched him drop his head and pull on his boots.

"S'OK. I get it."

She smiled at him, feeling her heart tug. "Love you."

He met her eyes. "Me too."

Having spent an hour with her parents, Eve guided the car homeward. She was revisiting her earlier conversation with Dan as she negotiated her way around a Sunday driver who was out to gaze at the scenery rather than get from point A to point B in any particular timeframe. She raised a hand as she passed the car, seeing an elderly couple with matching silver heads smiling at her. Eve watched them shrink in her rearview mirror and she thought about Ken. She had always imagined that they'd grow old together, spend the rest of their lives together. It had been a touchstone in her life that she'd rarely questioned since the day they'd been married. Now, as she waited at a traffic light, she wondered how likely it was that any two people could make a relationship work for a lifetime. Best-case scenario – there would be bumps.

Her eyes went to her phone, which she'd slipped into a slot in the central console. Dan's offer to go with her to Fort William was beating down her other thoughts. Was it totally out of the question? He was a professional, after all. It was what he did for a living. There would be nothing personal in it if he did come. She was just another client.

Even as the thought was twirling, she knew that she was deceiving herself. She might be naïve in some respects, but she'd picked up the distinct body language of attraction when she'd been in Dan's office in Edinburgh. She'd recognized her own heart rate quickening, the film of sweat gathering on her palms, losing her words and her inability to stop smiling at him. As she recalled the meeting, Eve was embarrassed that she'd been so overt that even Jess had noticed.

She glanced in the mirror again, but the old couple's car had vanished. As the traffic light changed, she tutted at herself. It was time she got home.

CHAPTER 14

Jess stood at the living room window. The white plastic wand was lying on a sheet of kitchen paper on the windowsill and Ram was in the kitchen banging around as she stared down at the test stick.

"A watched pot never boils." He called from the other room.

"Shut up," she said. "Or I'll come in there and throw up on you."

Ram came into the room carrying a cup.

"Here. My mum's remedy for nausea. Hot water, fresh ginger, and honey." He shoved the cup toward her.

Jess took the cup and sniffed.

"It smells nice." She sipped.

"So, anything yet?"

Jess looked down at the wand where, since she'd last checked, two narrow pink lines had darkened in the window.

"Oh god. Ram."

She turned to face him. He was smiling, his handsome face radiant. She looked for any sign of concern, of questioning or fear, but saw none. Ram was all but incapable of hiding his feelings from her, so Jess felt the knot of fear she'd been harboring loosen slightly. Perhaps he was right. It might be all right.

He leaned down and kissed her.

"Here we go then." He grinned. "Shall we call your parents?"

Jess felt the slap of reality. "Maybe we should wait? What if we get bad news?"

Ram's smile faded. "Well, this is real now so, what are you saying?"

Jess took a steadying breath. She'd had a sleepless night and had given the possibility of this happening a lot of thought. Now she needed to share her fears.

"I'm just saying that if the blood test results don't come back the way we hope, we might need to rethink."

He dropped his arm and stepped back from her. She missed the contact with him instantly.

"So you're saying that you might not want to go through with this?" He scrutinized her face and then her flat stomach, as if there were a sign on it saying, "Baby in here."

Jess took a breath. "Just listen to me."

He took another step back. "I'm listening."

She moved to the sofa and sat down, beckoning to him.

"Are we ready to cope with a child that could be seriously ill. In chronic pain? Have a condition that prevents him or her from having a full life? Or even worse – have a truncated life. Have you actually thought about it?"

Ram circled the sofa and sat next to her.

"Of course I have. My cousin on my mother's side had CF. We were around him most of my early childhood. He was a great guy." He looked at her.

Jess felt herself redden. She hated to be a doom-monger, but Ram's perspective seemed somewhat simplistic considering the reality they might be facing.

"I'm sure he *was* great. But how much pain was he in? How debilitated was he? How often was he hospitalized? How much care did he need on a daily basis? Were you around for all that?" She paused. When Ram remained silent, she continued. "How old was he when he died, Ram?"

Ram's eyes flashed. "In his thirties."

Jess nodded.

"So, all I'm saying is that we need to have all the facts, talk it through, and be sure we know what we're doing before we tell anyone else." She felt a tiny prick of guilt, knowing that her mother had been party to her suspicions in Braemar and yet she was forbidding Ram from confiding in anyone.

He looked away from her.

"I hear you. You're right. Let's wait a bit." He glanced over his shoulder at her. "But Jess, I don't want to talk about termination. It's not an option."

Jess pulled in a breath. Was he actually dictating that to her? His mouth was tense, his face looking closed, something she'd rarely seen since knowing him. As she tried to quell a surge of anger, she took a deep breath and spoke deliberately.

"What do you mean it's not an option? I don't recall this being an autocracy." She swept the room with her hand.

He looked startled.

"Since when do you make decisions, as major as this, for both of us?" She studied his face as he took in her words. His jaw jumped, the skin twitching as he chewed his lip.

"I'm not doing that." His eyes flashed. "I just don't..." He stopped himself.

Jess recognized the signs. He'd heard her loud and clear, so she softened her voice.

"Look. I don't want to let my mind go there either, but we'll talk about it all, when we've heard from Doctor James." Her hand sought his fingers. "Let's not think about anything until then."

She felt a stab of hurt as rather than take her hand, Ram leaned back and laced his fingers in his lap.

"OK. Let's wait until then."

The following morning, Jess kissed Ram goodbye and then immediately went back to bed. She was feeling queasy, and as she was working the afternoon shift at the shop, she had time to let herself slip back under the duvet and close her eyes against the day, for a little longer. The fact that she hadn't called her mother was tugging at her conscience, but by delaying getting up, she could excuse herself that task for now.

Not sure of how much longer she'd slept, Jess rolled over in the bed. There was a faint smell of coffee floating in from the kitchen, which was making her nauseous, so she turned back into her pillow and exhaled. Picturing Ram's expression from the previous evening had kept her awake for a good part of the night.

Over the course of their relationship, she had seen him respond to her in numerous ways, but she'd never experienced him dictating to her. Could her tolerant, sensitive husband really have all but closed the subject of a potential termination? He'd never forbidden her to talk about anything before, so the concept of him laying down the law had shaken her. The idea that she may not know him as deeply as she thought, or could have somewhat romanticized their relationship, was leveling.

Despite the time of year, the bedroom was chilly, so she sat up and yanked Ram's half of the duvet over herself, then curled back up like a clam under the heavy covers. As she counted her breaths in and out, trying to force down the steady swell of nausea, snippets of the conversation she'd had with Eve a few days earlier came back to her. She'd often seen her mother frustrated, over the years, by her father's dismissiveness.

As she extended her legs, her toes finding the edge of the wooden bed frame, Jess wondered if the blueprint for her parents' marriage and the manner of their interactions had been established from the very beginning, and whether that would hold true for her and Ram. She too had married young, and to someone older, and while that could potentially create the dynamic she'd witnessed between her parents, it was not what she wanted for herself.

After a few moments, she lifted her head and thumped the feathers into a flatter platform for her face. The question of this pregnancy was the first truly challenging thing that she and Ram had faced as a couple. She understood his position, but he wasn't the one who'd have to carry this baby to term, all the while afraid of the life that lay ahead of it – or worse – didn't.

They might have to live with the fact that their bodies had betrayed them by creating and then damaging something so precious – albeit unconsciously. There might never be a decision more important to them both, and therefore none that needed to be as deeply considered.

Jess flopped onto her back and stared at the ceiling. The noise of the street below awakening to the new week was familiar and comforting. The tinkle of breaking glass made her swing her legs over the bed and get up. At the window, she looked down as a stocky woman in an apron brushed some shards of what looked like a beer bottle into a pile at the edge of the pavement.

She pressed her hand into her stomach, her fingers rippling as if picking out a tune on a piano.

"Are you OK in there?" She dipped her chin to her chest. "Little one?"

The kitchen was tidy. Ram always cleaned up after himself before leaving for work, unlike Jess, who would toss her cereal bowl into the sink and leave the milk sitting on the counter. She crossed the narrow space and pulled out a cup. The thought of her usual milky coffee made her draw her lips together so instead, she reached for a lemon-and-ginger teabag and flipped the kettle on.

Her phone lay next to the toaster, and as she checked for messages, Jess knew that there was only so much more time she could delay calling her mother, before it became cruel.

CHAPTER 15

Eve hit Send and closed the laptop decisively. The email to her boss requesting the following week off had been succinct and, she hoped, plausible. The term *personal issue* seemed loose and yet encompassed so much that Eve felt sure there'd be little, if any, pushback from the understanding department head.

Ken had gone into the shop to take inventory for the coming week. As she'd stared at the clock, feeling anew the sharp edge of hurt over the fact that it had been two days since they'd got home and Jess had still not called her, Eve forced herself to swallow the last mouthful of cold tea. She knew that it was wrong, and yet she couldn't shake the sensation that she had some proprietary right to Jess's news.

Outside, the midday shadows were dividing the patio into a Battenberg pattern. A cat sat under the metal table licking its paw as Eve sluiced her empty cup out with hot water. As she watched the cat, elegant and oblivious to being observed, she considered the previous afternoon's conversation with Dan. She wondered how many of his clients he'd offered such a level of personal assistance to. She suspected very few. The idea that he'd singled her out in some way, while flattering, was discomfiting. He hadn't said much more once she's told him she was going to Fort William alone and, for Eve, the subject had felt suitably closed.

The phone rang, yanking her out of her daydream. Seeing Jess's name on the display, Eve grabbed the phone.

"Hi, love. How are you?"

"OK."

Not wanting to sound petulant or to dive right to the epicenter of the issue that had kept her up most of the night, Eve tried to divert.

"It's gorgeous outside today. What've you been up to this morning? Are you doing an afternoon shift?" she gushed.

"Mum." Jess sounded breathless.

"What?" Eve wound a tendril of hair around her finger.

"So, you can't tell Dad, OK?"

"OK." Eve was suddenly afraid of what she might hear.

"It's positive."

Eve released her breath. "Oh, Jess." Her eyes instantly blurred. "Darling."

Jess sniffed. "So we need to keep a lid on things until I get the results from Dr. James."

"Of course. Mum's the word."

Jess let out a laugh. "Well, I suppose that's true now."

Eve heard the harsh edge to Jess's voice and recognized it as fear.

"Jess, you need to try to think positive. Don't get into a funk until you have all the facts." She slid onto a stool at the island.

"Easier said than done." Jess paused. "Ram basically told me last night that he doesn't want to discuss termination – even if we know the baby could be affected."

Jess's ragged voice tore at Eve's heart, and while she was rocked by the word Jess had just used, Eve knew that her daughter needed her to maintain an even keel right now. As Eve watched the cat slink into the lavender bushes, she wondered if Jess could have in some way misinterpreted her husband's position. While he would often counsel Jess, a dictatorial Ram wasn't something Eve had ever witnessed.

"I'm sure he'll talk anything through that you need to."

"I hope so. He's not the only one to consider in this."

"Just try not to panic yet, Shorty. It'll all work itself out. You'll see."

Having sworn, again, to keep the news to herself, Eve hung up the phone. She'd told Jess that she'd pop into the shop, mid-afternoon, so that they could talk.

It was twelve twenty and she had no idea when Ken would be home. Not that she could share this with him.

Less than two hours later, Eve had walked into the shop. Two customers had come in while they talked, and Jess had served them both with a smile, swiftly slicing blocks of cheese and wrapping them in wax paper as Eve watched from the corner. The last person had left a few moments earlier, and mother and daughter now sat at a small table.

"There's no way that Ram won't be open to hearing your concerns." Eve leaned forward on her elbows. "But this line of thinking could be a knee-jerk, fear-induced reaction from you too." She eyed her daughter. "Could you really consider not keeping this baby?" Despite herself, Eve looked down at Jess's stomach. Eve had always balked when people had addressed her pregnant stomach rather than look her in the eye.

Jess's eyes were hooded.

"You know how I feel about children. It's a dream." She shoved the hair off her forehead. "I just don't want this little one's life to be that hard." She placed a hand on the front of her white apron. "And as for Ram's reaction – it really rocked me." She paused. "It made me wonder if there's a whole side to him that I haven't seen yet." She blinked several times, then shrugged. "I mean, should I be worried?" She eyed her mother.

Eve shook her head.

"I don't think so. You're both just finding your way as a couple. There's bound to be things you still have to discover about each other. That's normal." She paused. "Ram's the salt of the earth. He's compassionate and intelligent and he adores you. You'll make the right choice, and you'll do it together."

Jess shifted in the chair. Her hair had worked loose from the knot at the back of her neck, a golden ponytail now covering one shoulder.

"Anyway, it sounds as if you dealt with it in just the right way." Eve leaned back in her chair. "Head-on." She smiled at her daughter. "Do as I say, not as I do."

Jess's chin lifted, and she snapped her eyes to Eve's.

"I've never heard you say something like that before." She frowned. "I'm worried about you and Dad."

Eve shook her head.

"We're fine. It's normal in a marriage for there to be friction and for things to feel a bit stale sometimes." The words out, Eve wanted to snatch them back.

"God, Mum. Do you feel that way?"

Frustrated with her lack of sensitivity, Eve ran a hand through her hair.

"No. Not really. Maybe a little constrained at times, but we're really fine. Honestly. Don't worry."

Jess was biting her thumbnail, looking younger than her years. Eve smiled at her daughter.

"Look – why not call the doctor? It's been a while since your blood was taken. Perhaps he could call the lab and jildy them along a bit, under the circumstances."

Jess shook her head.

"I can't." She spoke around her thumb as she chewed the cuticle. "I'm scared."

Eve reached over and gently pushed Jess's hand down.

"I can stay with you, if you want?" Having offered, Eve recalled Jess's reaction the last time she'd injected herself into this situation, but to her surprise, Jess's face brightened.

"Would you talk to him?"

Eve shook her head. "He won't talk to me, Shorty. But I'll be here if you want to call him."

A few moments later, Eve watched her daughter pacing behind the display cabinet, the phone pressed to her ear. Her hair was uncharacteristically messy, and when Eve had arrived earlier, she'd noticed that Jess wore no makeup.

The gossamer string that had never fully detached Jess from Eve's core vibrated, and she felt the tension in Jess's back seep into her own. Mothers and daughters were intrinsically linked, or at least that was general opinion. As she observed Jess's cat-like progress back and forth, Eve's mind went to her birth mother, Fiona. With that invisible string being severed so early, by physical separation, she wondered if the young girl had experienced any residual connection, a clanging of some sixth sense, perhaps that her child needed her, was in pain or distress – much like twins were reported to do. The idea made Eve frown. An image of a girl pushing her baby's basket under a table and walking away sent a jolt through her middle. No. Chances were that Fiona had primarily felt relief.

Jess's head snapped up, and she glared at Eve.

"Yes, uh huh." She widened her eyes. "I'd rather hold on, if that's OK?" She crossed the flagstone floor and leaned against Eve's shoulder.

Eve whispered in Jess's free ear, "What's he saying?"

Jess turned and mouthed, "He's calling the lab."

Eve chewed her lower lip. After what seemed like an interminable few minutes, Jess jerked away from her mother's side.

"Yes, I'm here."

The next handful of seconds that passed felt weighted, each one like a bird's wing laboring to catch an updraft. Eve could hear her heartbeat in her ears, pervasive and disconcerting.

"Oh, thank god. Thank god." Jess's face was glistening as she beamed at her mother. "Yes, I'll make an appointment. Thank you, Doctor. Of course. Goodbye then."

Jess was instantly in Eve's arms. The apple scent of her daughter's hair and the weight of her torso against her chest made Eve press her eyes closed. It was OK. Her daughter was OK, and now her grandchild would be healthy too.

She'd agreed not to say anything to Ken until Jess and Ram could come over that evening to share the news. On her way home Eve had stopped at the supermarket and picked up the makings of a simple meal and had left a message on Ken's phone telling him that the kids were coming for dinner. Dan's curious offer and all thoughts of Fort William, and everything that entailed, had been happily relegated to the back of her mind as she homed in on the fact that her daughter – her young, headstrong and often impulsive daughter – was going to have a child of her own. The thought was both exhilarating and grounding.

Ken's car was in the driveway, so Eve parked next to it and carried the bags into the kitchen.

"Anybody home?"

The silence was disconcerting as she walked through the house, looking for telltale signs of her husband's presence – the ever-present gardening boots left at the sliding door, the discarded gloves on the counter with crumbs of soil radiating from each distorted finger. Nothing. The place was clean and empty of Ken's trademarks.

"Ken?" She leaned against the stair post. "Are you up there?"

Deciding that he must be in the shower, Eve mounted the stairs, but the bathroom was empty, as was their bedroom. Puzzled, she went into the hall and saw that the door to her studio was ajar. She pushed it open and soundlessly stepped inside.

Ken was facing the wall, hunched over her work table. A collection of photographs was fanned out between his fingers like a hand of cards. His long back was moving slightly, and his checked shirt had worked loose from the top of his trousers. Eve caught sight of the narrow strip of skin showing above his belt and felt her throat catch. Ken's dark hair was peppered with grey these days.

His socked feet were planted widely under the desk, and his elbows formed a triangle on the tabletop. She stood still, not wanting to startle him. As she took in his shape, she found herself caught up in confusion – juggling her deep feelings of love for this man and her decision to exclude him from her forthcoming journey.

"What're you doing?" She whispered.

Startled, Ken spun around on the stool.

"Oh, I didn't hear you come in." He closed the hand of photos as a magician might and laid them on the table. "Sorry. I wasn't snooping. Just looking at some oldies."

Eve moved in next to him and looked down at the photo on the top of the pile. It was of the two of them sitting on a drystone wall. From the length of her hair and what she was wearing, she deduced that it had been taken before Jess was born, when they'd visited the Isle of Skye. She smiled at their slimmer, youthful faces.

"Nice one, that. Remember the old shepherd who took it?" She reached past Ken's arm and spread the pile out across the table.

"Aye. He was none too pleased at being asked." Ken laughed. "Nice old duffer though, in the end."

Eve nodded. Despite the laugh, she'd heard the sadness in his voice.

"You OK?" She rested her hand on his back.

"Aye. Just feeling a bit nostalgic these days. Must be getting old." He turned to face her, and Eve was surprised when he reached out and cupped her cheek.

"Is there anything wrong?" He searched her face. "Anything you're worrying about?"

Eve forced herself to swallow.

"No. Why?" She glanced at the carpet.

"You're awfully quiet. Not really here even when you're here, if you know what I mean?"

She met his gaze.

"Ever since all this started with your birth mother. You're different."

"I'm not different." She frowned. "It's just a lot to take in, that's all. I need time to work through everything."

Ken's shoulders slumped. He walked over to the door and then glanced at her. "Whatever you say."

Eve felt her face redden.

"Don't be like that, Ken. It's not easy, you know." Feeling trapped by her own deflection, she eased past him, stepping out into the hall. "I'm doing the best I can."

He walked toward their bedroom and without turning around muttered, "I suppose you are."

Jess and Ram were sitting in the living room as Eve slid the plates into the dishwasher. Unable to contain themselves, they'd blurted the news out before even taking off their jackets and to Eve's surprise, Ken had been emotional.

"My wee girl." He'd crushed Jess into his chest. "Holy hell, you're going to be a mother." His eyes had been full as he'd sought Eve's.

Ram had been laughing like a loon as Jess, sniffing, had kissed Ken's cheeks.

"Watcha, Granddad."

Now, Eve listened to the melded voices filtering into the kitchen. Jess's was lilting, underscored by the two men's, speaking in rounds, providing the bass and tenor to her daughter's alto. Eve, picturing an orchestra, wondered where her own voice would fit into the score. As she wiped the countertops, she felt the nibble of self-pity that made her lips pucker in distaste. What on earth was wrong with her? The news couldn't be better, and yet there was something about the knowledge that Jess was pregnant that made her want to sneak out into the garden and light a cigarette – something she hadn't done in over two decades. She imagined the cool filter between her lips, the sharp tug of smoke drawn into her lungs, and the tension leaving her body as she pushed the toxic vapor out into the cooling night.

Ram came up behind her, startling her.

"God, Ram. You scared me." She spun around and flapped the cloth at him.

"Sorry. Just wanted to see if you needed any help." He flashed her a smile. "Granny."

Eve rolled her eyes.

"No Granny, please." She smiled. "Gram or Nan, maybe."

Ram's eyebrows twitched.

"Granny's too real?" He laughed.

"Yes, I think so."

They settled back in the living room with coffees. Jess was chatting while Ram smiled at her, tucking a strand of hair behind her ear and pushing another cushion down her back. Eve appreciated the way he took care of Jess, and all the tiny gestures of love that oozed out of him. She glanced over at Ken, who was grinning and nodding at his daughter, taking in each word as if it were coated in gold dust – the entire picture in sharp contrast to that of Eve's own announcement to her parents almost twenty-four years before.

As she tuned out the joyful noise around her, Eve saw herself at sixteen, her face round and flushed, her grey eyes wide and full of fear as she stared at herself in the mottled bathroom mirror in the cottage. She'd heard Russell moving around outside the door, speaking in a low, agitated voice to Mary, who'd whispered back to him. Eve had washed her mouth out several times but had still been able to taste the sourness of vomit. She'd wiped her face with a flannel and brushed her mussed-up hair before easing open the lock on the door and facing their disappointment.

Shaking off the memory, she refocused on her daughter's rapturous face, feeling the grip of happiness recapture her. This was momentous. This was good. This was her life now, and she was grateful for it all.

Jess was talking about names. Her choices were surprisingly traditional.

"I like Emma for a girl and Charles for a boy."

Ram laughed. "Charles? Something less regal, maybe?"

Eve remembered the way she and Ken had come up with Jessica for their daughter. Seven names on slips of paper in a bowl. Jessica had been Ken's selection, and so it was their daughter's brand had been born.

"What if it's twins?" Ram widened his eyes comically and nodded at Ken. "Or triplets."

Jess groaned. "Don't even say it. I'd be terrified."

Eve folded her legs up under her in the armchair. "You'd cope beautifully."

Jess shook her head. "Um, I don't think so. One's quite enough to be going on with."

Ken crossed his ankles on the coffee table.

"One was quite enough for us too." He winked at Eve. "Right, love?"

Eve nodded, feeling her breath seep away. "Right."

Half an hour later, Jess and Ram were in the hallway gathering jackets and bags. Eve had put together some leftovers for them and handed Ram the dish before wrapping her arms around Jess's shoulders.

"Goodnight. Get some sleep and remember to take your vitamins in the morning." She patted Jess's cheek. "I love you."

Jess leaned in and kissed her mother's forehead.

"I will. Thanks, Mum." Jess took the dish from Ram and opened the door. "I'll be in at twelve tomorrow. OK, Dad?"

Ken patted the air. "Aye. Whenever you like. I'll be there early for deliveries anyway."

Jess turned back to Eve. "We need to talk about Fort William. When are we going?"

Eve was aware of Ken's gaze shifting to her.

"Oh, we'll talk about it." She stepped away from the open door.

Jess frowned. "I thought you wanted to go next week."

Eve nodded.

"Yes, probably. But there's things to sort out first." She glanced at Ken, hoping for support. He looked at her blankly.

"What things?" Jess moved back inside the door, lifting the dish up to her middle.

"I think that under the circumstances, perhaps you should stay at home."

Jess's brow folded. "What circumstances?"

"Well, with the pregnancy and everything. You don't need to be traipsing around the country with me." Eve tried to smile.

"What are you talking about? I'm not ill, I'm pregnant." Her face flushed as Ram's steadying hand slid under her arm.

"Sweetheart, your mum's probably right." He focused on Eve's face, his dark eyes questioning her even as he reassured his wife. "It's early days, and perhaps you should stick close to home, just for a few weeks until things are further along." He leaned down and picked up his gym bag.

Jess was intelligent, intuitive, but her youth still led her to question herself at times. Eve saw the doubt cloud Jess's eyes as she looked up at Ram and bit down on her top lip. It occasionally worried Eve to see her daughter defer to her husband, anxious that Jess was mimicking her own passive behavior, but in this instance she was relieved.

"You're making too much fuss."

Ken stepped forward and hugged Jess.

"Might as well admit defeat, Shorty. Three against one." He eyed Eve over Jess's shoulder.

Jess let out an exasperated sigh.

"God, you lot. OK. OK. I'll wrap myself up in cotton wool until I'm twelve weeks." She glared at Eve. "But watch out after that."

Eve's relief made her feel lighter as she held the door wider for them.

"Night." She smiled at Ram, who nodded as he turned toward the driveway.

Eve closed the door and faced Ken, who was leaning against the wall, his socked feet jutting out from the bottoms of his fraying jeans. His face was blank, and yet Eve could clearly read the accusation there.

"What?" She passed him and made her way into the kitchen.

"Nothing." He spoke to her back, but she felt the word prick her skin.

CHAPTER 16

Jess stacked the small rounds of cheese on top of the counter. Ken had told her not to lift the large ones for the moment, and while thinking he was worrying too much, she was indulging him. Dinner the night before had been fun, but then her mother's pronouncement about Fort William had taken her by surprise. Eve had seemed odd, avoiding Jess's eyes, and the point about her staying at home hadn't felt like a genuine concern for her well-being – more an excuse.

As Jess lifted a baguette and began slicing it, she considered whether she was more hurt at being left behind, or concerned about her mother's true motive for wanting to go on with the next phase of her search alone. The serrated blade cut easily through the crust, and golden crumbs sparked off on either side forming a layer of dust on the wooden board. Jess arranged some slices on a platter and then set it on top of the counter next to a perfect disc of ash-covered goat cheese.

She glanced at the door as a customer walked in. The woman nodded at her, then began browsing the shelf filled with preserves and chutneys, so Jess carried on with her work. After a few minutes, the woman approached the counter holding a bottle of aged balsamic vinegar.

"Got everything you wanted?" Jess smiled at the woman, whose dark eyes were buried behind thick glasses.

"Uh huh. Thanks."

Having wrapped the item and taken the payment, Jess watched her leave the shop, following the shape of the broad back receding along the alleyway. Feeling an odd emptiness that momentarily felt like hunger, Jess picked up a slice of baguette and bit into it.

When they'd arrived home the night before, she and Ram had talked about their altercation over the pregnancy. Jess had been careful how she'd couched her position but, within a few moments of bringing it up, Ram had crossed the room and pulled her into his arms.

"I'm so sorry. I should never have said what I said – at least, the way I said it." He'd swept her hair off her face and kissed her eyelids. "Even if we don't agree on something, you can talk to me about anything, at any time, and I'll never shut you down that way again."

"It just surprised me, that's all." She'd leaned back from him. "I didn't mean to snap at you."

He'd simply nodded as she moved in closer, buried her face in his chest, and let the worry she'd been carrying subside.

Ken clattered into the back room, startling her. He was shifting a small barrel of olives across the floor with his foot.

"What're you up to? Eating the merchandise?" He laughed.

Jess shrugged.

"I know the boss. He won't mind." She grinned at her father's kind face. She'd always known that she'd marry a man who reminded her of her dad and in many ways, Ram did that. She watched as Ken lifted the dark barrel easily, placing it on a middle shelf, and wondered if he was aware of Eve's occasional struggles with his tendency to parent her. Jess knew it was her father's way of showing his love, but the fact that Eve had voiced frustration about it on the way into Edinburgh had unnerved Jess.

"Dad. Can I ask you something?" She eased between the counter and her father's back and sat at an empty table.

"Yep, what's up?" He spoke to the wall as he positioned the barrel and then began levering the circular top off it.

"Is Mum really OK?"

Ken didn't turn around but halted his movements. Jess watched as he slowly and deliberately rearranged the tidy contents of the shelf.

"Dad?"

Finally, he turned to face her.

"She's fine." He dipped his chin. "This is all a bit overwhelming for her, that's all."

Jess pursed her lips. "What, me? I mean, the pregnancy?"

Ken smiled.

"Well, that, and the whole Fiona business too. It's a lot to deal with at once." He leaned his elbows on the counter, his stomach splaying out against the polished glass. "I'll help her find her way through. We'll get there."

Jess saw a shadow cross his face.

"We just have to give her what she needs and, for now, that seems to be space to do this her way." He shrugged.

Jess felt the truth in the statement, but the nut of worry over Eve's decision hadn't left her.

"Suppose so. It just seems strange to me."

Ken shrugged.

"Well, I realized years ago that there's no understanding women." He beamed at her. "And that goes for you too."

Jess laughed.

"Funny man." She crossed her eyes at her father. "You and Ram don't know how lucky you are to have us."

Ken's smile faded.

"Actually, we do."

CHAPTER 17

Eve shoved her makeup bag into the hold-all. The thistle broach and note were in an envelope which she'd tucked into a side pocket. She'd over packed, taking enough casual clothing for five days despite her plan to stay only two or three. At the last moment, she'd included a silk blouse and a straight skirt which was tailored and hugged her hips, the hem skimming the top of her slim calves. Having kept it for special occasions, she felt good in the skirt, and the wool was soft under her palm as she pressed it down then pulled the zip closed on the bag.

Ken was downstairs waiting to say goodbye, and she knew that he'd been making an effort not to pepper her with questions about her plans for Fort William. She'd been aware of him moving around the bedroom the night before and had closed her eyes in the pretense of sleep rather than ask him what was wrong.

She glanced around the room, then carried the bag downstairs and set it at the door. Ken was in the kitchen on the phone.

"Yes. I'll be in at two. Don't touch those big boxes now, do you hear me?" His back was to her as he leaned against the island. "I'll move them when I get there." He slid the phone back into the cradle and his head dipped forward as he pulled his trousers up at the waist. Eve frowned. Had he lost weight? Before she could speak, Ken turned around and saw her.

"Oh, right. Ready for the off then?"

"Yes. I suppose so." She walked over to him.

"I meant to ask if you'd heard anything from that adoption register?" He frowned.

"No. Nothing yet." She took in his hangdog expression. "You'll be all right, won't you? There's plenty of food in the freezer."

"Of course. I'm not that feckless." He tutted.

"I know you're not. I'm just…"

"Just get this stuff done and get home. Everything else'll be fine."

Having followed him outside, Eve tossed the hold-all onto the back seat and got into the car. Ken closed the door and then leaned in the open window. His eyes were glittering as he kissed her, his mouth insistent on hers. Eve kissed him back, surprised to feel the tip of his tongue meet hers.

"Bye, love. I'll phone you when I get there." She clipped the seatbelt on and rolled up the window as Ken turned and walked back into the house.

As she drove north, leaving Perth behind her, nerves over

what the next few days held began to get the better of her. She hadn't wanted breakfast before she'd left home and suddenly her stomach turned sour. Checking her mirrors, she pulled the car into a layby. Throwing the door open, she dived out and walked into the long grass. As she leaned over, her stomach clamped down with a series of empty heaves until the nausea finally eased.

She wiped her mouth with her palm. What was she doing this for? She should turn around and go home to her life. Fiona had made her own choice all those years ago, and now Eve wished that she too could so easily abandon this entire quest. As she walked back to the car, she considered it for a moment. One simple U-turn and she could leave this all behind her. There would be no Fiona, past or present, and she could save herself the pain that was beginning to feel inevitable.

After a few minutes of letting the breeze cool her face, she got back into the driver's seat and twisted the rearview mirror around. Her hair was disheveled, and to her surprise she realized that she had forgotten to put on any makeup. Pulling the hold-all from the back seat, she rummaged around for the small bag that Ken had given her for her last birthday. Swiping on some powder and rouge and a lick of mascara, she felt her stomach begin to settle. One way or another, she was going on with this. There were long overdue questions to be asked and, given the chance, she intended to ask them.

Eve had chosen a low-key chain hotel close to the center of the town, with a view of both Loch Linnhe and Ben Nevis. It had looked unthreatening, and anonymous enough for her to get lost in. When she arrived, the car park had been half empty and once inside, she was pleased to see that the lobby was comfortingly bland. Hitching her bag higher onto her shoulder, she approached the front desk.

As she introduced herself, she felt her phone buzzing in her pocket. Having handed the receptionist her credit card, she answered it.

"Hello?"

"Hi, Eve."

This time, she recognized Dan's voice.

"Dan?"

"Oui, c'est moi."

She tucked the phone under her chin and signed the registration form that the young man had pushed across to her.

"How was your drive?" Dan sounded bright.

"Uh, fine." She frowned as she slid the credit card back into her wallet. "How are you?" She picked up her hold-all and turned in the direction of the receptionist's finger, looking for the lifts.

At the far side of the dimly lit lobby, she spotted him sitting on a low sofa. Her stomach flip-flopped as she stopped dead in her tracks. He held a paper travel cup and was waving at her. His skin was lightly tanned, and his silver-shot hair feathered thickly above his ears.

"What the hell?" She frowned.

"I hope you don't mind?" His voice was reverberating in her ear as she started walking toward him.

"Hello." He dropped the phone to his lap and smiled up at her. Despite her shock, she instantly felt herself floating as the intense blue of his eyes took her in.

"What're you doing here?"

He stood up. "May I?" He leaned down as if to kiss her cheek.

She hesitated and then felt the brush of his lips against her skin. Something in her core shifted, and Eve was aware of her heart working overtime.

"Seriously, what are you doing here?" She let the hold-all slip to the floor and sat down next to him.

"I know you said you wanted to come alone, but with your daughter not being well and everything, I thought you needed some moral support." He shrugged, his smile mesmeric.

"But I..." She forced herself to swallow. "I don't understand. How did you know where I was staying?"

"You told me, when we spoke." He slid the phone into his breast pocket.

Eve tried to recall their conversation of a few days earlier, frantically searching for the precise dialogue. Had she mentioned the name of the hotel?

"Look, I don't mean to intrude but this is tough stuff you're dealing with and I just thought..."

She cut him off. "Well, I don't need you here." She pressed her lips together. "I mean, I'm fine on my own." She leaned away from his magnetic shoulder.

"Why not let me help? I'm here now." He held his palms up.

Eve took in the charismatic face, the magical smile and those maddening eyes.

"I wish you'd not just turned up like this." She hesitated. "It's unfair."

The smile slipped from his face.

"Oh, I'm sorry. I thought you'd be glad of the company."

Eve tutted.

"I'm not one for surprises, Dan." She watched as he ran a hand through the thick hair at his temple. "This feels wrong, in so many ways."

He shook his head.

"There's no agenda here, Eve." He frowned. "I just want to help."

He sounded genuinely concerned and, for the first time since she'd spotted him, Eve considered whether his presence might in fact be a good thing. He had so much experience with these situations, he could guide her, particularly as she had no specific plan as to how to proceed. She frowned at him.

"Well, I suppose you could be helpful." She wagged her finger at him. "But on my terms, OK?"

He nodded in surrender and the ready smile was back.

"*Absolutment.*"

Having discussed a basic plan of action, they'd agreed to get settled into their rooms and then meet up again. As they made their way to the lifts, an elderly couple walked past them, heading for the front desk. Eve watched them link arms, their pale heads inclined toward each other. She smiled, noticing that Dan was watching her.

"Sweet." She shrugged. "They make it look easy."

He looked surprised, and she felt her cheeks redden. She hadn't meant to be so candid.

Dan lifted his own leather hold-all and gestured toward the lift. "Have you got your key?"

Eve waved the plastic card she'd been given. "Yep."

Their rooms were on the same floor but several doors apart. As Eve opened the door to hers, the blast of over-cool air conditioning chilled her. She dumped the bag on the bed and looked for the thermostat. Adjusting it up, she caught her reflection in the mirror above the chest of drawers. On a reflex, she fluffed her hair, wiped under each eye with her fingertip and added a fresh coat of lipstick. Satisfied with her reflection she blanched. She should call Ken, but even as she considered it, she wondered how on earth she'd explain this odd turn of events. He'd be understandably furious and the thought of trying to explain herself to him was daunting. If she handled this correctly, she could accomplish what she was here for and he need never know. Nodding to her reflection, she resolved to spare him the knowledge that Dan had followed her here. It would ultimately be for the best.

Dan was waiting in the hall as she emerged. He had changed, and the icy green of the fresh polo shirt made his eyes even more intense. She tried to avoid looking at him as they made their way back downstairs.

Their plan was to go to the local police and check whether there had been any record filed for a missing person fitting Fiona's description in mid-1976. Dan had suggested it, and it made sense to Eve. On an impulse, she had asked if they could take a quick walk before driving out to the police station, and as they made their way down the High Street, passing a collection of bakeries, outdoor equipment stores and gift shops, Eve made a mental note of the places she wanted to come back to.

As they paused at a pretty lead-paned window, the gentle

scent of lavender seeping out from the Highland Soap Factory made her think of Jess. She knew that her daughter loved the company's wild nettle body wash, so she made a mental note to get her some before leaving.

Dan was talking but Eve was distracted by the surroundings, taking in the packed display case in the window of the Fort Bakery. Ken would love this place. Next to it was the House of Clan Allan, their window full of an eclectic mixture of miniature whisky bottles, furniture, cushions decorated with artful stags' heads, and local paintings and photographs. As Dan moved on ahead, Eve stopped to look. Mounted on a simple easel was a framed print of a baby swaddled in a gauzy cloth. The child was sleeping on top of a loosely woven sack, which had been artfully draped over a gnarled wooden crate. Eve took in the image, the familiar warm light, the dust motes sparkling around the baby's profile. She looked down at the bottom right-hand corner, and there was the signature that she'd seen numerous times on similar work. Eve leaned into the window and let her forehead press against the cool glass. If only she could capture images that way. As she squinted, bringing the photograph back into focus, she realized that she'd left her camera at home. Annoyed at herself, she straightened up and looked around for Dan's outline. He had stopped up ahead and was peering at his phone.

Her decision not to call Ken raised its head. She couldn't possibly not talk to him at all, so she took out her phone and searched for the number in her contacts.

"Hello? You made it then?" Ken sounded tired and she instantly felt diminished by what she was intending to withhold from him.

"Yes. No problems." She noticed that Dan had turned around and appeared to be looking for her. "Everything OK there?"

Ken tutted.

"No. I burnt my toast, locked myself out and ran over the dog – all in the last three hours."

Eve laughed, despite herself.

"Funny. Especially as we don't have a dog." She raised a hand in response to Dan's wave. "Listen, Ken, I've got to go. I'm going to the police station to ask about a missing persons report."

"OK, Sherlock. Good luck. Let me know how it goes."

She slid the phone into her pocket just as Dan, having made his way back to her, dodged a young mother pushing her child in a stroller.

"Sorry, I didn't notice you'd stopped." He looked behind her at the window display. "Some interesting stuff?"

Eve nodded.

"I love that print." She jerked a thumb over her shoulder.

Dan stuck his chin out and scrutinized the photograph, then his smooth face folded into a frown as he stepped back from the glass.

Puzzled at his reaction, Eve also moved away from the window. "I'm a bit of a photographer myself, that's all."

Dan nodded.

"Ah. I think I've seen that kind of thing before." He pointed at the glass. "At least, it could be the same photographer."

"She's pretty well-known."

"That'll be why then." He smiled again. "And I can understand the attraction – the subject matter I mean." He appeared suddenly embarrassed, which made her want to touch his hand.

Rather than succumb, Eve switched her handbag to the opposite shoulder. "Shall we go?"

The police station was a short drive out of town, across the River Lochy. Along the way, they took a quick detour to see the exquisite thirteenth-century Inverlochy Castle ruins crouching on the bank of the river, a sight that made Eve even crosser that she'd forgotten her camera.

A few minutes later, they pulled up outside the low building.

They'd taken Dan's car, and the new-leather smell of the BMW lingered in Eve's nostrils as she crossed the path to the black front door. Dan followed a few paces behind her, and she felt his presence like a pleasant breeze at her back.

At the desk was a young police officer, her short auburn hair tucked tidily behind her ears and her white uniform shirt sagging across her concave chest. She looked up as Eve approached.

"Hello?"

Eve noticed that Dan had hung back, scrutinizing a curling notice that was pinned to a board by the door. He was giving her space, and she appreciated his sensitivity.

"I'm here to find out if there was a missing persons report filed sometime in mid-1976." Eve noticed the slight lift in the pinkish eyebrows. "It would be for a young woman called Fiona."

The police officer's badge read Morrison, and Eve wondered what her first name might be. As Eve ran through several potential names in her mind, the younger woman closed a folder on the desk.

"And you are?"

Eve pressed her lips together, embarrassed that she hadn't introduced herself.

"Oh, sorry. I'm Eve Carruthers. I'm actually trying to trace my birth mother. We were told that she was probably a runaway – from Fort William." She jerked a thumb over her shoulder in Dan's direction. "This is Dan Patterson from Family Connections. He's helping me with my search."

Officer Morrison nodded. "Oh, I've heard of them." She paused. "So, mid-1976, you said?"

Eve nodded. "Yes. Anything you have that might help would be wonderful."

Officer Morrison lifted half of the split countertop and walked out from behind it. Eve looked down at the sturdy shoes that swam around the young woman's spindly ankles.

"Our Missing Persons Coordinator's located in the Highlands and Islands division. I'll need to contact them and see if he can help you."

Eve's shoulders sagged. "Oh. You can't help me yourself?"

Officer Morrison shook her head. "Nope. But it'll not take a sec. I'll give him a ring now, if you want to wait?"

Eve glanced back at Dan, who was nodding at her.

"Sure, of course."

She sat down next to Dan, and leaned her head back against the wall.

"All right?" He pressed his shoulder into her and she could smell the faint musk of his hair.

"Uh huh. Just tired, suddenly." She closed her eyes. Perhaps if she didn't look at him, she could focus her energy on the phone call that was being made in a back office somewhere. A phone call that could, in some small way, possibly change her life forever.

Dan patted her thigh, the contact sending a spark down her leg.

"This is good. It's all progress."

She opened her eyes and took in the greying white ceiling, and linked her hands in her lap.

Ten minutes later, Office Morrison walked back into the reception.

"So, he can be here later today, if you can come back after lunch?" The young woman smiled at Eve. "Probably around two."

Eve stood up.

"We can do that, can't we?" She turned to Dan.

"Of course." He was close to her side, his hand flat across her shoulder blade. The proprietorial gesture made her jump, and she stepped away from the disarming buzz that was permeating her shirt.

Back in the car, Eve clipped her seatbelt on. The day, while chilly, had a cloudless sky as she looked out her window and wondered what Jess was doing. An image of her willowy daughter, her flat stomach slightly distended and the angular lines of her face softened by a new layer of flesh, made Eve miss Jess's presence. She would be beautiful pregnant, Eve had no doubt about that.

As they headed back into town, Ben Nevis looming green and purple ahead of them, Dan suddenly slowed the car to a stop. Nervous, Eve glanced over at him.

"What're you doing?"

"How about we go to the distillery?" He grinned. "It's just over there, and we can kill an hour or so."

Eve looked over at the cluster of buildings. A slash of stark white against the dark green of the hills behind them, the distillery sat behind a row of thin, red maple trees. A handful of remaining leaves clung to each branch as the wind whipped up, bending the narrow, elegant trunks. Eve's mind ground through the prospect of sipping whisky with this man she barely knew. She turned to him.

"Well I suppose it could keep my mind off things."

"Charming." Dan laughed as he pulled back out into the road.

"Oh. That's not what I meant."

"Forget it. I understand." He steered into the parking area. "I understand more than you think, Eve."

She felt his eyes on her as she fumbled with the seatbelt. Then his hand was over hers easing the clip open, the back of his fingers sending another shard of heat into her thigh.

"We'll find out whatever we can, and if this lead comes up empty, we'll regroup. We'll get there, just relax."

She shouldered the door open, instantly feeling the welcome brush of the breeze in her hair. Relax? That was easy for him to say. He appeared to be enjoying this, even to be in his element, while she felt as if her own skin didn't fit anymore.

As she stepped out into the wind, Eve recalled having had the same reaction when Ken had kissed her for the first time. They'd been at the cinema in St. Andrews soon after her fifteenth birthday. Russell and Mary had given her until 8:30

p.m., and Ken had assured them he'd have her home. In the dark theater, he'd pulled her close and tried to slide his hand inside her cardigan. She'd batted him off, but then, after the film, Ken had taken her hand and led her around to the back of the building. He'd asked her if it was OK and, at her silent nod, had leaned down and kissed her. Her knees had locked, and Ken had held her under her arms to stop her from toppling forward into his chest. They'd both laughed, running hand in hand back out into the yellow glow of the streetlights. He'd taken her home on the bus, his big hand over hers the entire time, and Eve had felt like the luckiest girl alive.

Dan was holding the door open.

"Madame. *Aprés tu.*" He bowed as she passed. "Let the tasting begin."

By the time they walked back into the police station, it was close to 3:00 p.m. and Officer Morrison was gone from behind the desk. In her place, a burly, balding man glared at them over his glasses. She explained who she was, this time introducing herself immediately.

"Aye, Morrison told me you'd be back. Wait there." He pointed a nicotine-stained finger at the row of plastic chairs that lined the wall opposite the desk. Both Dan and Eve slid onto a seat, as if having been reprimanded by an irate parent.

Dan leaned over and whispered, "Don't want to mess with that one."

Eve caught a waft of whisky. The tour of the distillery had been interesting, and the tasting quite informative. Eve wasn't a huge whisky fan, but she'd enjoyed the experience and, perversely, the obvious interest that the young woman guiding them had shown in Dan. Eve had felt proud to be with him, his casual manner, the confident voice, and the way he carried himself seeming to give her more significance. She'd smiled and nodded and let him touch her back as the young woman had explained the distilling process.

Eve watched as the policeman came back into the room with a younger man, not in uniform.

"This is Callum. He'll help you with your inquiry."

Eve stood and extended a hand.

"Pleased to meet you."

Callum had a shock of orange hair and red-framed glasses. He smiled, revealing a gap between his two front teeth.

"Hullo. It's Mrs…?"

"Carruthers." Eve shook his warm hand. "Eve."

"Right. So, I understand you're looking for an old missing persons report?"

Having followed him into a back office, handed him her driving license, and filled in an information request form, Eve sat across a narrow desk from Callum as he scrolled through a screen filled with lines that she couldn't make out. Dan was seated next to her, and she noticed that his knee was twitching. She frowned at him, and in response he gave her a silent thumbs-up.

"From January to September of 1976, there were three missing persons reports filed. Two were for women."

Eve leaned forward, her elbows on her knees.

"One was a woman in her forties. Went missing on her way home from work one night in May of that year." Callum shook his head. "Not your teenage runaway." He pursed his lips and continued to scroll down the list.

Eve couldn't stay seated any longer, so she stood up and walked to the far side of the room.

"Ah, this could be it." Callum nodded at the monitor. "A young girl reported missing by her father in September 1976. A local family. He was a doctor, looks like."

Eve snapped her eyes to Dan's as Callum continued.

"Dr. Francis Grant reported his daughter Fiona missing on September 12th 1976. She'd apparently left for school that morning and then not come home. They didn't think anything of it until her mother, Mrs. Sally Grant, discovered that some of her daughter's clothes were gone, and the money that they kept in a tea caddy was missing too."

Eve sat back down. "Does it say anything else?"

Fiona Grant. Her birth mother's name was very likely Fiona Grant. As she tried to stay focused, the name tugged at her subconscious.

"Seems she eventually turned up some months later. No info on where she'd been though."

Eve closed her eyes, trying to picture a tweed-coated doctor standing in the police station describing his daughter, when they'd last seen her, and what she'd been wearing, twisting his hands into a knot as he waited for a nugget of reassurance.

Callum coughed, and her eyes flew open.

"I have an address for the Grants at the time. Not sure if it's much use after all these years, but I can give it to you."

Eve swallowed.

"Yes, please."

Callum wrote the details on an index card and handed it to

her.

"Good luck."

Outside, Dan held the car door open for her. "Do you want to go over there now?"

She glanced at her watch. The idea of knocking on these people's door suddenly seemed ludicrous. What on earth would she say, if they were still there after all these years? What if they had no idea that their daughter had even had a baby? What if they were frail or ill and her questions distressed them?

"No. I need some time to think." She pulled the door closed and watched as Dan walked around the front of the car, then slid into the driver's seat. She wondered how many hours a week he spent at a gym in order to achieve the taut musculature. Her hand went to her middle. While still slim, she was definitely not as firm as she had been a few years ago.

They were both silent during the drive back to town. Eve stared out of the window, taking in the impressive outline of Ben Nevis. The mountain soared behind the jagged rooflines of Fort William. Even in the distance, it was an ominous sight, the slopes like rough pyramids of rock stacked one behind the other with swaths of rich green-and-tan carpet crawling up their sides like giant bodies of moss. Above all that, the summit had been dipped in icing sugar. Years ago, she and Ken had talked about climbing it. But everyday life had inevitably, and necessarily, got in the way. A newborn and a routine had pushed many such plans back, behind reality.

Eve glanced at Dan, who was concentrating on the road ahead. What was she doing with this stranger? What was she doing here without her partner, her best friend? She turned back to the window and swallowed down a surprising swell of tears.

An image of the photograph she'd seen earlier that day, of the baby lying on the old crate, came back to her. Jess had been a perfect baby. The kind of perfect that you saw in catalogues and on baby food jars. Eve had regularly been stopped in the street as neighbors, and even strangers, commented on her beautiful child. She had basked in the flattery, her blonde-haired, blue-eyed accomplishment carefully wrapped in a crocheted shawl, beaming at the myriad faces hovering over her. Once again, Eve tried to imagine leaving that perfect little human under a table and walking away. It was beyond comprehension.

She tried to picture Fiona, and herself as an infant in her young mother's arms. Suddenly, the presence in her handbag of the piece of paper with the Grants' address on it became caustic. All she wanted to do now was go to the house on Fassifern Road, ring the doorbell, see a face that might – in some bizarre way – look familiar to her.

She turned to Dan.

"I've changed my mind. Can we go now?"

Dan's eyebrows arched toward his hairline. "Um, yeah. Sure. What's the address again?"

The peak-roofed semi-detached house sat on a rise. It was set back from the road, and a narrow stone staircase rose through a beautifully kept garden densely packed with lavender, hostas, azaleas, and a red flowering plant that Eve couldn't name. The trees on either end of the house were tall, mature firs reminding her of those that lined her own garden.

Dan switched off the engine. "Ready?"

Eve forced a swallow. "I suppose so."

Gathering her resolve, she left the car, mounted the stairs two at a time, pressed the doorbell, and stepped back. Dan was hovering near the car and gave her a wave as she glanced back at him. After a few moments, the door opened. A young girl, perhaps nine or ten, wearing enormous fluffy slippers, eyed Eve.

"Yes?"

Eve forced a smile. "Hello. My name's Eve. I'm looking for the Grant family?"

The young girl frowned. Her long dark hair was caught up in a ponytail, and her hazel eyes flickered.

"Who?"

Eve repeated herself. The girl began to shake her head when a voice behind her made her turn back into the house.

"Can I help you?" A woman with deep frown lines and tightly curled fair hair stepped out onto the front doorstep.

"Sorry to bother you. My name is Eve Carruthers. I'm looking for the Grant family. I believe they lived here at one time?"

The woman shook her head and scowled.

"Dunno. Not heard of them." She paused. "We've been here eleven years. I can't remember the name of the people we bought from, but I don't think it was Grant."

Eve nodded.

"Is there anyone else who might've known them? A neighbor perhaps?" Eve used the line that Dan had given her should this scenario arise.

"You could try Mrs. Hennessey." The woman jabbed a thumb to her left. "Been there decades. She might remember."

Eve felt a lifting in her diaphragm, unsure whether it was disappointment or hope.

"Thanks. I appreciate it." She extended a hand, which the woman accepted.

"No bother." Finally, a smile cracked the ruddy face. "What's it about, anyway?"

"Oh, it's nothing really. Just some personal business."

The woman had already stepped back inside her house.

"OK, then. Bye." She raised a palm as she closed the door, not waiting for a response.

Eve made her way down the stairs, passed a smiling Dan, and immediately went up the set at the far end of the building. This side of the long house, in contrast, had a messy garden with a jumble of overgrown shrubs and browning grass. Outside the door was a dead potted plant, and next to it sat a small stone boot with some scrubby heather cascading out onto the step. Eve rang the bell.

An elderly woman opened the door. Inside her long green cardigan, her back was bent at an awkward angle, which spoke to Eve of years of carried pain. The face was remarkably smooth of wrinkles for what Eve guessed were her seventy-plus years. Eve introduced herself again and asked her question.

"Yes. I'm Mrs. Hennessey. I've been here fifty-three years now," she said proudly. "Seen a few families come and go from next door." She rolled her eyes. "Some good. Some not so." She winked at Eve. "So, the Grants is it you're asking about?"

"Yes. I'm trying to trace the family. Well, the daughter actually. Fiona."

The old woman moved out onto the step, and Eve noticed

that she walked with a pronounced limp.

"Well, they're gone." She grimaced. "Years ago now."

Eve felt the sink of disappointment.

"Oh. Do you know where they went?"

The old woman laughed.

"No, pet. I mean they've gone. Passed on. Shuffled off, you might say." She held Eve's gaze. "First Doctor Grant, oh, more than fifteen years ago, of cancer. Then Sally a couple of years later. Heart issues, I think."

Eve nodded, mentally recalling the tips Dan had given her in the car on the way over about how to keep a dialogue going.

"Right. Well, I don't suppose you know where the daughter might've moved to, do you?"

Mrs. Hennessey's eyes ran the length of Eve's body like an x-ray machine looking for a swallowed key.

"I might." She frowned. "I don't know you, though. I mean, what's your interest?"

Eve gathered herself. "I am Fiona's daughter."

The old woman's eyes widened and she cocked her head, absorbing the words.

"Daughter?"

Eve nodded.

"Well, I never."

Eve shifted her feet. Mrs. Hennessey was obviously reliving something as her eyes took on a distant look and her face moved in an animated way, as if she were silently having a familiar conversation over again.

"Mrs. Hennessey."

"Aye. Right. The last I heard some years ago was that wee Fiona had settled in Spean Bridge." She paused. "Never married, you know."

Eve tried to look impassive. Spean Bridge was a picturesque village less than half an hour from Fort William. She'd just taken a giant metaphorical leap closer to Fiona Grant. She turned and sought Dan's eyes as she gave him a thumbs-up.

"He was a tough nut." Mrs. Hennessey said. "Hard on them both."

Eve swung back around.

"He ruled that house wi' an iron fist. Just like he ran his surgery. Sally was fear't of him, I'm sure." She tutted. "Nasty piece of work."

Eve felt her heart rate pick up.

"Afraid of him?"

Mrs. Hennessey nodded. "Never said boo to a goose, poor Sally. Made jams and chutneys for a local shop. Worked all hours in that kitchen, barely went out. But we'd talk when we were hanging out washing." She gestured behind her. "Women do, you know."

Eve nodded, not wanting to stem the old woman's flow of memory.

"Wee Fiona was a timid thing too. Quiet as a mouse." She kicked her slippered foot at the curling heather and then met Eve's eyes again. "She bolted. No one knew where she'd gone for ages."

Eve swallowed.

"Then, months later, she just came back. No explanation, no nothing. Her mother was beside herself. There was some gossip. But he quelled it as soon as you like. No one in town would cross him, so the stories stopped quickly."

"Gossip?" Eve hoped she sounded casually interested.

"Aye. About why she'd gone." Mrs. Hennessy stepped back and steadied herself against the doorframe. "It was none of our business anyway." She shook her head.

Eve felt the tide of information ebbing. What had Dan said to do?

"Mrs. Hennessey, do you know why Fiona ran away?"

The old woman shook her head.

"No, lass. But I could'a guessed."

Eve nodded.

"There was a boy. A local lad, a year or so older than her. Dr. Grant didn't approve and Sally, well, she just kept quiet about it all." She shifted her weight to the opposite leg, her back curving even more unnaturally. "There was a big ruckus, and then, the next day, Fiona was gone." She raised her eyebrows. "Doesn'y take much to work it out."

"Right. I see what you mean." Eve moved to the edge of the step. "I wonder, do you have her address in Spean Bridge?"

The old woman's eyes snapped brighter.

"Och no, pet. She never kept in touch wi' me." She frowned. "But Spean Bridge isn't that big. I'm sure it wouldn't be too hard to track her down."

Eve and Dan had arranged to meet in the hotel lobby before going to dinner. As she passed the mirror, Eve took in her reflection. The wool skirt was looser on her than it had been the last time she'd worn it, the silk blouse clung to her torso and as she turned, she caught sight of the line of her ribs under the flimsy fabric. She tucked her hair behind her ears and checked her cheekbones for any stray dots of mascara. Then, grabbing her jacket, she headed for the door.

Dan was standing in the lobby, his back to the fake fireplace. He'd put on a tweed jacket, and his hair was freshly washed. As she approached, he beamed.

"You look *merveilleuse*." He reached out a hand and lifted hers to his lips. "Madame, shall we?" He swept his hand toward the door, and she felt herself redden.

"It's just a skirt." Self-conscious, she slipped her jacket on.

"Apparently there's a pretty good seafood place at the pier. I booked us a table."

"Fine." She passed him, emerging into the cooling night.

The red-roofed restaurant sat at the end of a low pier, the white stone walls in stark contrast to the wash of darkening sky and the gentle, shadowy folds of the hills hunched behind it. Their table was at a window overlooking the loch, and Eve watched a couple pass along the wooden boardwalk outside. A small fishing boat was moored next to the pier, and its flag-topped mast tipped from side to side as the water beneath it folded with the breeze. Across Loch Linnhe, a row of tiny lights sparkled, spraying white dots across the blackness of the water.

"It's very pretty here. It must be gorgeous in the daytime." Eve glanced at the menu, then back out of the window.

Dan had ordered a bottle of wine, and as the waiter poured some for him to taste, she slipped her hand into her bag and pulled out the phone. There were two missed calls, one from Jess and one from Ken. Feeling another dip of guilt, she switched it to silent. She'd call home later, let them know her plan for the next day.

She watched Dan swirling the big glass, sniffing and sipping the ruby liquid.

"What is it?" He was staring at her.

"Nothing. Just lost in thought."

His eyes were luminous in the dim restaurant. The silvered temples and broad jaw, the way his lips curled unevenly when he smiled, the long fingers on the stem of the glass all sent a ripple through her.

"So, tomorrow. What's the plan of attack?" He lifted a bread roll and tore it in two.

"Not sure." The warm burn of the wine was welcome at the back of her throat as she swallowed.

Dinner passed pleasantly. The food was marvelous, and the wine, rich, smooth, and spicy, had gone down well – if too quickly. Dan had ordered them each a brandy after the meal which she'd tried to refuse, unsuccessfully. Together with the whisky earlier in the day, Eve now felt herself as close to drunk as she could ever remember being. She was not a heavy drinker, and the sensation was both foreign and exhilarating.

"Shall we head out then?" Dan was smiling at her.

She focused on his eyes, trying to make them stay in one place.

"Um, yes. Better get to bed." The words out, she instantly felt her face heat up. "I'm tired, I mean."

Dan laughed.

"I get it. C'mon." He stood up and reached for her hand. "Steady as she goes."

The hotel lobby was dimly lit. A few people were milling around the small bar in the corner, and a receptionist smiled wanly at them as they passed. Dan held the lift door open for her.

"*Aprés tu.*" He laid a hand on her back.

"Why do you do that?" She pressed the button for their floor.

"What?"

"The whole speaking-French thing." She leaned her head back against the stainless-steel wall of the lift.

"Uh, it's a habit. I suppose I miss being there."

She glanced at him, noticing that for the first time since she'd met him, he seemed less than confident. She tried to imagine her stalwart, home-loving husband speaking French in an attempt to impress. The notion was ludicrous.

"It's a bit of an affectation, don't you think?" She clamped her mouth shut, shocked at her own nastiness. This was not who she was.

Dan stepped to the side, creating distance between them.

"Sorry you feel that way." He glanced at her. "It's not intentional."

Eve was riddled with embarrassment. The alcohol had loosened her tongue, and she couldn't take it back now.

"I'm sorry. I didn't mean to be so rude. It's just that you don't need it." She waited for him to meet her gaze. "It's not what impresses me about you."

Dan flicked his eyes to hers.

"OK." He waited.

"I mean, you're an impressive person. You've achieved so much. You're well educated. You've travelled and opened yourself up to more than I ever will." She paused.

Dan was frowning. "You're an impressive person yourself, Eve."

She let out a harsh laugh.

"Oh yes. Little Eve. Same old life, same old stuff, same old job, same old same old for as long as I can remember." She felt her throat thickening. "I've never been anywhere. Done anything out of the ordinary." A tear broke out and trickled down her cheek.

Dan was next to her, his thumb wiping under her eye. "Stop it. You're not doing yourself justice."

She leaned into the pressure of his touch.

"You have raised a wonderful daughter. You have a really responsible job. You have a husband who loves you. You're there for your parents. You're a photographer."

She lifted her head.

"That's not nothing." He said.

Eve sniffed.

"It's not about where you've been, Eve. It's about how you live. And you live broadly."

She met his eyes. His face was close to hers, and she could smell the brandy on his breath. Her eyelids felt heavy, and just as she thought she could feel the pressure of his lips on hers, the lift jolted to a halt, making her eyes fly open.

He held her under the arm as they weaved down the corridor. At her room, she fumbled with the key card until he took it from her and opened the door.

"Come on. Let's get you to bed."

Eve let him help her onto the bed. He slipped off her shoes and then unzipped and slid her skirt over her hips. She lifted her arms like a child to let him pull her shirt off, and then she lay on her side, her legs curled up against her stomach as he tucked the covers over her. Her head was swimming. Where was her pillow? Where was Ken? She needed to phone him.

CHAPTER 18

Jess turned sideways and looked at her reflection in the bathroom mirror. Her stomach formed a minute round under her palm. Her sickness had become obnoxious and, according to her mum and the books she'd been reading, she could expect it for at least a few more weeks. She pulled her hair up into a rough ponytail and secured it with a band. Then, after cleaning her teeth for the third time since she'd woken up, she rinsed out the sink.

Ram was at the corner shop getting some things for breakfast, and she was supposed to be making a pot of coffee. The coffee grounds had been what had sent her charging to the bathroom. She could no longer tolerate the smell of them. As she emerged from the bathroom, she heard his keys in the lock.

"Hey." He walked into the living room.

"Hi." She stood on tiptoe and kissed him. "Sorry. No coffee yet. Had a bit of a quick call." She jerked a thumb over her shoulder. “Me and coffee, not a good combo at the moment.”

Ram smiled at her.

“No problem. I’ll see to it.” He dumped the plastic bag on the counter and shrugged off his jacket. “Want eggs?”

Jess considered. Eggs had been safe, so far.

“Um, yeah. OK.”

She pulled the newspaper from the bag and flipped to the classifieds. They’d been searching for a car seat, and Jess checked the *For Sale* section each day to see if there were any bargains. Eve had been horrified when Jess had said she’d consider a secondhand seat if it was in good condition.

“No. Dad and I will get it for you.” Eve had looked offended. “No secondhand anything for this baby.”

Jess turned the page, scanning the ads. Eve hadn’t been in touch since leaving for Fort William a day and a half ago, and Jess was fluctuating between being hurt about the lack of contact and being anxious about her mother. She looked up at Ram, who was putting butter into a pan.

“Why do think she hasn’t called?” She slapped the paper on the counter and slid onto a bar stool.

“Dunno.” Ram shrugged. “Probably just busy.”

Jess frowned. “Not buying that. It takes five minutes to call.”

Ram laughed softly.

“You sound like she did when you moved in here.” He lifted a bowl and began cracking eggs into it.

Jess remembered Eve turning up on the doorstep one evening when Jess had only been living with Ram a few days. She’d been surprised to see her mother standing there.

"Well, if the mountain won't come to Mohammed," Eve had huffed, and Jess, embarrassed, had asked her in. Since that event, Jess and Eve spoke almost every day, so the absence of that customary contact was uncomfortable.

"Yes. I remember." She picked up a slice of bread and nibbled at the crust. "But this is different."

Ram widened his eyes at her. "Just leave her another voice-mail and don't worry. I'm sure she's fine."

Jess slid off the stool and grabbed her phone from the coffee table.

"Mum. It's me again. Just checking in. Can you call me back please? I'm getting worried."

After a few minutes, Ram pushed a plate of eggs and toast across the counter.

"Here. Come and eat."

Ram made the best eggs. In fact, Jess thought he was a great cook all around. She loved to sit on the stool and talk to him as he threw ingredients into pots without measuring anything. She marveled at the skill, not having mastered it herself.

"These are good." She shoveled more egg into her mouth. "Do you think I should go up there?"

Ram's eyebrows bounced. "Where?"

"Fort William."

"No, I don't, Jess."

"Why not?"

"Because if she'd wanted you there, she'd have asked you."

Jess felt the sting of the truth.

"Well, her leaving me behind wasn't anything to do with me

being pregnant." She pouted.

Ram lifted the pan and set it in the sink. "Well, you probably just need to try and respect her reason, whatever it was."

"All right. Thanks for that, *Sensei*." She pulled a face at him.

Having finished her food, Jess padded into the living room and curled up in the armchair. "I'm going to pop over and see Dad later. Do you want to come?"

Ram shook his head. "No, you go. I've got some paperwork to do."

She watched his lean form from across the room as he finished cleaning up.

"Can you come and snuggle me for a bit?"

Ram hung the towel on the hook and crossed the room.

"Oh, yes. A snuggle, is it?" He nudged her thigh until she lifted herself up from the seat, just enough for him to edge underneath her. She settled on his lap, tucked her face into his neck, and slid her fingers into his hair.

"I love you."

He ran a hand down her back.

"Me too."

Jess turned into the driveway. The garage door was open, and the wheelbarrow, full of grass clippings, was sitting on the path.

Rather than go to the front door, she made her way around to the back garden.

"Dad?" She called out.

Ken emerged from behind the greenhouse.

"Hi, Shorty. Nice surprise." He pulled off his gloves and hugged her. "No Ram?" He looked over her shoulder.

"Nope. Just me." She shrugged. "Sorry."

Ken slung an arm around her shoulder as they walked back to the house. "So, what brings you out to see the old man? Are you checking up on me?"

"Kind of. You doing all right?"

Ken slipped off his boots and left them outside the patio doors.

"Aye. I'm fine. Are you?" He eyed her as she slipped past him and circled the kitchen island.

"Yep. All good." She gave him a double thumbs-up.

"So. What's going on then?"

She leaned into the cabinet. "Have you spoken to Mum?"

Ken filled the kettle with his back to her. "Uh huh. She called me yesterday when she got there." He turned to face her.

Jess chewed the skin around her thumbnail. "Oh. Good."

Ken frowned. "Has she not phoned you?"

Jess shook her head. "Nope. *Nada*. Nix. *Rien*. Nuttin." She used her mother's phrase. "I'm worried about her."

"She sounded fine when I talked to her." Ken took a biscuit out of the tin. "Why're you worried?"

Jess pulled her mouth down at the corners.

"Look, it's her decision." He hooked a finger through the handle of his mug.

Jess carried her tea into the living room. The late-afternoon sun was pooling on the floor next to her, the paned-glass window creating a shadowy crisscross shape on the carpet.

"I think I might go over. Just to make sure she's all right."

Ken shook his head.

"I wouldn't. You know what she's like when she's made her mind up about something."

Jess cupped the mug in her lap. The warmth of the china felt good in her palms. Her dad always protected her mum, and this situation would obviously be no different. Resolving to change the subject, she swung her legs up and crossed her ankles on the coffee table.

They talked about her morning sickness and the upcoming week's schedule for the shop. Ken shared some ideas he'd had for additional merchandise, and they laughed about one of their suppliers from Ardnamurchan, a reed-like man with milk-bottle-thick glasses who insisted on driving the racks of blue-veined cheeses over to St. Andrews himself lest they get "jostled" on the way.

Having established that her father had something in the fridge for dinner, Jess left her cup in the kitchen and hugged him goodbye.

"So, when's she coming home?"

Ken shrugged. "Not sure. Maybe tomorrow, or the next day. She said that she'd got an address for the parents."

Jess frowned. "So is she going there?"

"Apparently."

She hefted her bag onto her shoulder and pulled her cardigan closer around her chest.

"Well, please tell her to bloody well call me back if she phones you again." She grimaced. "Daft old cow."

Ken laughed. "Now, now. Off you go – and say hello

to Ram."

The night had passed slowly, and Jess hadn't slept more than a few hours. Her mind was spinning as she watched Ram snoring, his face half submerged in his pillow. He looked like a little boy when he slept as his cheeks puffed out with each exhale and his hair stuck up from his head. He was leaving for work at 8:00 a.m. and planned to ride his bike in that day. Ken had said that she could have the day off, as he was closing early to do some bookkeeping, as he did the last Tuesday of every month.

The dawn was sending a creep of pink up the wall opposite the window as Jess turned onto her side and pulled her legs up closer to her chest. September mornings in St. Andrews were chilly, and the old building took a while to warm up once the heating came on.

She stared at the wall and calculated. If she left at 8:30 a.m., she should get to Fort William around noon, which would mean she could surprise her mother. Maybe take her for an early lunch. She'd spend a couple of hours with Eve and drive back to St. Andrews before Ram even knew she'd been gone. He wouldn't be home until after 6:00 p.m. so, with no disasters along the way, she could just make it.

Next to her he stirred, a fist pulling the duvet up closer to his jaw. She held her breath. She didn't want him to wake just yet. If those dark-chocolate eyes looked at her – if the mellow voice asked her what she had planned for today – she didn't think she'd be able to carry off the deception for more than a few moments.

Slipping from the bed, she tiptoed into the living room.

She checked her phone and, seeing no messages, grabbed a blanket from the back of the sofa and wrapped it around herself. Her feet were freezing, so she curled up on the seat and shoved them under a cushion. Her stomach churned and as she pressed a hand into her middle, her phone buzzed on the coffee table. Jumping up, she grabbed it, hoping it was her mother. Instead it was a text from her phone carrier informing her that she had five days left to upgrade her plan. Disappointed, Jess dropped the phone onto a stack of magazines and returned to her blanket cocoon.

Within a few moments, Ram appeared in the doorway.

"What're you doing up?"

She pulled the blanket tighter around her shoulders.

"Just restless and I didn't want to disturb you."

He settled next to her and pulled the end of the blanket over his thighs.

"It's cold out here."

Jess opened her arms, the blanket spreading like a cape.

"Come in then." She smiled at him.

The front door clicked shut and Jess glanced at the clock. It read 8:16 a.m. so she had a few minutes to throw on clothes and grab her stuff. She trotted to the window and watched Ram's long back undulate, curving over the handlebars of his bike as he pedaled away from her. The blue helmet she'd bought him with the white saltire on it looked overly bright and incongruous in the diffused morning light. She loved that he wore it despite telling her that it wasn't necessary.

Seeing him turn at the end of the road, she spun around and

headed for the bedroom.

After pulling on her jeans, a sweater, and sheepskin boots, Jess trotted downstairs to the car. She had a bottle of water, a packet of salty crackers, and an apple in her bag, none of which she expected to keep down until she reached Fort William. She let herself into the car and lifted her phone. Seeing no messages, she searched for her father's contact.

"Hello there." Ken sounded surprised. "I thought you'd be sleeping for Britain, having a day off."

"Did Mum call you last night?"

"Em, no. I left her a message though, so I'm sure she'll ring this morning."

Jess tucked the phone under her ear and pulled away from the curb.

"And you're not worried?" she snapped.

"A bit, but she'll call."

Jess tutted as she maneuvered the car into the lane and waved to thank the person in a rainbow-colored van who'd let her in. How could her dad be so laid-back? The more she thought about her decision, despite the twinge of guilt at hiding it from Ram, the more convinced she was that she was right to go to Fort William. Eve was going through something, and Jess wanted to be there for her mother as Eve had always been for her.

"Are you still there?" She squinted and reached for her sunglasses as the clouds cleared and a spear of light shot through the windscreen. "Dad?"

"I'm here."

"Sorry. I didn't mean to bite your head off." She indicated at a junction and waited for the lights to change.

"Then don't." Ken sounded cross.

It didn't happen often, but she knew she'd made him angry.

"Sorry."

"Just try to put yourself in her shoes, Shorty. It can't be easy to navigate all this."

Jess moved out into the lane.

"Where's she staying again?"

Jess glanced in the rearview mirror. She was speeding and wanted to make sure there were no police cars lurking along the A9, as they were prone to do. She'd left Dunkeld, Pitlochry, and Blair Atholl behind her and was now skirting the edge of the Cairngorms National Park. It was close to 10:00 a.m. and she calculated that she was over halfway there.

The day had lightened the farther west she drove and to her right, beneath a bright blue sky, the land fell gently away from the road. Slopes of mauve and pink heather formed circles of color that dotted the landscape leading up to thick swaths of trees. Behind that, the mountains formed a dark ridge along the horizon as far as she could see. She'd only stopped once to use a bathroom, and she'd been able to eat a few crackers without throwing up. Her stomach felt more settled than earlier, despite her mounting nerves. She had one more hour to go.

Fort William was busy as she negotiated her way along the High Street. According to her navigator, the hotel was only a few feet away and she squinted, searching for the sign. Spotting it up ahead, she turned into the car park. As she looked for a space, she scanned the row of cars for the familiar shape of Eve's. It was almost noon and she hoped that she wasn't too late to catch her mother before she set off.

Her father had said that Eve had the address for Fiona's parents, but that he hadn't spoken to her since, so he had no idea if she'd actually gone there the previous day. For a moment, Jess imagined her mother knocking on a mangled door at a huge, ramshackle house, an old crone opening the door and dragging Eve inside as she screamed for help. Jess shook her head and laughed out loud at herself. Spying her mother's car, she exhaled.

The lobby was quiet. No one but the receptionist was around, and she had her nose buried in her phone.

"Excuse me. I'm looking for my mother, Eve Carruthers. She's staying here." Jess stood at the desk, her bag between her feet.

"Oh, right." The young woman dropped her phone and turned to the computer. "What name again?"

"Carruthers. Eve." Jess tried not to sound irritated at having to repeat herself.

The girl chewed her cheek as she looked at the monitor. Jess was on the point of speaking again when the girl nodded.

"Right. Yes. She's here."

"Can I have her room number, please?"

The girl shook her head.

"No. I'm not allowed." She shrugged. "I can call her room for you."

Jess shook her head.

"No. I want to surprise her. Look, I'm her daughter." She

smiled at the girl. "Honest. I just want to surprise her."

The girl frowned.

"I'm really not allowed."

Jess sighed. It was time to bring out the big guns.

"Listen. I just found out that I'm pregnant. It'd be so much cooler if I could just knock on her door and say ta da, guess what, Mum? Don't you think?"

The girl was smiling now.

"Well, if you can show me some identification, I suppose it'd be OK. Just don't tell anyone."

Jess carved an X on her chest. "Hope to die."

A few moments later, she walked along the dingy corridor. The tartan carpet was faded, and some of the wall lights weren't working. As she looked for the room number the girl had given her, Jess wondered why Eve hadn't chosen somewhere nicer to stay. She recalled their lovely room in Braemar and then pictured the rather bossy Mrs. A. Perhaps this impersonal place was better, for her mother's purpose.

Up ahead a door opened and a man walked into the corridor. He was tall and slim and had thick, silver-shot hair. There was something about his shoulders, the way he held himself, that was familiar and he was speaking quietly to someone behind him. Not noticing Jess, he moved farther out into the hallway and there, following no more than a step or two behind him, was Eve.

Jess's breath caught in her throat. Eve looked tired, but she was smiling. She let her hand rest on the man's forearm and then, as she turned to close the door, she spotted Jess.

Time stood still. Jess could hear her heart in her ears, and her feet felt as if they were burning through the floor beneath her. The walls were leaning inwards and there was a hissing in her ears. She sucked in another breath.

"Mum?"

Eve was moving toward her, her face a mask of shock.

"Jess, what're you doing here?"

Jess felt Eve's hand on her arm and jerked away.

"Don't," she spat.

Eve stepped back as if she'd been stung. She looked stricken.

"Sweetheart, you're so pale. Come and sit down."

Jess heard the words *sit down* above the clatter of her heart, but all she could see was Dan Patterson, the annoying, boastful guy from Family Connections, standing behind her mother. What the hell was he doing here? What was Eve doing here with him? Why had he been in her mother's room?

Jess felt clammy all over. Eve was trying to speak to her, but Jess couldn't take anything in. She had to get out of here. She had to get home to Ram. Turning her back on them both, she bolted for the lift. She could hear Eve shouting her name as she forced her way through the sluggish doors. She thumped the button over and over, willing the doors to close on the picture that she couldn't bear to see any longer.

CHAPTER 19

Eve wiped her mouth on a damp towel. She'd emptied herself of everything she'd eaten and drunk the night before, and now all that filled her was fear over the encounter that she'd just had with her daughter. Jess's face had been ashen. She'd been shaking, and when Eve had tried to touch her arm, she'd felt Jess's skin tacky under her fingertips. Her daughter's expressive eyes had been vacant, as if she'd been on a different plane.

Eve looked in the mirror and saw Dan behind her, sitting in the chair that he'd spent the previous night in. His clothes were crumpled and his hair unkempt. He had a dark shadow on his chin, and he looked older this morning. She checked her face and then walked into the room.

"You need to go, Dan."

He looked up at her.

"But I want to help fix this." His face sagged. "Please, Eve."

She shook her head. "My mess. I have to sort it out."

He stood up and reached for her hand but she pulled hers back and moved to the opposite side of the bed.

"Please just go. I'm all right. I'll go home and explain everything. It'll be fine." She kept her voice even.

His eyes looked cloudy, as if their intensity had been diluted by his concern. She shut her own eyes, closing her mind to his face, to his voice, and the way he affected her. She had to focus on her family. She'd done serious damage, and she could only hope that Jess would forgive her.

"I feel so responsible…"

She held a hand up.

"I made the decision to keep your being here from my husband, and daughter. I've made a fool of myself." She felt her voice give way. "To indulge in some stupid…" she halted. "When I should've been focusing on why I'm really here."

Dan looked startled.

"I need you to go. Please, Dan."

She turned away from him.

"I'm so sorry, Eve. This was my fault. I invited myself here. I was totally selfish. I wanted…" He stopped.

"What?" She perched on the edge of the bed. Every part of her was exhausted.

"I wanted to spend time with you. Really spend time with you. I knew it would be risky for you – a bad choice, but I pushed it anyway."

She stood up and folded her arms across her chest.

"We're both adults. You're taking too much responsibility."

He shook his head.

"No. For once in my life I'm taking on just the right amount."

"Bye, Dan. Thank you for all your help." She extended a hand, a formal gesture which felt cold and yet wholly appropriate.

"Good luck with the rest of your search." He enclosed her fingers in his. "Will you please let me know if you find her?"

Eve took in his frazzled expression, the heavy shadows under his eyes, and the genuine note of caring in his voice.

"I'll email you."

Less than three hours later, Eve pulled into her driveway. She'd called Ken from the road and left him a message that she was on her way home. Despite having ignored his calls for the past day and half, she felt oddly hurt that he hadn't called her back. His car was in the driveway, and as she walked to the front door, her stomach dipped. How much would he know? Would Jess have told him what she'd seen earlier that day? Would Ken let her talk, explain? Would he believe that nothing had happened with Dan, other than a drunken flirtation that had ended with her passing out in her underwear?

Whatever else Dan might be, he'd been a gentleman. He'd slept in the armchair rather than leave her alone in her inebriated state. She'd woken to see him crunched in the chair, his head at an awkward angle and his shoes neatly sitting at the door. Despite her shame at her behavior the night before, she'd lain and watched him sleep for a few minutes realizing that this would be the only time she'd get to do that. Eventually, as if sensing her surveillance, he'd opened his eyes and stretched. His long frame had unfolded slowly from the impossibly small chair.

"Morning, gorgeous." He'd grinned as she began to acknowledge the searing pain behind her right eye. "How are we feeling?"

She'd groaned. "Mortified and hung over."

He'd laughed and suggested room service, but Eve had refused, insisting that he turn his back so she could get up and dress herself. They'd been on their way downstairs for much-needed coffee when they'd bumped into Jess. The thought of her daughter staring at her, mute and horrified, made Eve feel sick to her stomach again.

As she tried to put her key in the lock, her hand was shaking so badly she dropped it. She bent down to pick it up, and then the door opened.

"Hi." Ken was smiling. "Welcome home."

CHAPTER 20

Two days had dragged by, and Eve had neither spoken to Jess, despite leaving her several messages, nor told Ken what had happened. He'd questioned her as to why she'd come home without going on to Spean Bridge, but she'd deflected, saying that she needed time to regroup before taking that on. He seemed satisfied with her response, and the more understanding he was, the worse she felt.

Now, as she stood in the kitchen ironing his best shirt, she noticed that the cuffs were worn, small threads easing their way out of the fold at the wrist. The sight of the frayed material sent a needle through her heart, and a tear plopped onto the pale blue cotton, followed by another. Then, she couldn't stop. Her insides were crushing together, making it hard to breathe. Her hands were shaking so badly that she held onto the iron with both of them, clenching the handle as her body rocked back and forth over the wobbly table.

It took a few minutes for her to slow her breathing down. The shirt had become speckled and the iron, drained of water, had stopped spurting its steam into the garment. She set the iron on the counter, scrunched the shirt into a ball and shoved it into the bin. Ken wasn't due back for a few hours, and as she checked her watch again, Eve knew precisely what she had to do. She dumped the rest of the ironing back in the basket and folded the table away. Glancing around the room, she grabbed her keys and headed for the door.

Getting into town was quick, despite being stuck behind a tractor for the first few miles. As she pulled into a parking space adjacent to Jess and Ram's flat, Eve's hands were still shaking. It was almost 10:30 a.m., and knowing that her daughter would most likely be home, she looked up at the stone-fronted building. She couldn't let Jess avoid her any longer. She had to clear the air, and then she must talk to Ken.

Having been let in the lower door by a neighbor coming in with his shopping, Eve mounted the stairs to the second floor. She glanced at her rumpled reflection in a mottled window before ringing the bell.

Ram was in a baggy track suit. His hair stood up in a cone at the back, and he looked like he'd been asleep.

"Oh, Ram. You're home."

He massaged his head and yawned.

"Eve. Hi." His eyebrows jumped. "Yes. I've got a cold."

Now that she heard him speak, it was clear that he wasn't well. She tried to read his face for any signs of disapproval but was unable to gauge his expression.

"I'm sorry to disturb you. Is Jess here?"

"No. She's gone for a walk at the Old Course." He dropped his gaze to the floor and stepped back. "Are you coming in?"

"I don't want to hang about if you're resting. Can I just leave her a note?"

He nodded and shuffled back into the living room. His track bottoms dragged on the floor, and Eve noticed that his feet were bare.

"You should wear slippers." She couldn't help herself. "You'll catch your death."

Ram picked up a writing pad from the coffee table, handed it to her, then flopped onto the sofa. He hadn't said more than a few words, but now something in his demeanor indicated that Jess had told him everything.

Eve checked her watch. "When did she leave?"

"Only about twenty minutes ago. She'll be another hour, I'd think." He tugged the blanket over his legs. "Do you want to wait for her?"

Eve met his gaze. The gentle eyes had a clear message. He was wary, but open to hearing her.

"No, I won't wait, but I do want to talk to you quickly. Is that OK?"

"Sure. I'll make us some tea." He made to get up.

"I'll do it. You stay put. In fact, go and put some socks on while I do this."

He tutted but got up and disappeared into the bedroom.

Being opposite her son-in-law, preparing to defend herself, Eve was so self-conscious that she couldn't sit still. With her mug in hand, she paced back and forth in front of the window.

"So, what's going on?" Ram spoke through his nose. "Are you OK?"

She nodded. "I'm fine, Ram. Thanks for asking. I've made a huge mess of things, but I'm all right."

He sipped his tea as Eve continued.

"I'm worried about Jess, though. What she saw…I mean, what she thought she saw."

Ram's eyes locked on hers, but he remained silent.

"It wasn't anything, Ram. I mean, nothing happened." She squeezed the mug between her palms. "I'd had more to drink than I'm used to and I pretty much passed out. Dan – Mr. Patterson stayed with me in case I was ill in the night. I was in the bed and he was in the chair – all night."

Ram eyed her.

"I swear on my life." She stopped pacing. As she waited for a reaction, what made her more uncomfortable than being condemmed for her poor choices was the potential of losing his respect.

Ram set his cup on the table.

"Eve, I'm not judging you. I think it was an odd thing you did, but you have to understand why Jess is so upset." He wiped his nose on a crumpled tissue.

"I do understand." Eve thumped down into the chair opposite him.

"Actually, I'm not sure you do." He frowned. "It wasn't just the fact that she saw you with that guy. It was that you deliberately shut her out. She thinks you used her pregnancy as an excuse to exclude her from something she felt a part of." He coughed, a rattling sound that made Eve wince. "She doesn't want to believe that anything happened with that Dan person, but what she saw…" He paused. "She's understandably pretty cut up about it all."

Eve felt the weight she'd been carrying across her chest increase in intensity. What Ram said was true. All of them deserved so much better from her.

"I understand that completely, but to be fair, I felt she should stay here because I was genuinely worried about her being away from home. She fainted in Fort William you know, and…" Her voice trailed as Ram nodded and then pulled a new tissue from the box.

"Have you told Ken yet?" He blew his nose. "I don't mean to intrude, but Jess is finding it hard to be at work because she's keeping it from him. She feels dishonest."

At that, Eve gave way to the tears that had been bubbling up to the surface since she'd walked in.

"God, Ram. I've ruined everything." She leaned over and took the tissue he offered her. "I'm such a fool."

"Can you tell me why you did it?" He spoke quietly. "Why you went with him?"

She swallowed over a lump. "I'm thoroughly ashamed of myself but, in my defense, I didn't go *with* him." She paused as Ram's eyes narrowed. "He just turned up there. I had no idea he was coming." Even as she said it, she heard the weakness of her position.

He shifted in the seat.

"I told myself that I didn't need to tell anyone because his being there, even uninvited, was purely to help me professionally." She swallowed. "But if I'm honest, I was flattered by the attention. He's a handsome man, and I behaved like a fool with a crush." She paused. "But when it came down to it, it wasn't about that at all."

Ram leaned forward, his elbows on his knees.

"What was it about then?"

She shrugged. "I just felt the need to continue searching alone. I wanted the chance to figure out something this significant, by myself. To prove that I could." She paused. "The flattery was nice. It was a boost to my ego, but I never intended to betray Ken. I think I was just curious what it would feel like to be admired by a man like Dan. Someone worldly and sophisticated." She sniffed. "I'm just so ordinary."

Ram stood up, the blanket falling to the floor. He walked around the table and perched on the arm of her chair.

"The other thing is that for a while I'd been feeling that Ken and I were simply floating around each other – not really connecting." Eve watched him shake his head, a motion so small it was almost imperceptible. "He's all I've ever known. The only man I've ever loved." She felt her face heat up.

Ram frowned. "So, this Dan guy…"

"No. That's not what I'm saying." Eve held a palm up. "But Ken's always protected me from everything, paved the way and fought all life's dragons, but that feels like smothering at times. He's not one for change either. I mentioned it to Jess a few weeks ago."

He squeezed her shoulder. "Eve. You're an amazing woman. You underestimate yourself so much."

She shook her head.

"You do." He patted her shoulder. "I think you need to just

come clean with both of them. Tell them exactly what you told me, and then everyone can move on."

She shoved the damp tissue inside her sleeve.

"What if they can't forgive me?" She felt the press of new tears.

"They will. It might take time, but they will."

Ten minutes later, she stood in the doorway. Ram held the note she'd written to Jess and was keeping the door open with his toe.

"Drive carefully and let me know if there's anything I can do." He smiled at her.

Seeing the genuine kindness in his face, she leaned in and kissed his cheek. "Thank you, Ram. You've been so good to me."

He shook his head.

"Not at all. You and Ken are my family. This is a glitch. You'll get through it." He hugged her. "Now go home and talk to him."

She nodded.

"I will." She gestured toward the note. "Please tell her that I love her."

"Will do."

As she drove through the town, eventually passing the Old Course Hotel on her right, Eve scanned any passersby, looking for the familiar outline of her daughter. Knowing that she wouldn't see her, Eve made her way home. By the time she got back to the house, she'd worked through several potential conversations with Ken, and she was surprised to see that he was home already. She walked steadily up the front path. This was fate. Kismet. Call it what you will. He was here and it was time.

Ken was in the kitchen eating a sandwich.

"Hello." He spoke around a mouthful. "Just popped back for a quick sarny." He lifted the bread up as evidence.

"You hardly ever come home for lunch. Anything up?" She tossed her keys in the dish on the counter and slid onto a stool opposite him.

"I wanted to see how you were. You've been a bit quiet since you got home." He shrugged. "Just checking up on you."

Eve looked at the man whom she'd loved since she was a young girl. He had given her a life that was full of caring, security, laughter, and affection. His face was thinner than it had been in a while, his eyes seemed to droop a little, and his round stomach had retreated inside his shirt – another of the changes that she'd noticed over the past few days.

"I'm all right." She pulled the soggy tissue out from her sleeve. "But I do need to talk to you."

CHAPTER 21

Jess sat with her feet under Ram's thigh. The room was warming up, but she still felt shivery.

"I hope I don't get your cold." She wrinkled her nose. "Not that I'm unsympathetic."

He laughed. "Oh, right. You're my personal Florence Nightingale."

She pouted. "Hey. I just made you a honey lemon drink." She poked her toe into the flesh of his thigh, then settled back against the cushion, feeling the warmth of her husband's leg begin to seep through her thick socks.

"Listen, Jess, I need to tell you something."

The change in his tone surprised her. "Sounds serious."

"Your mum came round today while you were out."

Jess clamped her lips together.

"Before you flip your lid, just listen."

She folded her arms across her chest. "I'm listening."

"She was really upset. Wanted to explain about everything." He paused. "She told me what happened with that guy."

Jess twisted a tassel on the blanket around her index finger. She was furious with her mother, and the whole Dan thing was utterly shocking, so much so that she still felt the weight of it in her heart. She wanted nothing more than to believe that it had been innocent – a misunderstanding – but the disturbing scene in the hotel was etched on her mind. She'd been avoiding her mother but, now that Ram had seen Eve, Jess was afraid to hear the truth of the situation.

"Wait. I'm not sure I want to hear this."

He took her hand in his. "It's not what you think."

She wound her fingers through his. "So tell me."

Having listened to him for a few minutes, Jess considered his account of Eve's story. Eve had mentioned to her weeks ago that she felt that she and Ken needed to shake things up, but Jess couldn't imagine her mother taking a step, however misguided, toward Dan Patterson. Even if Eve was frustrated with Ken, Jess couldn't imagine her terminally sensible and caring mother actually thinking that Patterson was anything other than a pretentious show-off.

"So she admitted that she liked him. All that French crap?"

Ram nodded.

"She said it was flattering. Not that she really intended to act on it, but that it boosted her ego." He shrugged. "I can kind of understand that."

Jess frowned. "You're far too understanding."

Ram shook his head.

"She also mentioned that they'd been a bit disconnected recently – her and Ken."

Jess nodded.

"I think this whole incident was a culmination of lots of little things." He paused. "She's had a lot on her mind."

"And what about all the nonsense about me needing to stay here?" She knew she sounded petty, but Jess rarely felt the need to censor herself with Ram.

"She genuinely felt that you should rest and take care of yourself after what happened in Braemar." He paused. "She knows that she should've told you both that what's-his-name had shown up there, but she was just trying to figure things out by herself."

"Oh, right. Just herself and Dan Patterson, you mean." She raked her fingers through her hair and twisted it into a messy knot.

"Well, like I said, he was just on the periphery. Nothing more. And I suppose he did know how she should move forward with getting information. Go from point to point, etcetera." Ram rubbed his palm along her calf.

"Well, it's not rocket science. It was *my* idea to go to the police in Braemar."

Ram nodded. "I know." He squeezed her leg to get her to look at him. "I think you need to let this go. She's devastated that she's hurt you." He reached into his pocket and pulled out a piece of paper. "She left you this note." He held it out to her. "And she was going home to tell your dad everything that'd happened."

Jess pushed herself up in the seat.

"Don't let this become a real rift between you." He flapped the piece of paper.

"I'm not sure I care what she has to say." Jess sniffed.

"Come on. This is your mum. She'd do anything for you. She adores you." He held his palm up. "So she screwed this up, but how many times has she forgiven you your mistakes? Picked up the pieces and helped you get through stuff?"

Jess saw a tiny wrinkle form across his brow. The dark eyes were waiting, willing her to be the bigger person that he knew she could.

"Oh god. You're such a…"

"What?" He smiled and Jess felt her anger seep away.

"A big pain in the arse." She let herself laugh. Leaning forward, she snatched the paper from his hand. "OK. I'll call her tomorrow."

CHAPTER 22

Ken had only slept in the guest room twice in twenty-three years: once when he'd had a bad flu and once when Jess had come home after an argument with her senior-school boyfriend. She'd been crying hysterically, and Ken had volunteered to vacate their bed so Jess could sleep in with her mother.

Now, having watched him take his pajamas from under the pillow and leave her crying as he went down the hall and quietly closed the door of the tiny guest room, Eve could hardly breathe. She lay under the covers fully clothed and stared at the ceiling, trying not to close her eyes. Every time she did, she saw his face the moment she'd told him about Dan showing up. She hadn't even been able to finish telling him what had happened or explain herself properly, before his face had drained of color and he'd walked away from her, mounting the stairs two at a time. She'd called after him, pleading that he hear her out, but the pain that had been evident in his face had paralyzed her and the effect of that had remained in her throat, as if she'd swallowed glue.

He hadn't come out of the little room for a few hours, and now that it was past 3:00 a.m. Eve hoped that he was sleeping. She turned to face the window, but the sight of his smooth pillow made her turn back to face the door. If only he'd been angry with her, shouted, or at least let her finish speaking so that she could assure him of the innocent nature of her time with Dan, she might have had a chance to at least begin to mend things.

Ken's silence was purgatory. While not exactly an orator, he only became silent when he was either extremely angry or, as she'd seen only once or twice over the years, deeply hurt. Eve knew that all she could do now was wait for him to work through the information she'd given him and then hopefully emerge from his cave. Once he would talk to her, listen to her again, she'd lay herself open to whatever he had to say. She deserved it.

The room was cold, and the tip of her nose was freezing as she pulled the duvet up over her face. As she felt the heat from her own breath, a creaking floorboard made her throw off the covers and sit up. Ken stood in the doorway. He was fully dressed, even wearing shoes.

"Where are you going?" She stood up.

He held up a palm. "Don't get up. I'm going to a hotel."

"Ken. Listen to me, please." She moved toward him.

"Eve, I'm telling you to stay here. I've got to get out of the house." He turned away from her. "I'll ring you tomorrow."

Eve felt her insides collapse. He was leaving her. He was actually going.

"Ken, please don't go. Nothing happened," she shouted at his broad back.

He halted momentarily, hovering in the doorway for a few seconds, and then continued walking.

Eve's feet were stuck, her bare toes clawing the carpet. She should run to him, hang onto his arm until he heard her, but instead she sank back onto the bed, grabbed the duvet in both fists and listened to him clatter down the stairs. She heard the chink of keys, the slam of the front door, and then the rumble of the engine as his car pulled out of the driveway.

She sat on the edge of the bed for a few minutes, then stood up on unsteady legs. The room was dim but she could see the doorframe clearly. She squinted, imagining that she could still see him standing there, his back to her as she shouted. Willing herself to put one foot in front of the other, she walked slowly down the stairs and into the kitchen. She flipped the light on, and the starkness of the room made her flinch. She glanced around, looking for some sign of his presence, a shoe or one of his ubiquitous dirty gloves. The place was tidy, empty of any sign of him. She filled a glass with water from the tap and drank deeply.

By 6:00 a.m., Eve had dozed on the sofa for only a few minutes, her phone close to her hand. There had been no calls, no messages. As she filled the kettle, a movement outside caught her eye. The cat that she'd seen a few days earlier was back. This time it was stalking something, its stomach low to the stone of the patio and its ears pricked up. She set the kettle on the stove and watched the animal move, sleek and controlled, until it darted into the lavender bushes. Rubbing her eyes, she wondered what had been hiding in there. A bird, perhaps, or a mouse, or some other small creature that had fallen prey to the stealthy cat. Suddenly, pictures of Dan jumped before her eyes: his mesmeric eyes, the flash of a smile, and then the memory of him scrunched into the armchair in her room. She shook her head. She had fallen prey to the charm of a man she hardly knew, and she'd deceived her love, her best friend and partner, in the process.

By 11:00 a.m. Eve was beside herself. Having called in sick to work, she'd taken a quick shower and changed her clothes. The washing machine now hummed under the kitchen counter as she paced back and forth in front of the sink. What if he didn't come back? He'd said he'd call and yet, so far, there hadn't been any word from him. Just as she reached for her phone, it buzzed on the counter. Grabbing it, she saw a text message. *At shop. Will call later.* Eve felt her legs buckle. Even this dry message was something. With trembling fingers, she tried to compose a response when the phone rang in her hand, making her jump. Flooded with relief, she answered Jess's call.

CHAPTER 23

The coffee shop on Market Street was busy. Jess had arrived first and had grabbed a table near the counter at the back of the overly warm room. She was oscillating between anger and tearfulness and was apprehensive about seeing her mother after everything that had happened. Wanting the meeting to take place on neutral territory, Jess had suggested this café. The fact that they made the best millionaire's shortbread in St. Andrews was just an added benefit.

Jess had developed a craving for the crumbly caramel-and-chocolate-topped biscuit, and was having a slice almost daily. Ram had begun bringing it home for her on his way back from work and now, as she eyed the glistening square in front of her, her mouth filled with saliva. She'd just have one bite, then she'd do her yoga breathing while she waited.

Moments later, Eve pushed through the glass door and glanced around the room. Jess grudgingly raised a hand and

Eve, unsmiling, wove her way through the tightly packed tables. As she reached Jess, it was clear that Eve had been crying, and the harsh speech that Jess had rehearsed felt a little less firmly justified.

Eve's face was ravaged, her eyes red-rimmed, and her nose swollen. Jess tried not to notice, but the sorry image chipped away further at her finely honed anger. She didn't stand to hug her mother as she would usually have done. Instead, she pointed at the spare chair, the coldness of the action feeling unnatural.

"You look terrible." She slid the cup of coffee she'd bought for Eve across the table.

Eve nodded.

"Yes. Deservedly so." She shrugged her coat off and pulled the cup closer. "Thanks for meeting me." She glanced around her. "Have you heard from your dad?"

Jess nodded.

"He called me this morning. He sounded dreadful."

Eve wiped her eyes with a crumpled tissue.

"He went to a hotel last night." Her voice cracked, and Jess fought the impulse to reach across the table and grab her mother's hand.

"Well, what do you expect, Mum?"

Eve nodded silently and wiped her nose. She looked like a lost child, and even as Jess recognized the irony of that imagery, she steeled herself against the natural instinct to comfort her mother. While she hated to see Eve in pain, there was a tiny part of Jess that wanted to let Eve swim for a while longer in this quagmire she'd created. She'd done this to herself.

She'd deceived them, and Jess wanted her to feel the impact of that. Pointedly silent, Jess pressed her thumb onto the plate, mashing some crumbs of biscuit into a pile which she dropped into her mouth.

Across the table, Eve was staring at her cup, letting tears run unchecked down her face. Jess felt her remaining anger crumble and so extended a leg and tapped Eve's calf under the table.

"He'll be back. He's just doing his big hurt bear thing." She tried to smile as Eve sniffed loudly and shoved the tissue in her pocket.

"I know. I just can't stand that I've hurt him. Or you."

"You did hurt us both." Jess frowned, recalling the tearful night she'd spent at home with Ram on returning from Fort William. What she'd seen in the hotel corridor had rocked her to her core, raising all her hidden fears about her parents' relationship to the surface, and even as she'd recounted the events to Ram, she'd had to dash to the bathroom twice to throw up. He'd finally managed to calm her by persuading her to take a warm bath.

Eve shoved the hair from her forehead as Jess checked her phone for messages. Eve said nothing, sipping coffee and wiping her eyes between sniffs while Jess watched the face of the woman she admired most in the world twitch in pain. The cheeks were more heavily lined than usual, and lank fingers of hair stuck to the broad, capable forehead. The silence between them was a prickly and uncomfortable space. Unable to stand it, Jess spoke.

"So, Ram says it was all a misunderstanding, at least the Dan part." She waited for her mother to meet her gaze.

Eve's eyes remained glued to the tabletop.

"Nothing happened, Jess. On my life." She pressed a palm to her chest. "It was all a stupid mistake." She looked up. "I owe you an enormous apology."

Jess pressed her lips together, a gesture which she knew to be Mary's and one her mother also employed to indicate displeasure. Suddenly, the image of Eve stepping out of the hotel room behind that ridiculous man flashed bright again, and Jess felt her anger resurge. The notion that her mother could even consider spending time with another man was inconceivable.

"I have one question, Mum." She frowned. "How could you do that to Dad? He's so…"

"So what?" Eve locked eyes with her.

"So kind, and so good. He totally adores you. He'd do anything for you, and he trusts you implicitly." Jess felt her throat tighten. "He didn't deserve that."

Eve's face had flushed pink.

"I know that. I have to live with what I did, which is bad enough. But do you know what's almost worse than that colossal mistake?" She hesitated. "The fact that I was less than honest with you for the first time in your life. It breaks my heart to think that I've lost your trust and respect." Eve's shoulders rolled forward, and her voice gave way to a sob.

Glancing around to see if anyone else had noticed Eve's distress, Jess shifted in the chair. She couldn't do this to her mother any longer.

"Mum, it's not that bad." She whispered. "Yes, I'm angry, but Ram explained what you said about Dan just showing up, and the flattery and stuff, and while it makes me question everything I know about you, I'm doing my best to understand why you did it."

Eve pinched her nose and dragged the tissue back out of her bag.

"Are you really?"

Jess nodded. "It was a misguided thing to do, but I'm trying to make some sense of it."

Eve nodded. "Thank you. I'm not sure I believe you, but thanks."

An hour later, they walked along Market Street, heading for the flat. Knowing that Ram was still home not feeling well, Eve declined Jess's invitation to come in.

"No. I'll go home in case Dad comes back."

"Right." Jess nodded.

"I just hope he does."

"He will. You know him, Mum."

Jess watched her mother cross the road and head toward her car. Eve's back was curved under her coat, as if an unaccustomed weight were dragging her shoulders down. As she waited for Eve to get in, Jess noticed a puff of her mother's breath float up into the chill of the early evening. Autumn was almost at an end, and then winter would come and go and then, with the spring, would come the tiny person Jess was creating inside her, a melding of her and Ram's characteristics. As she laid a hand over her stomach, she hoped that this baby would have its father's compassion.

As she watched Eve's car pull away, Jess imagined how hard it must be for a mother to ask for her child's forgiveness, and with that thought, the last shreds of her anger dissipated. Ram was right. Eve had been an exemplary mother, and Jess hoped that she'd be half as good at it herself.

CHAPTER 24

Ken had stayed away for three nights. He'd texted each day but hadn't called, and Eve had waded through her work. She'd gone to the shops, called her parents and pretended all was well, done laundry and stared at the TV in a fog of fatigue. Nothing tasted right, worked properly, or made sense. This fractured reality was nothing like what she wanted.

Dan had phoned a couple of times, and each time she'd seen his number, she'd declined the call. He hadn't left any messages, which she was grateful for, and eventually she'd texted him saying that she was fine and to please stop. Since that, mercifully, she'd heard no more.

Now, her untouched dinner had congealed on the plate in front of her, and the headache that had been building all day increased in intensity. She scraped the food into the bin, stashed her plate in the sink, and lifted her handbag in search of some aspirin. As she pulled the pill bottle out, stuck to its side was the yellow note with the Grants' address in Fort William. The letters had been smudged but were still legible, and as she pulled the note away from the bottle, Eve knew what she would do.

Up in her studio, she sat at the work table with a pad of paper and a pen. She'd started typing the letter on her laptop but then had deleted it in favor of a handwritten message using the heavy, bonded paper that she kept for thank-you notes and invitations. The pen felt cumbersome in her hand, but as she started to write, the words came easily.

My darling Ken,

I know you don't want to hear from me, but I have to write. "Sorry" isn't adequate. In fact, there are no words that are. When you're ready to listen, I will gladly tell you everything. I think you may have imagined things to be worse than they truly are.

I know how much I've hurt you. I know that I will have to earn back your trust, but all I ask is that you give me that chance. For everything that we've been to each other, I ask you for that one thing.

I've decided to go to Spean Bridge. I'm going alone and will text you the hotel information. Until I have closed the door on these questions I have – this quest, such as it is – I think I'll be better off alone. I'm sure you'll appreciate the space too, so this will hopefully help us both.

Keep an eye on Jess. We met and talked, and I think she will eventually forgive me.

You know how much I love you both. I have no future without you in it.

Eve

Eve sealed the envelope and propped the letter up against the hall mirror. She glanced at her reflection and winced. Staring back at her was a shadowy face. New lines were etched underneath her eyes, and the skin around the grey pools was puffy and pink. Her hair was dirty, clinging flatly to her head, and her neck was swamped by the collar of her sweater. She shoved the oily strands off her face and sighed.

Later that night, having washed her hair, booked a place to stay in Spean Bridge, and texted both Jess and Ken about her plans, she emailed her boss asking for a temporary leave of absence and apologizing for her recent, erratic behavior. As she slid into bed, pure exhaustion took over, shoving the myriad thoughts that had kept her awake for the past few nights to a place deep enough inside that she was able to sleep. When she woke to the alarm at 7:00 a.m., Eve felt, for the first time since she'd come home from Fort William, that she had a purpose – something worth getting up for.

Rather than a hotel, she had booked a small, self-catered cottage attached to a beautiful stately home in the center of Spean Bridge. She was looking forward to a few days of the kind of quiet that could only be found in a Highland village during a quiet season. She longed to be left to her own devices and to melt into an environment where no one knew her, her history, or her mistakes.

Having often read about the Great Glen, the first thing she'd put in her bag was her camera. Whatever else came out of this trip, she'd promised herself to make time to take some photographs of the stunning Lochaber region.

The drive had been uneventful, and as she entered the village of Spean Bridge, she felt the sense of peace that had been missing for some weeks now, returning. The homes she passed were characterful and tidy. Clustered in groups, some sat close to the road with low stone walls around them while others were set back behind smooth lawns and intricate garden gates. Eve soaked up the serenity as she followed the navigator north to her lodgings, and before long she was turning into the driveway.

The house was impressive. An ivory-colored, nineteenth-century structure with Victorian architectural features, it was surrounded by mature shrubberies. Manicured lawns on either side disappeared underneath dense strips of tall trees. A breathtaking view of Ben Nevis served as the backdrop, and Eve blinked at the white-topped mountain she'd seen just a few days earlier from Fort William.

On the left of the drive was the most spectacular row of crimson-colored hydrangea that Eve had ever seen. As she headed for the guest parking area at the back of the house, she made a mental note to photograph all of this for Ken.

The owners, a friendly but discreet middle-aged couple, spoke in hushed tones as they conducted her quickly down a curved gravel path to the guest cottage. Having accepted the key and thanked them, Eve closed the heavy front door behind her.

The cottage was everything she'd hoped for. Downstairs was a high-ceilinged, light-filled living room with a rose-colored sofa and a leather armchair both facing an ornate fireplace. The room was warm, smelling mildly of cinnamon, and on the narrow counter that separated it from the brightly lit galley kitchen beyond was a small vase of flowers and a welcome note.

Upstairs, the bedroom was dreamy. A large four-poster bed sat next to a double-wide window which was framed by floor-length, sheer curtains. The afternoon light shone golden through the gleaming glass, and outside was another spectacular view of the mountain.

Eve exhaled and, throwing her bag onto the floor near the bed, pushed the door open to the en-suite bathroom. A huge claw-foot bath sat across one corner of the room. Wide ceramic tiles covered the floor, and a heated rail draped with pristine white towels was mounted on the wall next to the deep pedestal sink. Without thinking, Eve crossed the room and began running water into the bath.

With her scarf knotted loosely around her throat, her coat and woolen hat on, Eve walked down the long drive and out onto the road. It was getting close to 5:00 p.m., and while it was not quite twilight, the evening was threatening to crawl in from the surrounding moors. She loved this time of year, the time of heather and the vivid colors of autumn that blanketed the Highlands, paving the way for the dark starkness of winter to come.

As she walked away from the house, she noticed the woolen mill on the opposite side of the road. She crossed over, intending to go inside, but then spotted, set back and to her right behind the village shop, the distinct Highland Soap Company sign. It hung outside a pretty, whitewashed building and Eve smiled at the irony. She never had gone back to the one in Fort William for Jess's gift. Deciding that she'd venture in the following day, she turned right and began walking in the direction she'd come from earlier. She'd seen a Tourist Information Office on her way into town, and it seemed like a good place to gather some local facts, and pick up a walking map.

Within a few minutes the distinctive, pebble-dashed building appeared on her left. Eve let a car pulling a caravan go by, then crossed the road and went inside. Behind a dark wood counter, a grey-haired woman sat with her back to the door. On hearing Eve come in, she swung around and smiled.

"Well, hello. You're just in time. I was about to close." She stood up and brushed some invisible crumbs from her skirt. A badge pinned to her cardigan read *Iris*.

"Oh, I don't want to keep you." Eve smiled back. "I can come back tomorrow."

Iris shook her head.

"Not at all. I've got a few minutes. What can I help you with?"

Eve moved closer to the counter and glanced at the long display shelves stacked with colorful leaflets touting various Highland tours, fishing trips, and ski and mountaineering instruction. Next to the display was a separate stand holding brochures on the Scottish engineer Telford's famously constructed Spean Bridge, and next to that several different leaflets about the Commando monument that sat on a panoramic viewpoint a mile or so outside the village. Eve knew that these elite Green Berets had trained here during the Second World War, and the memorial had been erected to commemorate the fallen.

She leaned an elbow on the counter.

"I was looking for a local walking map and perhaps some

info on Leanachan Forest. I was hoping to walk some of the trails and take pictures."

Iris nodded and, coming around the counter, began pulling leaflets from the wall display.

"These are good for the forest. This one has a map of all the trails, and this one's the best for local history, info on Ben Nevis and such." She thrust a handful of flyers into Eve's hand. "Oh, and there's the map you'll want." She pointed to a low table next to door.

Eve turned to follow the direction of the crooked finger, and as she located the small stack of maps, she also spotted a revolving display rack holding a cascade of postcards. She moved closer, trying to focus on the images. There were many of Ben Nevis, the lochs and highlands of Lochaber and, of course, the famous bridge, but on one side of the rack were several cards that stood out as different from the rest. She pulled her hat off and squinted, taking in the various images. In one, a baby in a tiny pair of dungarees was lying in a wheelbarrow on top of a checked blanket, surrounded by a tumbling English -country-style garden. Another was set on a riverbank, the child poking its head out of a soft canvas bag with a spray of gypsophila behind it. Eve tried to control her breathing. Next on the rack was the same print she'd seen in Fort William of the child in a barn. She spun around to see the older woman putting her coat on.

"Why do you have these in here?" Eve croaked.

The woman frowned.

"Why not? We support all our businesspeople here." She lifted a small shopping bag from behind the counter and flipped off a light.

"I'm sorry, I meant…"

"Fiona's local. She has as much right to have her stuff in here as anyone else."

On an impulse, Eve slid one of the postcards of the baby on the hay bale from the rack. "Can I buy this?"

The woman pursed her lips. "I'm closing."

Eve reached into her handbag for her wallet. "Please. I'd be so grateful."

After being treated to a few exaggerated sighs, Eve tucked the postcard into her pocket and followed the older woman outside. As Iris turned a large key in the lock, Eve waited behind her.

"May I ask if you know her – the photographer?"

Iris buttoned her coat and then slid her handbag onto her shoulder.

"Aye, I do. Fiona Grant. She's local, like I said."

Eve heard the name, and with it came a rushing in her ears that made her rock on her heels.

"Fiona Grant?"

The woman moved past Eve and began walking toward the road.

"Uh huh. She's quite famous, you know. Has books and calendars and stuff all over the country in various places – so I hear."

Eve nodded mutely.

"Well, I'm off. We're open tomorrow from ten if you want to come back." Finally, Iris smiled again. "Sorry, I'm in a bit of a rush. My son's coming for his tea."

"Oh, sure. Of course. Thanks," Eve managed to respond and then, as the woman's narrow back moved away from her, Eve looked around for a sign of what to do next. There was little question now that Fiona Grant was indeed the same Grant whose work she had admired for years. The same diminutive woman she'd become tongue-tied in front of in Edinburgh. But could this woman, who had dedicated her life's work to capturing stunning images of newborns, be the same person who had given birth to her thirty-nine years ago and then callously left her under a table at the mercy of strangers?

Eve found that she couldn't fill her lungs properly. Seeing a bench a few feet away, she headed for it, the postcard now clutched in her hand.

After stopping to buy some food at the shop, Eve had walked back to the cottage, pulled the heavy curtains in the living room, and lit the fire. A bowl of untouched soup sat on the low table in front of the sofa, and the TV was burbling in the background. She lifted the postcard from the table and flipped it over. There was one tiny line of text at the bottom of the space for writing in. It said "Photography by Grant ©2016." She ran a finger over the name, as if trying to divine more information about the person named, then tossed the card onto the table, lifted the warm bowl, and, despite her lightheadedness, went into the kitchen and threw the soup down the drain.

The following morning, after a disturbed night, Eve splashed water on her face, dressed quickly, and went downstairs. The cottage was chilly, but rather than light the fire, she'd turned up the thermostat a few degrees. After a rudimentary online search for Fiona Grant, which kept sending her back to a generic website filled with images, the majority of which were familiar to her, Eve's plan for the morning was to go back to the Tourist Information Office and ask more questions – after she texted Ken and Jess. She lifted her phone, tapped a message to them both, and then drained her teacup. Since arriving, she'd heard from Jess, but not from Ken.

She sighed and looked out of the window. The sky was bright blue, and she was eager to get out into the fresh air.

As she passed the narrow table that sat inside the front door, Eve noticed an old-fashioned telephone. On a shelf underneath was a local directory, its pages fanned at the corners like wings lifting the cover from the front of the book. She smiled, not sure when she'd last seen one of these.

As she pulled her coat on, the seeds of an idea sprouted. She shook her head. It couldn't be that simple, surely? She lifted the heavy phone book and carried it back to the sofa. Flipping through to the Gs, she scanned the page. There were several Grants listed, but only one with the initial F. The name, address, and telephone number of F. R. Grant were there, right in front of her. Eve pressed her eyes closed against the tears that had suddenly blinded her.

Fifteen minutes later, with the thistle broach and the note in her pocket, she was driving toward the top of town. According to the map program she'd checked, Fiona's house was only a matter of minutes from the guest cottage. Distracted by the navigation screen, Eve had to brake sharply to let a child on a bicycle pass in front of her. As the little boy waved, she pulled away slowly, her heart banging in her chest. Within a thin strip of time, the navigator's tinny voice was telling her that she'd reached her destination.

She parked the car in the street and looked around, trying to spot the low bungalow that she'd seen on a satellite image less than an hour ago. Behind her, set back from the road, was the opening to a narrow driveway. Locking the car, she walked up to the wrought-iron gate and peered between the two tall firs that framed the entrance to the home. There it was, the white stone house, the twin bay windows and the dark slate roof. A single chimney split the house in two, the roof evenly sloping away on either side of it. On one corner, a dark red Virginia creeper decorated the wall, crawling from the ground up to the roof line, and several spindly trees that had lost their leaves were scattered across the front lawn. Eve took it in, the pretty but unassuming house that could be home to her birth mother.

Suddenly overwhelmed, Eve backed away from the gate. Her car was only a few paces away, and she wanted to feel the safety of it again, protecting her from whatever was to come next. Turning quickly, she trotted back and let herself in. As she slipped into the seat, her legs were shaking so she pressed a hand onto each thigh to quell the involuntary movement. If only she could talk to Ken, ask him what he'd do. No sooner had she entertained the thought than Eve was annoyed with herself. After everything that had happened, everything that she'd done, learned about herself, and risked, why was she questioning whether she could do this alone?

She twisted the rearview mirror toward her. While still tired, she looked less traumatized than she had for the past couple of weeks. Grabbing her lipstick, she swiped some on, wiped dark dots from the corners of her eyes, and then zipped her bag closed. She was going to walk down that drive and ring the bell. What did she have to lose?

Eve's hand was on the door handle when there was a movement in the corner of her eye. She twisted around to see someone emerge from behind the gate. She took a deep breath and watched as a woman, carrying a large bag on her shoulder, walked toward the car. Eve was frozen to the seat as the figure came closer, the face emerging as a gently lined oval with wide-set eyes surrounded by short, dark-blonde hair. She wore a green wax jacket, the kind that Eve had seen in country-life-type magazines, and the thin, denim-clad legs tapered down into clumsy Wellington boots. Eve calculated that the woman was around five feet five, her slim build reminiscent of Jess's frame.

There was something in the way this woman walked, the way she looked at the ground and let her head lean to the right as if avoiding a low-hanging branch, that made Eve catch her breath. She knew that she did the same thing, as Ken had teased her about it in the past. The closer the woman came to the car, the realization that this was indeed the photographer that Eve had met in the bookshop two years earlier threatened to choke her.

As she watched, the green jacket came level with her window. Eve sat motionless, not sure whether to throw the door open and say something or to let the woman pass unassailed. As she moved by the window, Eve recognized the brand of the camera bag. She thought her heart might stop, so she leaned her head forward onto the steering wheel. Forcing herself to breathe slowly, she sat upright again.

The woman's back was shrinking in the rearview mirror. Either Eve had to act now, or she might never find the nerve to do this again.

She started the engine and turned the car around. Creeping as slowly as she could, she steered along the quiet road. The woman was walking briskly, the bag pulling her left shoulder down under its weight. Within a few moments she dipped right, walking down the steep slope that led to the woolen mill. Intrigued, Eve drove into the car park behind the building and climbed out of the car.

As she stood in the entrance to the mill shop, surrounded by rows of colorful cashmere and cream Arran sweaters, tins of shortbread, flat caps, and tartan scarves, Eve could smell the distinct tang of coffee. She moved forward, following the scent as it took her through the cheerful displays around her.

At the back of the space, a single step down led to a bright, glass-roofed conservatory. Eve looked around, taking in the various occupied tables. Eventually she spotted the woman near the back of the café. She had shed the jacket and was sitting with her back to the door. She appeared to be flipping through a magazine and had a large frothy drink close to her hand.

Rather than head to the counter, Eve pulled her shoulders back and walked toward the wax jacket that now hung on the back of a chair.

CHAPTER 25

Jess walked into the back of the shop, trailing behind her father. Ken had seemed so quiet when she'd arrived that morning that she'd insisted on staying on for the whole afternoon. She'd invented a work event that Ram had to go to in Dundee, and Ken, having made it clear that the subject of Eve was off the table, seemed happy to have Jess's company as he worked silently around the storeroom.

She picked up a stock list and scanned the items, not really taking in what she was seeing. Ken was stacking large cans of stuffed vine leaves onto a high shelf, and she watched his tartan back curve and straighten as he lifted and adjusted the cans.

"Can I help?" She tossed the list onto the scrubbed stainless counter.

"Oh, that'll be right. You hefting these in your condition." He winked at her over his shoulder.

"I'm pregnant, not dying." She rolled her eyes. "You lot are all daft."

Ken lifted the last of the cans and then kicked the empty pallet away, sending it smacking into the wall.

Jess jumped. "Take it easy, Rocky."

Ken flinched.

"Sorry. Didn't mean to give it such a whack." He wiped his forehead with his sleeve. "Don't need a gym, me." He smiled at her. "It's built in, just running this place." He drew a circle around himself with open palms.

Jess caught the shadows under his eyes which seemed to have deepened, even since she'd arrived that morning. Her father was paler than usual, and his jeans were loose on him.

"Dad. Are you going to talk about it?"

He shook his head. "What's there to say?"

She hefted herself up onto the counter and stuck her chin out.

"Talking won't fix anything." He shook his head.

"It might help you not implode."

He assessed her, his face appearing to relax as the mask of tension he'd been wearing all day cracked.

"If I talk, I might say things" – he paused – "that wouldn't be good."

She nodded. "Look, I know you're hurt and angry."

"Furious," he snapped.

The force of the word shocked Jess. "OK. You're furious."

He leaned back against the shelves and dragged his hand over the crown of his head.

"Jess, this is between her and me. There's nothing you can

do, and I'm beginning to think there's nothing I can do either."

Jess felt something inside her shift. She'd never seen her father look so defeated, and rather than evoke sympathy, it made her angry.

"For god's sake, Dad. You sound as if you're giving up." She slid off the counter.

Ken eyed her.

"This is you and Mum we're talking about. You're seriously saying that there's nothing you can do?"

He shrugged.

"Dunno. Whatever I've been doing has obviously been wrong, up to now." His eyes flashed.

"Oh, stop it. That's ridiculous and, frankly, a bit pathetic." She frowned. "You need to at least let her explain. She said you wouldn't listen to her."

He nodded.

"Aye. She's right. I don't need the details." He moved across the storeroom and, with his back to her, lifted an envelope from the small desk in the corner.

Sensing her moment, Jess dived in.

"Nothing happened with Dan. He basically stalked her. Just turned up. She made a bad decision by not telling you he was there, had too much to drink and passed out." She paused. "I was angry with her too, it was a stupid situation to get into, but I believe her, Dad." She walked over and stood behind him. "She loves you. She just got a bit confused by everything that's happening to her, and then was distracted by a fake tan and some stupid flattery."

Ken turned to face her. To Jess's surprise, he looked calmer.

"It's more complicated than that." He shoved the tail of his shirt back into his waistband. "Yes, she deliberately excluded me from this whole Fiona thing, and then hid that guy's presence from me, which was bad enough, but the fact that she was so dissatisfied with her life…" He jabbed himself in the chest. "Her life with me – that she was open to that arsehole's advances," he paused. "That's the worst part."

Jess felt her throat thickening as her father's face slid back under a tense film. He was staring at the floor.

"I feel like I've failed her." He lifted his chin, and she saw his eyes fill.

Jess crossed the space between them and hugged him.

"That's enough. Just stop it." She stepped back. "Self-pity really doesn't suit you."

He sniffed.

"Do you want to know what I really think?" She poked his arm.

"Um, yes." He frowned.

"You need to back off a bit. Give her more credit and stop treating her like a child." Jess paused, anxious that she may be crossing a line.

Ken held her gaze, but remained silent.

"Aside from being your wife, and my mum, she's a highly intelligent, capable, professional woman. Sometimes you forget that."

Ken's brow folded.

"I know. You're right." He wiped his palm across his face. "I'm so proud of her, too. I need her to know that. And I need to think before I speak, sometimes." He paused. "But she's hurt me, Jess."

Jess nodded.

"I know that, but you just have to let her talk to you. Really listen to her and then you'll both figure out how to fix things." She smiled. "She made a mistake, but you can get past it. I know you can."

"OK. I'll try." He patted her cheek. "Since when did you become so wise?"

Jess laughed softly.

"Like father, like daughter, I suppose." She crossed her eyes at him. "Well, up to now, anyway."

CHAPTER 26

Eve cleared her throat, and the woman swiveled around in her seat. She looked startled, and as she assessed Eve, Eve looked down into a reflection of her own dove-grey eyes.

"Excuse me. I don't want to disturb you." She sidestepped, moving closer to the table. "Do you have a minute?"

The woman frowned, her broad brow and high hairline striking Eve dumb. So many elements of her own face looked back at her.

"Um, I suppose so. What is it you need?" The woman shifted back in the seat as if to see Eve better.

"May I sit?" Eve gestured toward the empty chair.

"Eh, all right. I'm not here for long, mind you." She glanced behind her as if looking for an exit, or a friend who might rescue her from being accosted by this stranger.

Eve shrugged off her coat and shunted the chair closer to the table.

"So, Miss." The woman paused. "How can I help you?" Her tone was all business.

"Well, it's a little delicate. I need to ask you a question about something that happened many years ago."

The woman blanched. "Look, I'm not sure who you are, but I..." She shoved her chair back and made to get up.

Eve pressed on. "I think... I mean there's a distinct possibility that I'm..."

"You're what?" The woman sounded afraid now, a trace of pink creeping across the finely lined cheekbones.

"Your daughter."

The words out, Eve leaned back against the chair, feeling its wooden ribs clash with her own.

The woman stared, her mouth slack.

Rather than go on, Eve watched as the grey eyes darted from her face to the surrounding café and back again. It was as if the woman was simultaneously trying to absorb what Eve had just said while checking if anyone around them had overheard the conversation. After a few moments, she shook her head.

"I don't have a daughter. I'm sorry to disappoint you, but there it is." She reached behind herself and tugged her coat from the chair.

Eve, sensing that her momentum was slipping away, reached into her pocket.

"Please, don't go. I promise I won't keep you. I just have one thing to ask you."

The woman was standing now, buttoning her coat with quivering hands.

"I don't see what you could possibly have to ask me." She

looked down at Eve. "So if you'll excuse me."

Eve laid the back of her hand on the table. On her palm was the thistle broach. She kept her eyes on the woman's face, not flinching when there was an audible gasp. The woman's hand went to her mouth.

"Please sit down. I just want to ask you a couple of questions. I don't mean to alarm you. I mean no harm." She gestured toward the chair. "Please."

The woman looked around her once again and then slowly pulled the chair back out. As she sat, Eve caught the glint of tears in her eyes. Eve moved her hand farther out across the table.

"Do you recognize it? It was left with me in my basket. This and a note."

The woman's head moved so fractionally that Eve wasn't sure whether she'd nodded or was simply trembling.

"Is your name Fiona Grant?" Eve closed her fingers around the broach.

The light streamed through the window behind, turning the woman's hair into an ethereal halo around her ashen face.

"Yes. I'm Fiona."

Eve nodded.

"I thought so. It's nice to meet you." She extended her free hand.

Fiona hesitated, then took her hand, and Eve grasped the icy fingers.

"Seems an odd thing to say, but I've no idea how to do this." Eve shrugged.

Fiona nodded, mutely.

"I don't want to upset you." Eve repeated herself. "I just…"

Fiona withdrew her hand. "What do you want?" She exhaled the words.

"Nothing. Well, maybe to learn a little about what happened. Why you…"

"Why I what?" Fiona tugged at the collar of her coat and then shoved a strand of hair away from her forehead.

Eve took a slow, cleansing breath. This was it. This was the moment.

"Why you abandoned me?"

Fiona closed her eyes. Both cheeks were now gleaming. Eve felt a mixture of sympathy and calm indifference as she waited for her mother to look at her again. When Fiona finally met her gaze, there was such obvious pain there that Eve second-guessed the decision to confront her this way.

"Listen. I'm sorry, um, what's your name?" Fiona leaned forward on her elbows.

Eve let out a nervous laugh. "God, sorry. I'm Eve."

Fiona nodded.

"OK, Eve. I'll talk to you, but not here." She gestured around herself. "It's not the best place for a private conversation."

Eve nodded. "Right. What do you have in mind?"

Fiona stood up again and slung the camera bag over her shoulder.

"If you can walk a little way with me, I live nearby. Maybe we can go to my house and talk there?" She gave a half smile, then pulled a tissue from her pocket.

Eve pushed her chair back. "Yes. Of course. I'm sorry. I…"

Fiona shook her head. "Don't be. I just need to pay and I'll meet you outside." She gestured toward the door.

For a moment, Eve pictured Fiona dashing into the ladies' room, shimmying up onto a cistern, and sliding out of the window in order to get away.

"I'll wait over there." Eve pointed at the door she'd come through just a few minutes earlier, the moment before she had spoken to her mother for the second time in her life.

As Fiona walked away from her, heading to the counter, Eve wove between the tables, keeping her eyes on the narrow green back. She was going to her mother's home. The thought was bizarre, and as she played with it in her mind, she felt a rush of nerves. Grabbing her phone, she tapped out a text to Jess. *I've found her. More later. xx*

The house was warm, and as she hovered in the bright, sparsely furnished living room, Eve could smell wood smoke. Fiona had dumped the camera bag inside the front door, and her coat was slung over the stair post. She'd gone into the kitchen, leaving Eve to pore over the wall of photographs hanging behind the sagging leather sofa. Image after image, some of them familiar and some new to her, made Eve's chest ache. Infants in various stages of early life, states of awareness or sleep, all in ethereally lit outdoor scenes, crowded the wall. Eve scanned them, looking for something. She wasn't sure what she sought, but the sense of searching was overwhelming. She squinted at a print of a tiny child, the fingers so miniature that Eve was sure the baby must have been premature. The perfect little fingernails, clamped onto the corner of a fluffy blanket, made Eve gulp.

A noise startled her and she swung around. Fiona held a tray and, jutting her chin out, gestured toward the twin armchairs that flanked the brick fireplace.

"Sit down. Please."

Eve moved to one of the chairs and sank into the wrinkled leather.

Fiona set the tray down and handed Eve a mug.

"There's milk and sugar there." She pointed. "Help yourself."

Eve noticed that Fiona appeared to have brushed her hair, and there was a hint of rose on her lips. Eve was instantly concerned about her own appearance. If only she'd thought to check herself in the hall mirror.

"I'm sorry about what I said in the café." Fiona inspected her cup. "About not having a daughter." She picked at the china rim, her fingernail working at an invisible mark. "You just caught me off guard."

"It's OK. I did rather spring it on you." Eve smiled and tried to assess her feelings about the surreal scene that was playing out. She glanced back at the picture wall. "You know what's funny? I've always loved your work. I have some of your prints. A calendar on my desk at work." She paused. "There's something magical in the way you capture light. I've never been able to master it."

Fiona's face brightened. "You're a photographer?"

Eve shook her head.

"Amateur. A hobbyist really. I take pictures. Mainly landscapes. Not very good ones." She shrugged. "I'd like to be better."

Fiona nodded.

"I'm a career counselor at the university. I..."

Fiona cut her off. "Well, that's an important job."

Startled by the interruption, Eve blinked.

"You help young people find their way. There's no more important work than that."

Eve frowned. She'd never thought of her job in quite that context and yet, hearing it described that way, there was a dawning, a flash of realization. Before she could respond, Fiona went on.

"Where do you live?"

"St. Andrews."

"Are you married?"

Eve nodded, knocked off-kilter by having Fiona turn the tables and pepper her with questions. This hadn't been Eve's plan. She was the one with the questions. She'd wanted to drive this process.

"I am. Ken's my husband. Almost twenty-four years."

Fiona smiled.

"Lovely. I never married." She pulled her mouth down at the corners. "Never saw the point."

Eve heard sad resignation as opposed to resolve in the statement. Fiona's face was sagging as she stared into her cup.

"I was sixteen, you know." She lifted her chin and met Eve's gaze. "When it happened."

Eve, sensing that she needed to, remained quiet. Her mind was spinning. Sixteen. Her mother had been the same age as Eve when she'd fallen pregnant. The irony was striking.

"I was terrified, of my father mainly." She licked her lips.

"He was a bully, quick with his fists, and had no time for the weaknesses of humanity – or the vagaries of life." She set her cup on a side table. "My mother knew why I left. At least, I think she did." Fiona paused. "We never actually talked about it."

Eve wrapped her fingers around the teacup. "Not even when you went home?"

Fiona shook her head.

"No. They didn't want to know where I'd been. Dad was mortified that I'd run away at all, caused a ripple in his perfectly structured life. He was adamant that we tell people I'd been staying with cousins in Aviemore. He didn't want any gossip and, after he'd given me the beating of my life, he made me swear never to mention the entire episode again."

Eve took in the face opposite her. Fiona's eyes were slightly deeper set than Eve's own, and the once taut line of Fiona's jaw, the same jawline that both Eve and Jess shared, had been softened by time and a layer of loose flesh. As she scanned the features, Eve wondered if she was seeing her own fifty-something reflection.

"Mum went along with it, poor soul. But then, she never dared challenge Dad." Fiona shrugged. "She had no life, really."

The sadness in Fiona's voice was thick.

"But you think she suspected?" Eve forced herself to swallow some tea.

"I think so. I mean, I was different when I got home. I couldn't stop crying, and my shape had changed. I'd lost most of the weight by the time I came back, but I think any mother would know." She frowned.

Eve heard the words and felt a surge of anger. A mother would know. A mother *should* know. Perhaps a mother who hadn't shoved her baby under a table and bolted – would've known. She pressed her eyes closed and waited for her heart to settle.

"Are you all right?" Fiona was up and hovering next to her.

"Yes. I'm fine." Eve stood up. "It's just so strange." She paused. "I was sixteen too, when I got pregnant with Jess."

Fiona's eyebrows bounced.

"You have children?"

"A daughter. She's twenty-three." Eve turned her back on the grey eyes and scanned the photographs again. "She's married, and expecting." Eve faced Fiona. "She's beautiful."

"You're beautiful too. I always imagined you beautiful."

Eve, never having thought of herself as such, was taken aback by the statement. She tried to acknowledge the compliment but then, not finding the words, she sat back down.

"I pretended that it happened to someone else. I looked back at it and filed it away like a film script – a predictable, tragic kind of film." Fiona's face was contorting. "I fell for the boy. I was stupid and naïve and desperate for love."

Eve nodded, breathing shallowly.

"I asked what had happened to you. I was told you were adopted – nothing more. I tried to find out where they'd sent you, but all they would say was that you were fine." She paused. "There weren't the same resources then. It wasn't as easy to trace people." She searched Eve's face. "For everything I didn't know, what I *did* know was what I couldn't give you."

Eve swiped at her damp cheek.

"When you were born, I had no idea that I could love someone so deeply, so quickly. You were only mine for a few weeks, but it was profound. You were so perfect. I couldn't believe I'd made you." She paused. "But I was afraid of you. Of everything you needed from me." Tears were streaking Fiona's face. "I was a child."

Eve pulled a tissue out of her bag and held it out. Fiona took it and blew her nose loudly the same way Jess did, which had always driven Eve crazy.

"I met you once, a couple of years ago." Eve blurted.

Fiona stared at her.

"In Edinburgh. I bought one of your books."

"Did we talk?"

Eve shook her head. "Not really."

Fiona stuffed the tissue inside her sleeve. "I think I've been looking for you all my life. In every baby I photographed, I was searching for the shape of your cheeks, your perfect little elbows, the dimples I used to kiss on your knees. I was looking for a split second of recognition, perhaps a reflection of my own eyes." Her voice cracked.

Eve could not deny that in some respects she could relate to this. Whether she'd recognized the motivation or not, she also looked for life through her camera. It seemed to be more richly colored that way. She turned to face Fiona. She wanted to give her something.

"I had a good life. Wonderful parents."

Fiona looked startled.

"When I got pregnant, they rallied behind me. Ken and I got married and moved in with them. There was never any shame around it." She swallowed. "They adored Jess the moment they saw her."

Fiona was nodding.

"I never felt that I was missing anything. I mean, I never wanted to know about you." While the statement of fact was important to her, Eve hoped she hadn't sounded cruel. "It wasn't until my own daughter asked me about her medical history that I realized I needed to look for you. See you…if you still existed. It started out being more for her than for me, but then the more I searched the more I wanted to know that I'd get to see your face, just once. Whether I'm like you. Whether Jess is like you. I didn't think I cared. But I do. I did." Eve's throat clamped shut as tears began to course down her face. "I do."

The feeling of Fiona's arms around her was electric. Eve, wanting to resist but failing, leaned into the wiry embrace.

"I'm so sorry. I don't know what else to say."

An hour later, the two women sat on the floor. Fiona had poured them a brandy each and then, as the daylight faded, she'd lit a fire.

Eve felt the welcome burn of the alcohol in her chest as she watched the flames flicker in the grate. Fiona was quiet, also staring into the fire. Eve had asked most of her questions, found some answers, and then chosen to leave other things unsaid. Fiona had been open, emotional, and remorseful, and as Eve considered the few extraordinary hours they'd just spent together, she thought Fiona had handled an impossible situation with no small amount of grace.

As she watched the stranger who'd given birth to her sip her brandy, Eve felt a sense of deep peace flowing through her, like an ocean reclaiming the sand. There was just one thing left to ask.

"Fiona, who was my father?"

Fiona's eyes snapped to hers.

"His name was John. He lived in Fort William. We went to school together. He was two years older than me."

Eve nodded. "What happened?"

Fiona sighed. "The usual thing. He was scared rigid by the news. Ran away. He joined the navy and left me to pick up the pieces."

Eve shifted to her hip to relieve the pressure on her tailbone.

"He ended up working on an oil rig in the North Sea." Fiona sipped some brandy.

"Where is he now?"

Fiona turned to look at her.

"He was killed in a car crash in nineteen eighty-seven."

Eve felt the weight of the words as Fiona's face took on a new pallor.

"So you kept in touch after he left?"

Fiona nodded.

"Eventually. Just letters and such. He never came back to Fort William, though."

"Did he ever ask about me?"

Fiona nodded. "Yes. He did. I sent him some photos. I only had two or three of you."

Eve tried to picture the young man, in navy whites, on

board a ship somewhere, sitting on a bunk bed looking at faded snapshots.

"Do you have any pictures of him?"

Fiona shook her head. "I don't. I'm sorry."

Eve shrugged. "S'OK. I just wondered what he looked like."

"He was lanky, with dark curly hair and brown eyes. He was awfully shy, deeply intelligent, and could always make me laugh."

Eve knew that laughter could be highly intoxicating, and it was one of the things she loved most about Ken. Ken. She missed him so much that each time she thought about him, her breath escaped her. Could she really have brought them to a place where he wouldn't speak to her? She pictured his face crumbling and the hurt and disbelief she'd put there. She hadn't slept properly since she'd told him about Dan, and with that, plus her lack of any appetite to speak of, Eve knew that she had the look of a scarecrow about her these days.

Fiona had stopped talking. She'd stood up and was rubbing her palms together, her narrow shoulders hunched toward her ears.

"The evenings get cold so quickly at this time of year." She placed another log on the fire and then turned to Eve. "Can I get you something to eat?"

Eve hauled herself up from the floor.

"No, thank you. I need to go. I'm exhausted, and I want to call home." She looked around the room for her handbag.

Eve thought Fiona looked disappointed as she pulled her cardigan closer around her middle.

"I understand. It's been a hell of a day."

Eve glanced at the grey eyes.

"Oh, I didn't mean it in a bad way." Fiona's face was flushed. "Just that it's been…" She halted.

"Unexpected?" Eve smiled, wanting to dissolve any concern that Fiona had about her awkward use of words.

"To say the least." Fiona laughed. "It's been so good to meet you, Eve."

Eve nodded.

"Yes. Thank you for bringing me here, for sharing your story with me." She spotted her bag on the floor by the window.

As she was pulling on her coat, Fiona patted her arm.

"I'll do what I can about the medical history. I don't have any scary stuff to share, and John's parents have both passed, but whatever I have I'll send to you."

"Thanks. I'd appreciate that." Eve turned to leave.

"Just a minute. I have something for you."

Eve watched as Fiona trotted up the stairs. Within a few moments, she was back with a black case in her hand.

Eve frowned. "What's that?"

Fiona held the thin strap out toward her.

"It's a Leica. I want you to have it."

Eve shook her head. "I can't. Really."

Fiona pushed the strap closer to her.

"You can. I insist." She looked tentative, despite the statement. "Please, Eve. I've given you little enough. Let me do this."

Eve looked down at the camera encased in black leather. It swung between them like a heavy pendulum linking them in some esoteric way with its course back and forth.

"Please."

Eve reached out and took the camera. "Thank you. I don't know why..."

Fiona held a hand up.

"It's kind of you to let me give it to you." She smiled. "It's the one I got the best results with for a long time. Once you get used to the aperture settings, it'll see you right too."

Eve felt the weight of the camera in her hand.

"Don't you use it anymore?" She slung the strap over her shoulder.

"I do, but it's yours now."

After exchanging contact information and an awkward hug, Eve left the house behind and walked through the darkening streets. She passed a middle-aged man with a handsome Airedale terrier. The man tipped his cap at her as she passed, and the old-fashioned gesture touched her. The mill was only a short distance away, and with the streetlights already glowing, she felt quite safe as she made her way back to her car.

A few minutes later, as she approached the guest house, her mind was reeling with all that she wanted to tell Ken. She imagined their conversation, how she'd tell him about the day and how he'd respond.

In the darkness, the bank of hydrangeas had lost its rosy glow, now made up of various densities of black. She shivered as she reached the cottage door and let herself in, then flipped the light on and dumped her bag, the camera, and her coat onto the sofa. There was an envelope on the kitchen counter, and a single rose in a bud vase. She trotted across the room, hoping the offering might be from Ken, despite the logistics making it unlikely.

The note was from the owners, wishing her a pleasant evening and telling her that there might be a power cut the following morning for some maintenance work they were having done. Disappointed, Eve tossed the paper onto the counter and pulled out the second of the cans of soup she'd bought. She dumped it into a pot on the stove then texted Ken to say she'd met Fiona and to ask if she could call. Requesting permission to talk to her own husband felt ludicrous, but the text was a passive form of contact probably more appropriate for the circumstances. She hit send and held her breath. Eventually, she saw the telltale dots flickering in a cartoon bubble, indicating that he was replying. After what seemed like an age, the message bloomed on her screen.

Not just now. Heading to Jess & Ram's. Glad it went well.

She read it several times as if each time she might find something more, a subliminal message between the curt lines. Eventually, she typed back *OK – Talk tomorrow*, switched the soup off, picked up the camera, and climbed the stairs to the bedroom.

Eve lay on her side in the dark, the pillow bunched under jaw. She'd dozed off as soon as she'd lain down and now, not sure how long she'd been asleep, she checked her watch. The need to talk to her mum was overwhelming, so she grabbed her phone.

"Hi, sweetheart. Where are you?" Mary sounded tired.

"I'm in Spean Bridge. Did I wake you up?"

"Not at all. I'm reading. How's it going there?"

Eve reached over and switched the bedside light back on.

"It was an eventful day." She pushed herself up against the fat pillows. "I met her. Fiona."

She could hear Mary breathing.

"Oh, Eve."

"It was OK, Mum. She was pretty defensive to start with, but we ended up going to her house and talking for a long time." Eve chewed her cheek. The next thing that Mary said could be an indication of how she was truly faring with the unexpected tangent her daughter's life was now following.

"Was she kind to you?"

Eve smiled. This was typical of Mary.

"She was fine. It took a while for her to open up, but she told me what happened. Why she left me." Eve turned to look out of the window. The depth of the darkness was surprising, not a single light or star breaking through the blanket of night sky.

Eve talked her mother through the day's events and her conversation with Fiona Grant.

"Well, who'd have thought it. Her being that photographer too?" Mary paused. "That's where you get it, obviously."

Eve shook her head. "No, Mum. She's a real professional. I just play at it."

Mary was making tutting sounds.

"Not at all. You've a talent. That's obvious. If you took photos all day every day, you'd be just as good as she is." There was a defensive tone to Mary's voice that tugged at Eve.

"Thanks, Mum. You're always my biggest supporter."

Mary laughed. "We both are."

Eve nodded in the silence. "I know."

"Your dad's here. He sends his love."

"Give him a hug from me. I'll pop over when I get home and we'll have a long chat."

After getting her diary out to write down when Eve would be coming, Mary once again sounded tired.

"Eve, are you all right, darling?"

"I'm fine, Mum. Don't you worry. All's well."

"Well, get some sleep and phone me as soon as you get home. I worry about you driving on that road."

Eve set the phone on the side table and heaved herself off the bed. Her clothes were clinging to her back, and the claw-foot bathtub was calling.

CHAPTER 27

Jess sat opposite her father at the small dining table. Ken had agreed to come to the flat for dinner rather than go home to an empty house, and Ram had taken charge of the cooking, as usual. He stood at the stove stirring a pot of hollandaise sauce while a slab of local salmon, covered in wafer-thin slices of lemon, baked in the oven.

Ken had seemed in relatively good humor when he'd arrived, and now his nose was buried in the newspaper.

Jess looked over and smiled at the long back of the man she loved.

"How much longer? I'm famished."

Ram laughed. "For a change."

She tutted. "Less of that and more cooking."

He flashed her a smile and lifted the pot from the heat. "Sauce is done. Fish in five."

Jess walked into the kitchen and leaned against his side as he drained some asparagus from the steamer.

"You're the best," she whispered.

"You're absolutely right."

She patted his backside and shuffled back to the table.

"So, Ken, when's Eve back?" Ram served food onto three oval plates.

"Not sure." He shrugged. "Her text last night just said that she'd met her – Fiona." He folded the paper and lay it on the table.

Jess picked up a handful of peanuts from the bowl on the table.

"No details then?" Ram was frowning.

Ken shook his head. "No, but I didn't talk to her, so..."

Jess tutted loudly, as Ram set a plate in front of each of them.

"Seriously, after everything we talked about yesterday?" She scowled at her father.

Ken shook his head, then pulled the dish closer to him and began adding a liberal coating of black pepper.

"She wanted to talk, but I was in the car. We'll catch up tomorrow."

"Jesus, Dad." A tiny piece of peanut flew from Jess's mouth onto the placemat.

Ram looked at the mat and grimaced.

"What?" She glared at him, picking up the morsel with her fingertip.

"I was driving." Ken lifted his water glass.

Jess shook her head and stood up.

"I'm calling her now. She must be bursting to talk." She glared at her father. "And you just blanked her."

"Why not eat first." Ram caught her hand as she passed him. "Give her a call after dinner."

Jess caught his expression and hesitated. There was a subliminal message there that she was missing, but Ram's intuitive compass was infallible, so she slid the phone into her pocket and sat back down.

"I didn't blank her." Ken was glowering at her, a forkful of food suspended in front of his mouth. Without eating it, Ken placed the fork back on the plate. "OK. I was short with her." He dipped his chin. "I should've talked to her."

Jess gave a sharp nod and lifted her fork.

"Then we'll call her once we've eaten." She looked at Ram, who was about to say something. "And we'll both talk to her."

Dinner passed without further reference to Eve, as Ken and Ram talked about football, golf, and the impending sale of the premises next door to the cheese shop. Ken had, momentarily, considered taking it on as an expansion of his business, but having thought better of it, he'd learned that a high-end leather goods company had bought the place. Confident that it wouldn't create any conflict, Ken seemed pleased that the empty shop would soon be occupied.

Jess had cleared her plate of the second, smaller sliver of fish Ram had served her. He was collecting the dishes, and Ken was showing signs of leaving, so she pulled out her phone and texted Eve. *Are you awake*? Within a few moments, Eve replied. *Yes*.

"Dad, she's still awake." She waved the phone at Ken, who

appeared to be looking for his jacket. “I’m going to call her.”

Ken’s shoulders sagged as he crossed the room toward her.

“You talk to her, Jess. I’m going to go home.”

She grabbed his arm. “Seriously?”

Ken nodded. She took in his face. He seemed to have aged in the last week, and she was flooded with concern for him.

“Come on, Pops. Aren’t you being a bit petty now?”

Ram was standing in the kitchen, and as she glanced at him, he was shaking his head wildly.

Jess sighed. “OK. Can I tell her you’ll call tomorrow?” She raised her eyebrows at her father.

“Aye. Tell her that.” He leaned down and kissed her cheek. “Thanks for dinner, Ram. Another culinary triumph.” He shook Ram’s hand. “You’re a king among men.”

CHAPTER 28

Eve had spent almost half an hour talking with Jess the previous night. She'd been so glad of the contact that she'd become tearful, a response that had confirmed just how much she was missing her family. Jess had said that Ken had already left for home, and while Eve wasn't sure she entirely believed her daughter, she'd resigned herself to not talking with her husband for another day.

She'd given Jess a synopsis of the events and shared some of her conversation with Fiona.

"So she was sixteen too?" Jess had sounded incredulous. "What are the odds of that?"

"I know." Eve had shaken her head in the dark bedroom. "Amazing, isn't it?"

"Did you like her? I mean, was she nice?"

Eve had stared at the ceiling.

"She was nice enough." Even as she answered Jess, Eve

realized that she hadn't formed any specific opinion of Fiona, which struck her as odd. "She was obviously very nervous. She apologized to me."

Jess had tutted. "A lot of good that does you now."

Eve, to her surprise, had come to Fiona's defense.

"Well, it sounded like her father was a tyrant. She was terrified of him." Eve had then considered that situation and compared it to her own, with Mary and Russell. "We can't know what that's like, Jess."

Jess had conceded the point and then they'd talked about Jess's day, her next appointment for an ultrasound when they'd get a photo of the baby, and her persistent craving for caramel shortbread which, as she'd laughingly told her mother, was threatening to take over her life.

Having had the best night's sleep she'd had in over a week, Eve now lay in the four-poster bed. Her nose was cold and as she twisted to check her watch, she saw that it was just 6:15am, probably too early for the heating to have come on. She turned onto her side, rubbed her bare feet together, and then curled up into a ball. The day ahead was wholly unplanned, but having asked Fiona where her father had been buried, Eve intended on going to the cemetery in Fort William to find John Cameron. Fiona had been surprised at her asking but had given her the details before Eve had left the house.

"I could go with you, if you'd like?" Fiona had looked earnest, but Eve had instantly shaken her head.

"No. I'd prefer to go alone." She'd caught Fiona's obvious embarrassment. "But thanks."

When they had exchanged contact information, and Eve

had put Fiona's number into her phone, Eve had had such a deep sense of certainty that she'd never see this woman again that it had shocked her.

Now, as she lay looking out of the brightening window, she could picture the face that she'd been seeking for the past few weeks. She saw the expressive eyes, the wide mouth with the tinge of sadness at its gently lined corners, the tightly curled hair framing the broad forehead. The face, in its entirety, did nothing to evoke much emotion in her, but oddly, the camera that now sat on the bedside table seemed to be emitting an audible buzz. She moved higher up on the pillows to get a better look at it. The black case that was molded around the sophisticated equipment gleamed, the strap dangling down almost to the carpet. Eve reached out and wound the strap between her fingers. That was what she'd do today. She'd take pictures.

The Craigs cemetery sat close to the road and as she approached, Eve spotted several elegant headstones set behind a low stone wall. The mossy grass around them was pristine and cropped short.

Having parked nearby, she lifted the camera from the passenger seat and walked into the graveyard. Fiona's description had been detailed and now, as she held the handwritten instructions, Eve followed the simple map, making her way around a massive oak tree that dominated a broad but gentle hill in the center of the space. Checking the paper once again, she bypassed three stones that were enclosed behind a tall iron fence and then, as per Fiona's instructions, she counted four headstones on her left before stopping at an eye-level obelisk. The stone was dark, the engraving difficult to decipher, but as she leaned down and squinted, Eve could make it out. The inscription read *Johnathan Charles Cameron, March 3rd 1959 – April 2nd 1987 Beloved son, light of our lives. Taken too soon.* She stepped back from the headstone feeling suddenly lightheaded. The morning had been grey when she'd checked out of the cottage and headed back to Fort William, but now the sky was clearing, and while it was still cold, the sun was spearing through the cloud cover.

Eve shivered, letting the camera strap slip down her arm. She looked around her. She'd seen no one since coming into the cemetery and was apparently still alone. Without thinking, she slid the camera from the case and took the lens cap off. The light, while still weak, was behind her as she focused on the headstone, the letters of her father's name clarifying themselves as she twisted the lens casing back and forth.

Shifting her feet until she found the composition she wanted, she pressed the shutter. The sound was expensive, like finely honed metal blades slicing against each other, and it seemed to hang in the silence of the morning. She lifted her head and glanced around, suddenly aware that she might be disturbing the nearby souls lying under the carpet of green. Satisfied that she was doing no harm, Eve refocused and took another shot, then another, her eyes not leaving the words *Taken too soon.*

As she replaced the lens cover, she felt her knees buckle. Gravity taking over, she sank to the ground, her fist meeting the mound of grass that covered Johnathan's grave. The camera landed with a thud next to her hip. Struggling to focus, she read the inscription again, and the poignancy of the absence of the most critical piece of information from this man's epitaph, the word *father*, stripped her of her breath. She pressed her eyes closed and let the tears come, and as she gulped back sobs, Eve let herself be sucked into the painful and yet mystifying vortex of mourning a parent she'd never known.

As the pain coursed through her, causing her to wrap her arms around herself, she rocked gently back and forth on the damp ground. After a few moments, she took a deep breath and tried to sort through the mixture of feelings that were engulfing her. There was a sharp bitterness for the relationships she'd been denied and a dull, bone-crushing sadness that bore no resemblance to anything she'd ever felt before. As she tried to separate the tumble of emotions, underlying everything was undeniable shame.

She opened her eyes. She was ashamed of what she'd done to Ken, to Jess, and even to Dan. She'd fumbled through the past weeks disregarding their feelings, being secretive and narcissistic. She'd made bad decisions, absented herself both emotionally and physically from the people she loved most, and all for what – to track down a woman whom she had nothing in common with other than a few strands of chromosomes and a love of photography, then to crumble at the grave of a man who'd chosen to deny her existence for half of his truncated life.

Gradually feeling her breaths come more easily, Eve leaned back on her hands and extended her legs out in front of her. Her booted feet formed an open V, behind which Johnathan's headstone crouched, cold granite, the color of a winter sky.

"I'm sorry I never met you." She swallowed the last word, her throat raw.

As she stared at the inscription, a flutter of movement caught her eye. Afraid to move, she watched as a tiny robin landed on top of the headstone. The young bird appeared unperturbed by her presence as it proceeded to preen, running its miniscule beak along the length of its wing, separating the feathers into downy corn rows.

Eve's hand instinctively reached for the camera that sat on the grass next to her. She lifted it stealthily to her eye, slid the lens cap off, and focused on the bird. Just as she pressed the shutter, a gust of wind came up from behind the headstone, fluffing the bird's minky feathers out into a dramatic boa around the red thumbprint of its breast. Eve clicked several shots, the bird remaining still save for the movement of its feathers. The light bounced off the stone as the little creature inclined its head, assessing her before taking to the air. As she watched it fly away, with each beat of the perfect wings, Eve felt her sadness abate.

An hour later, having texted Jess to let her know what was happening, Eve steered the car toward home. Her path seemed clear for the first time in weeks, and as the miles ticked by and the landscape began to flatten out, the farther east she went, her spirit lifted. She'd be back before Ken got home from the shop, and her intention was to do whatever she had to to get him to listen to her.

The day was brightening and as the road unfurled, her determination grew. Only as she saw signs for St. Andrews did she feel the creep of anxiety again. She tried to picture Ken, his ruddy face cracking into a smile as she opened the door. Then, she saw him cold and unemotional as he told her that he didn't want her anymore. Eve pushed the image from her mind as she negotiated a roundabout. The familiar topography usually gave her a sense of calm, and yet her stomach was in knots as she passed the whitewashed bed and breakfast and then began counting down the driveways to the hedge-enclosed entrance to her home.

As Eve pulled up at the house, she was relieved not to see Ken's car. This meant she did indeed have some time to gather herself and prepare. As she walked into the house, she knew that if he couldn't forgive her, then nothing else mattered.

After she had unpacked, she stood at the window and watched Ken park and walk up the driveway. His shoulders were rounded and his clothes looked like they'd been borrowed from a bigger man.

Rather than open the door, she waited in the living room. The fire was lit, sending a glimmer of gold across the heavy curtains. To Eve, the house smelled of wood-smoke, and of her fear.

Ken's key clunked in the lock, and as the door swung open, she moved into the hall. He tossed his keys into the bowl on the narrow table and raised his eyes to hers.

"You're home then?" He slipped his shoes off and left them in a heap under the coatrack.

"Yes." She took a tentative step toward him. "How was your day?"

Ken shrugged. His eyes had dark shadows under them, and his face was more angular than she'd seen it in years.

"OK." He gave her a half smile and, without touching her, walked past her into the living room. The absence of any contact was surprising and painful to Eve, as she followed him into the dimly lit room. Ken had walked straight to the sideboard and was pouring himself a whisky. She watched as he replaced the stopper in the crystal decanter. He didn't habitually drink the moment he got in from work, but rather than comment, Eve went into the kitchen and poured herself a glass of wine.

When she came back, Ken was sitting with his feet up on the coffee table. His head was resting against the back of the chair, and as he crossed his ankles, she noticed that his socks didn't match – one being an argyle pattern and the other plain. The idiosyncrasy made her smile as she settled on the sofa.

"What happened with your socks?"

Ken blinked and then looked down at his mismatched feet.

"Dunno. I suppose I didn't notice." He looked over at her. "Or didn't care."

She nodded. He was obviously exhausted but, despite her concern over picking the right moment to present her case, Eve couldn't wait any longer.

"Ken, I need you to listen to me." She paused. "I know you're still angry and hurt, and disappointed in me, but you must hear what I have to say."

He closed his eyes and blindly sipped his drink. The fact that he didn't protest or shut her down encouraged her.

"I've let you down. I've made some terrible choices and I've hurt you." She watched as his jaw ticked, his heavy eyelids remaining closed. "I know I don't deserve your forgiveness, or even your understanding, but I'm asking for both."

He opened his eyes and assessed her. His cheeks were sunken.

"I don't know what happened to me." She clasped the glass

to her chest. "It's like I got totally lost or something."

Ken eyed her over the rim of his glass.

"I was so confused by the whole abandonment thing, the drama of my history." She watched him drain his glass. "I suppose it made me question the very essence of who I was, and then I just let that take over."

Ken put his feet down and leaned forward on his knees. She recognized his expression as one that preceded a well-considered thought, so she held her breath, willing him to speak. He blinked several times, then met her gaze.

"I know what happened. Or what *didn't* happen, with that guy." He shook his head. "Jess told me."

The sound of Jess's name was like a slap. Eve wasn't surprised that Jess had told him, but the fact that they'd had to discuss her ridiculous indiscretion made her cringe.

Eve nodded mutely.

"I'm sorry I didn't let you tell me yourself." His eyes were glassy. "I was just so…"

"I know," she blurted.

Ken raised a palm.

"I was going to say, I was so angry that I couldn't hear anything. Then, I was hurt and then…" – he paused – "then I was sorry."

Eve's heart was thumping. Sorry. *He* was sorry.

"I'm sorry that I didn't take it all more seriously, the whole Fiona thing." He twisted in the chair to face her.

"Ken…"

"Please let me finish." His eyes flashed.

Eve held her palms up, letting him go on.

"I'm sorry if I don't listen to you sometimes. Or if you feel dismissed. And I'm sorry that I didn't understand how unsettling what you were going through really was." He set his glass on the table. "I should've known how fundamental finding your mother was to you." He held her gaze. "If I had handled it better, then perhaps you wouldn't have felt drawn to…" He halted, his face beginning to color.

Eve shifted forward in her chair. The impulse to rush over and sit by his side or clasp his hand was overwhelming. Sensing that this was not the moment for such intimacy, she held herself back.

"It wasn't anything you did or didn't do." Her voice was low. "It was my own insecurities rearing their ugly heads."

Ken took her in, his dark eyes scanning her face.

"I don't think I knew I had so many questions about myself. Then when I found out about Fiona, I let all that cloud my judgment. I got wound up in the mystery." She shrugged. "As if it'd really made a difference to who I am now." She held her hands out wide. "I'm so ashamed of how I behaved." Her voice cracked. "Ken, I need you to forgive me. I don't think I can breathe if you don't."

He slid forward in the seat. His linked fingers dangled between his knees, and Eve pressed down the tears that threatened to take her voice as she waited for him to speak.

"I thought I'd lost you." Ken's eyes were full as he slipped awkwardly from the chair onto his knees. Seeing the movement, Eve lunged across the room and knelt down in front of him. His arms went around her, the firm muscles crushing her ribs against his. As the breath left her, she buried her head in his neck.

"I'm so sorry. I love you so much." She spoke against the rough skin of his collarbone. "Can you forgive me?"

They stayed locked together until Eve could feel the carpet begin to bite into her skin. The blood was tingling in her calves when Ken eventually released her, flopping back onto the floor.

"Sit with me." He held a hand out to her as he shifted back against the front of the sofa.

She took his hand and settled into the curve of his side, the space she'd occupied for over twenty years. The weight of his arm around her shoulder, the warmth of his breath, and the prickle of his chin against her cheek brought such a wave of peace and of gratitude that Eve closed her eyes to savor the moment. This was home. This was where she needed to be. Whatever the past had revealed or the future held, this was home.

EPILOGUE

December was closing in and with it had come snow. The rooftops of St. Andrews were covered in a picturesque crusting of white, and Ken's shop window, thanks to Jess, had been artfully decorated with holly wreaths and knots of fresh mistletoe suspended over the merchandise.

Eve had finished most of the faculty meetings that she had scheduled for before the end of the semester and was counting the days until the Christmas holidays began. She'd have two weeks off during which she planned on finishing the decorations in the house, doing some last-minute shopping, and then preparing to host Mary, Russell, Jess, Ram, and his parents for Christmas dinner.

The previous weekend, on their way back from their ballroom dancing lesson, she and Ken had stopped at a farm near Dunfermline to choose a tree, and now the sharp scent of pine greeted them whenever they walked into the house. Eve adored this time of year, but this Christmas felt even more special as Jess was well over her sickness and had entered the rosier phase of pregnancy. Her shape had noticeably changed, her stomach now a firm round, and her face fuller.

Ram smiled constantly, and even his parents seemed to have moved past any remaining reservations they may have held over their daughter-in-law. His mother had sent several adorable baby outfits, and since they'd found out that it was a girl, the pink bedding, mobiles, and toys were steadily accumulating in the tiny room at the flat that Jess and Ram had prepared for their daughter.

Eve had stuck the most recent ultrasound picture Jess had given her on the fridge door, and every time she passed it, she touched it with her fingertip. In just a few months, their granddaughter would be here, so cherished.

Since her return from Spean Bridge, after a few weeks of tentative quiet, Ken had gradually let her get close again. He'd moved back into the master bedroom and even rediscovered his sense of humor. Each time he sprang a childlike prank on her or cracked one of his bad jokes, Eve laughed heartily, reveling in their renewed connectedness.

Now, as she clicked off the desk light in her office and picked up her laptop, she checked the clock. Jess and Ram were coming for dinner, and she wanted to stop at the bakery on the way home to pick up some caramel shortbread. Jess's obsession with the sweet biscuit had not abated and, rather than tease her anymore, they had, as Ken aptly put it, decided to simply feed the Kraken.

With the sweet biscuits sitting on the passenger seat, Eve drove home. Many of the houses along Strathkiness Road were decorated with bright lights, and several of the front doors had decorative wreaths on them. Turning down her driveway, Eve smiled. Since she'd left that morning, Ken had hung lights around the front door and draped them over the twin holly bushes that flanked the entrance to the house. The bright little pops of gold against the glossy red of the door brought a lump to her throat.

Before she could put her key in the lock, Ken opened the door.

"Hi." He beamed at her. "Good day?"

She nodded.

"Not bad." She kissed him. "This is the best part of it though. The lights are gorgeous."

He nodded, seeming pleased, closed the door, and waited for her to shed her coat so he could hang it on the rack.

"I'll make you a cuppa." He turned toward the kitchen then, halting, turned back to her. "Oh, there's a parcel for you." He jabbed a thumb at the narrow table near to the stairs. "Came earlier."

Eve stared at the package. It was a large flat rectangle wrapped in brown paper and secured with liberal amounts of thick tape. Lifting it, she felt padding around the edges. She squinted at the handwriting, which was bold, the sender having used a thick felt-tip pen. She didn't recognize the hand.

"Wonder who it's from," she called into the kitchen.

"Only one way to find out," Ken called back.

Eve walked into the kitchen. The room was warm, and Ken had lit her favorite lavender-scented candle that sat on the windowsill. As she set the package on the counter, he handed her a steaming mug.

"Well, open it." He grinned. "Or I will."

Eve set her cup down and pulled the package toward her.

"I don't recognize the writing." She tugged at the tape on one corner. There were several layers of it, and after a few seconds of her picking ineffectually at an edge, Ken thrust a pair of scissors under her nose.

"For god's sake, woman, cut it."

She took the scissors and sliced through the outer paper. Inside, under a layer of bubble wrap, was a dark wooden frame. Initially all she saw was the back of what looked like a painting, with a thin loop of metal wire draped between two screws. She glanced up at Ken and frowned.

"What on earth?"

He shrugged.

She turned the frame over and caught her breath. It was a sepia print of a baby. The child lay in an old-fashioned Moses basket, wearing a pale-colored dress that skimmed the minute knees, and the tiny feet were encased in leather shoes. A lacy, broderie anglais bonnet all but obscured the infant's face, and a crocheted blanket was folded neatly under its feet. The basket sat on what looked like cobblestones next to a terracotta pot with long fingers of feathery fern trailing to the ground.

Eve stared at the image. The light was coming from the left, illuminating the down on the baby's arm and, as she focused on the perfect little limb, Eve saw them, the trademark microscopic dust motes glinting as they hung above the child.

She glanced at Ken, who was staring back at her.

"What is it?" He walked around to her side and then, noticing an envelope on the floor, he picked it up. "Looks like this fell out." He held it out to her.

Eve's hands were shaking as she lay the print down on the counter. Ken leaned over it, scrutinizing the image.

"It's one of those prints you like." He glanced at her over his shoulder.

Eve slid her finger under the flap of the heavy envelope and pulled out a single sheet of paper. She scanned the page as the letters jumped around. Finding it hard to focus, her eyes skipped to the bottom of the page, and the name she saw there shocked her.

"Well, read it." Ken was smiling.

"It's from her." She swallowed.

"Who?"

"Fiona."

She took a breath and read out loud.

Dear Eve.

I hope you and your family are well? Since we met, I've thought about you so often. Life takes on a certain shape and then, all of a sudden, the very outline of what we know as normal can be changed by a single conversation. Now that I have an image of you as you are now, I've heard your voice, shaken your hand, and been fortunate enough to have you tell me about your life, my 'normal' has been forever altered.

In case you're unsure, this picture is of you. It's the only photo I kept – the rest I'd sent to John. This was taken on the patio of the café in Braemar. You were nineteen days old. I crocheted the blanket myself, and the bonnet was a gift from a good friend called

Jean. When I look at this picture, so much comes back to me, but the most overwhelming feeling is one of loss. I don't tell you that to evoke your sympathy, but what I do want you to know is that I will live with the decision I took as a frightened child, and the regret of that choice, forever. Please try to forgive me for that.

I wish you only good things and, if you find that there is room in your life for a friend, please stay in touch. Merry Christmas.

Fiona Grant.

Eve folded the page and set it on the counter. She looked up at Ken, his face blurring in front of her.

"Well, there you go." Ken's arm went around her shoulder. "It's a great picture."

Eve wiped under her eyes with her thumb.

"I don't know what to say." She paused. "I never expected anything from her."

Ken pulled her closer.

"Of course not. But now she's done this, I mean, she seems to want to stay in contact. Do you think you'll see her again?"

Eve reached for a piece of kitchen paper and blew her nose.

"I didn't think I would. When I left Spean Bridge, I felt like I was done. Like I'd got everything I needed from her."

He nodded.

She pulled the picture closer and traced the outline of the basket with her fingertip. Mary and Russell had many photographs of her as a child that she'd seen over the years, but there was something in the quality of this one that made her feel whole. As she took it in, Eve tried to identify what it was that held her so transfixed. She looked at the fabric of the little dress, the edge of the lacy bonnet, the neatly crocheted squares of the blanket, and then it struck her. When she'd learned of her abandonment, the images she'd been inundated with were those of a mother's cold neglect. Over the weeks that she'd been searching for information, she'd asked herself numerous times how any mother could care so little as to leave her child out in the open and literally run away. Now, as she looked down at the baby in the picture, at herself, all she saw were the signs of care, pride, protection, and of love.

Eve breathed into the pain that had gathered under her rib cage. Whatever else Fiona had or had not done, whatever decisions that young, terrified girl had taken, she had cared about Eve.

Ken moved in close to her side.

"So what're you thinking now?" His chin brushed her cheek.

She pressed her face against his.

"I'm thinking I'll call her, just to wish her a happy Christmas."

ACKNOWLEDGEMENTS

My sincere thanks go to Bev Katz Rosenbaum and Amanda Sumner, for their insight and editorial prowess. Thank you to Lesley Shearer, Carly Guy, and Anna Marie Laforest for their consistent support and honest feedback, and to Sharon Erksa for her unfailing artistic sensibility.

A special thank you to Gaynor Egan, for her time and the depth of information she shared with me about the life of a university careers counselor.

Last, but never least, to my amazing husband Bob, without whom none of my books would have taken flight.

ABOUT THE AUTHOR

Originally from Edinburgh, Alison now lives near Washington DC with her beloved husband and dogs. She was educated in England and holds an MBA from Leicester University.

Made in the USA
Middletown, DE
01 September 2021

47293534R00191